On the 8th Day, God Created a Marine

Lewis Allen Lambert

authorHOUSE®

AuthorHouse™
1663 Liberty Drive
Bloomington, IN 47403
www.authorhouse.com
Phone: 833-262-8899

Published by AuthorHouse 12/10/2021

ISBN: 978-1-6655-4378-1 (sc)
ISBN: 978-1-6655-4379-8 (e)

Library of Congress Control Number: 2021923190

Print information available on the last page.

This book is printed on acid-free paper.

DEDICATION

On July 5, 2015, God welcomed another Marine into his kingdom of brave men and women. He was my grandson, Adam James Lambert. This book is dedicated to him and to those who have joined God's company of heroes.

We miss and love you AJ.

Semper Fi

This is a work of fiction; it is not Adam's story.

The Marine Corps Version of Genesis 1*

In the beginning was the word, and the word was God.

In the beginning was God, and all else was darkness and void, and without form. So, God created the heavens and the Earth. He created the sun, and the moon and the stars so that light would pierce the darkness.

The Earth, God divided between the land and the sea, and He filled these with many assorted creatures. And the dark, salty, slimy creatures that inhabited the murky depths of the ocean, God called sailors. And He dressed them according. They had little trousers that looked like bells at the bottom. And their shirts had cute little flaps on them to hide the hickeys on their necks. He also gave them long sideburns and shabby looking beards. He called them "squids" and banished them to a lifetime at sea, so that normal folks would not have to associate with them. To further identify these unloved creatures, He called them "petty" and "commodore" instead of titles worthy of red-blooded men.

And the flaky creatures of the land, God called soldiers. And with a twinkle in His eye, and a sense of humor that only He could have, God made their trousers too short and their covers too large. He also made their pockets oversized, so that they may warm their hands. And to adorn their uniforms, God gave them badges in quantities that only a dime store owner could appreciate. And he gave them emblems and crests and all sorts of shiny things that glittered, and devices that dangled. (When you are God, you tend to get carried away.)

On the 6th day, He thought about creating some air creatures for which he designed a Greyhound bus driver's uniform, especially for Air Force flyboys. But he discarded the idea during the first week, and it was not until years later that some apostles resurrected this theme and established what we now know as the "Wild-Blue-Yonder Wonders."

And on the 7th day, as you know, God rested.

But on the 8th day, at 0730, God looked down upon the earth and was not happy. No, God was not happy! So, He thought about his labors, and in His divine wisdom God created a divine creature. And this He called a Marine. And these Marines, who God created in His own image, were to be of the air, and of the land, and of the sea. And these He gave many wonderful uniforms. Some were green; some were blue with red trim. And in the early days some were even a beautiful tan. He gave them practical fighting uniforms, so they could wage war against the forces of Satan and evil. He gave them service uniforms for their daily training. And he gave them evening and dress uniforms, sharp and stylish, handsome things, so that they might promenade with their ladies on Saturday night and impress the hell out of everybody! He even gave them swords, so that people who were not impressed could be dealt with accordingly.

And at the end of the 8th day, God, looked down upon the earth and saw that it was good. But was God happy? No! God was still not happy! Because in the course of His labors, He had forgotten one thing: He did not have a Marine uniform for Himself. He thought about it, and finally God satisfied Himself in knowing that, well…not everybody can be a Marine!

*StrategyPage.com

Contents

1

CHRIS

May 25, 1962, was the hottest day of the year in Napa Valley, California and for high school seniors, it was graduation day. Unfortunately, the ceremony was held inside the school gymnasium which had no air conditioning. Sweat dripped down Christopher Harrington's neck and face as he painfully sat through the third speaker of the day; his shirt was soaked under his black gown.

When it was finally over, Chris threw his cap into the air and dashed to the rear of the gymnasium where his mother greeted him. Bonnie Harrington, was a widow whose husband was killed during the Korean War in early 1953. She never remarried. Bonnie and Chris managed to make a life for themselves. She was a bookkeeper for one of the largest wineries in the area. Chris worked in the packaging and shipping department since he was 14 years old. Since many of the workers were from Mexico, Chris made a lot of friends who taught him to speak Spanish.

Graduation was the turning point in both their lives. San Diego State University offered Chris an athletic scholarship. He was a two-sport high school standout in baseball and basketball. It was a tough decision to leave his mother but she urged him to continue his education and to make a better life for himself.

Chris continued to work for the winery until he left for San Diego in late August. He saw the Pacific Ocean for the first time, in fact he never traveled anywhere outside Napa Valley. He was a small-town boy awed by being in a large city with so many attractions and distractions. Though he was about to embark on a new life, especially as a college athlete, he knew the road to success was by earning his degree. He realized he couldn't make it as a professional athlete; he wasn't tall enough for professional basketball and probably not good enough as a baseball player. It wasn't difficult for him to excel in sports in high school considering the competition among small town high schools wasn't very formidable.

He managed to make the university's freshman basketball team which was required for him to keep his scholarship. In the spring, he made the varsity baseball team. The competition was stiff and only two freshmen made the team, Chris was one of them.

He managed to maintain good grades during his first two years despite the fact he played basketball and baseball, both required a lot of time away from his studies.

2

CHANCE ENCOUNTER

In his junior year, Chris met Camille; an encounter that changed his life in many ways. Camille was the daughter of a Marine Corps officer and a French-born mother. After high school, Camille lived in France for a year with her mother's family. She was a year older than Chris but a year behind in school. Chris's initial encounter with her was totally unexpected. While playing basketball, he was knocked off the court into Camille's lap by an opposing player.

It was awkward at first especially when she reached out to break his fall and he fell into her arms. They both looked into each other's eyes. He thought she was the most beautiful girl he'd ever seen. Before he returned to the court, he asked for her name and then thanked her.

After the game, Chris walked over to her and apologized.

"You don't recognize me, do you?" Camille said.

Chris was stumped. He had no recollection of meeting her.

"I'm in your psychology class. I sit two rows behind you," she said.

"I'm very sorry about not knowing you. You probably come to class after I'm seated," Chris quipped.

She acknowledged she usually came to class late. Chris asked if she wanted to go out for pizza. Camille accepted without hesitation. He told her to wait for him to get dressed.

Some of the other players razzed him about his opportune moment and follow up conversation with Camille. He pressed them as to why they seemed so critical of her.

"She is crazy, Chris. She sleeps around when she appears to be normal and then is a raving lunatic the rest of the time," one of the players said.

"She has severe mood swings. She is probably on some heavy-duty medication," observed another player.

Chris was not dissuaded and ignored the comments, though he was grateful for the warning.

Camille waited outside the gymnasium for him. They walked off campus to a local college hangout. She seemed to be quite normal as far as Chris was concerned. They had a very interesting discussion about her life as a military brat. She mentioned that her parents wanted her to live in France with her aunt and uncle for a year to perfect her French language skills.

Chris's life seemed totally mundane compared to what she experienced. The only thing they had in common was their respective father's military service. Camille mentioned she hardly ever saw her father during her childhood. He was quite strict with her when he lived with them. Since he was stationed at Camp Pendleton, he was home all the time which made her eager to spend a year in France.

Chris returned to his dorm feeling optimistic. Camille showed no signs of being out of control or coming on to him. Could his teammates have lied to him?

The following week, Chris made sure to say hello to Camille, in fact he changed his seat to sit next to her. They ate lunch together and spent time between classes talking about what they wanted to do after college. Chris noted her demeanor was normal, at least in his mind. She laughed and joked though her language was as salty as a Marine's.

Chris's friends asked what he did to her to make her seem so normal. Of course, he had no response because she was always appeared rational around him. Before the Thanksgiving break, Camille asked Chris to spend the holiday at her San Diego home. Chris really wanted to spend the time with his mother. He struggled with his decision. Surprisingly, Bonnie Harrington supported her son's desire to meet Camille's family.

Including the day, he arrived at Camille's home, Chris never witnessed any change in her behavior since the day they met. She hadn't been with any other guys as far as he knew. However, he got a dose of reality once he met her parents.

Camille's mom, Edith was very happy to meet Chris. When she had a chance to be alone with him, she admitted that he was the first boy she ever brought home to meet her parents. She explained that Camille suffered a condition that required her to be on medication to control her behavior. She said Camille suffered from a bi-polar disorder which she explained in detail.

"It's apparent, Chris, you've had a great impact on my daughter. She hasn't been off her meds for at least eight weeks. She seems to be quite happy having you as a friend. I am not trying to pressure you in any way, but if you decide to stop seeing her, I expect she will revert back to her previous behavior."

Chris listened intently and realized how much Camille depended on his friendship. He was also surprised she never acted improperly with him as she had allegedly done with other boys. Her mother's words rested heavily on him.

"I understand, Mrs. Iverson. When Camille is with me, she seems perfectly normal, I mean she hasn't exhibited any mood swings."

"It may happen someday. Don't be alarmed and don't desert her, try to be there for her. I don't know how you feel about her, but she talks about you all the time, that has never happened before. Please let me know ahead of time if you consider leaving Camille. There is so much I'll have to do to deal with her. I hope I haven't put too much pressure on you, Chris."

"I can only promise I'll be good to her and be sensitive to anything that changes in our relationship."

Chris noted a tear in Mrs. Iverson's eye. She looked at Chris lovingly as if she were his mother. She gave him a big hug.

When Chris was introduced to Colonel Harold Iverson, who looked like the stereotyped Marine officer portrayed in WWII movies; steely eyed, chiseled face and a square jaw, Chris was a wee bit intimidated. The colonel's strong handshake and grim appearance were really a façade. Once he spoke with Chris, he seemed to be a concerned parent.

"I come from a family of four brothers so I didn't have the skills to deal with a daughter and an only child at that. I was away from home most of her life and I dragged Camille and her mother all over the world. I never realized the impact on Camille of being uprooted from her friends so often and then becoming the new kid in another school. She never rebelled, but her therapist has told us that her emotions were tightly held inside and contributed to her vast mood swings," he said rather sadly.

"I understand, colonel. She seems rather normal since we've met and Mrs. Iverson has commented that she faithfully takes her medication", Chris replied.

"Whatever you've done to have such an enormous influence over my daughter is greatly appreciated young man" he said.

As Chris turned to look for Camille, her father grabbed him gently by the shoulder.

"What are you plans after you graduate college, if you don't mind me asking?"

"Camille and I haven't discussed it yet," Chris replied.

"What I meant to ask is what do you want to do after graduation as far as a career?"

I'm not sure yet. I still have another year so I'll have to wait and see. I just hope the draft doesn't get me before that," Chris said.

The colonel looked him square in the eye, a look that made Chris feel uneasy.

"So, you don't want to serve your country in time of need?" He gruffly stated.

"I probably would, but not as a grunt, sir." Chris replied.

"If you want to serve in another capacity after graduation, I can probably get you into officer training school. I'm sure as an athlete you can handle the physical training."

"Thank you, colonel, I'll keep that in mind. I appreciate the offer."

It was a tense fifteen-minute conversation that unnerved Chris. He never thought about the military as a career though his father served with distinction.

He caught up with Camille speaking with her mother. She rushed over to give him a hug as her mother smiled with a sense of relief.

"Isn't he wonderful, mother?" Camille said after the embrace.

"I think he's someone special," she replied.

During the two months Chris and Camille knew each other, they hadn't had any physical contact except for the surprised embrace in front Mrs. Iverson. Was it just for show or did Camille have feelings for him? Considering she'd allegedly had sex with lots of college boys, Camille surprisingly refrained from any flirtatious acts or any subtle indications she wanted to sleep with Chris. He was good with that, after all, he didn't want to be just another sexual encounter.

During Thanksgiving dinner, Colonel Iverson announced he was being promoted to brigadier general and assigned to the Pentagon as the Marine Corps commandant's deputy chief of staff. The announcement took his wife and daughter by surprise. He said he wasn't moving them to the Washington DC area because he didn't think he'd be there too long. He said he expected to be sent to Vietnam within a year as the Marine Corps increased the number of troops deployed there.

Everyone was silent for a moment. Chris thought the family was used to such announcements, considering Camille mentioned she hardly saw her father during her childhood. Mrs. Iverson said she didn't think it would've been a good idea to move again even if the assignment was for a longer period of time.

"You can retire after Vietnam now that you are being promoted to the rank you've been working so hard to achieve; moving again is just not in the cards for me," Mrs. Iverson said.

"If this war lasts more than a few years, I'll probably see another promotion. However, whatever happens, we'll make San Diego our permanent home," the colonel added.

Thanksgiving 1964, was the first time Chris spent the holiday outside of Napa Valley. After dinner, he asked Camille if she wanted to spend Christmas break with him so he could show her where he grew up and take advantage of the dozens of wine tasting rooms in the valley. Though she didn't require her parents' permission, she wanted to make sure her mother agreed considering she was on medication. That discussion was saved for another day.

Before Chris returned to his dorm room on campus, the colonel gave his recruitment pitch one last shot.

"I could probably delay you going into harm's way for a while. I have enough influence to have you assigned to a non-combat unit, though every Marine is a combat trained warfighter," he said.

"Colonel, if I joined the Marine Corps and became an officer, I'd like to become a leader serving with pride whether in war or peace," Chris said.

Where the hell did that come from, he thought?

"I knew you had the right stuff. I'll be waiting for your call about this time next year," the colonel said.

That was the last time Chris spoke with Camille's father before he graduated college.

The three weeks between Thanksgiving and Christmas went by very fast. Most of that time Camille and Chris didn't see each other much because they were busy studying for final exams. Camille was excited to spend a week with Chris at his home in Napa. Chris had to prepare his mother for her visit since Camille would be staying in their home. Mrs. Harrington wasn't a prude; she certainly thought her son would be responsible to do the right thing.

Camille drove them to Napa. It was her first visit there and she said it reminded her of France. Chris's mom was very welcoming to the first girl Chris ever brought home who didn't live in the valley. Chris didn't know what his mother's expectations would be when she had to go to work a few days at the winery to close the books before Christmas. Did she even consider that her son would sleep with his girlfriend in her home?

Chris wondered if Camille might try to come on to him. They never came close to doing anything in a sexual way. He was often puzzled as to why she hadn't tried anything, considering the stories he heard about her. On the afternoon of their second day in Napa, Camille grabbed

Chris's hand and said she wanted him to make love to her. She kissed him passionately on the lips and led him to the guest room.

After an hour of pleasuring each other, she looked at Chris in such a sincere way.

"I'm in love with you. I've never told anyone else that before, please believe me. I hated myself until I met you. I did a lot of things that I now regret. I'm sure the guys at school talk about me. I have a terrible reputation but I don't care. I have you in my life now," she confessed.

Chris was taken aback. He realized they had become very close friends and shared so much of each other's thoughts and feelings. He didn't consider she would actually fall in love with him. There were no signs that he was aware of.

"I don't know what to say, Camille. Perhaps I was too naïve to realize you had fallen in love with me. I'm so happy you told me how you feel. I sort of have the same feelings about you. I mean I'm trying to deal with these feelings I have for you. I never loved anyone before so it's new to me," he stammered.

"Stop talking, Chris and make love to me again before your mother comes home."

Over the next few days, they made love whenever they could. Camille slipped into Chris's bed on the night before they returned to campus. She made their time together something he'd never forget.

Over the next five months, Camille and Chris were inseparable. He even gave up baseball to spend more time with her. She won him over in a big way. During the summer break, Chris had to return to Napa to work. Camille went to France with her mother. The two missed each other more than either of them could have anticipated.

It was difficult to communicate with Camille since she was living in rural France. He tried phoning twice but he couldn't reach her. They exchanged a few letters. In one, Camille wrote she told her mother everything that happened between them. Chris was surprised her mother approved. What Chris didn't know at the time was that she told her mother she wanted to marry him, a subject they never discussed before.

Their reunion in San Diego, in September was spectacular. They spent a weekend in a hotel and never left the room. The anticipation of seeing each other again and what they missed all summer played itself out in a significant way. Two months later, Camille told Chris she was pregnant.

Both of them agreed to keep the baby but not how to tell their respective mothers? The colonel was in the Pentagon, heading for Vietnam in a few short weeks. Camille's mom, born and raised in France, would probably be thrilled and not at all judgmental. Chris believed his mom wouldn't be prepared for such a shock but would be secretly pleased as long as he graduated college.

The two of them spoke with Camille's mom first since she still lived at home and her condition couldn't be hidden for too long. As expected, she took the news quite well. She made a decision not to tell her husband who planned spend a few days at home on his to way to Southeast Asia. By the time he came and went, Camille's condition remained a secret.

Chris called his mom who fell silent at the news.

"You must marry Camille, I expect that is the honorable thing to do," she whispered.

Though Camille told her mother over the summer she wanted to marry Chris, they never discussed the subject even after she knew she was pregnant. Chris followed his mother's admonishment and asked Camille to marry him. He told her he planned to ask her after graduation, but in truth, he never really considered it until she became pregnant.

Chris and Camille married in early December in a small church in La Jolla, California. Bonnie Harrington attended the wedding and spent a few days at the Iverson's home. The two prospective grandmothers got along quite well since they were both wine experts.

Camille didn't enroll for the spring semester but chose to remain at home awaiting her baby's birth expected in June. In April, Camille's mom received a letter from her husband addressed to Chris who was living in the Iverson home. The colonel had been informed of the marriage and the pregnancy, and apparently accepted the news well.

The letter to Chris had more meaning now that he was the colonel's son-in-law. He wanted to know Chris's plans after graduation since he had a family of his own to consider. He informed Chris he had already alerted the Marine Corps of the possibility his son-in-law would take the necessary steps to apply for officer training.

Chris didn't feel pressured to make any decisions until after the baby was born. If he applied, he'd have to go to Officer Candidate School at Marine Corps Base in Quantico, Virginia. Unfortunately, he'd have to leave his wife and baby in San Diego for a few months.

Andrew Harrington was born on June 12th. Both grandparents were ecstatic as were his parents. Everyone decided to call him Andy. In July, Chris left for Quantico uncertain of his future or whether he'd even live to see the end of the war.

Officer training was rigorous both mentally and physically. Chris was challenged in both areas but managed to finish first in his class. He was trained to be a platoon leader. When he received his orders, he was surprised he wasn't assigned to a combat unit. Instead, he was selected to remain at Quantico to train new officer candidates. Somehow, he expected the general was behind it, but the truth was the Marines needed experienced officers for combat so they stripped their training units of senior lieutenants and captains.

3

THE ACCIDENT

As the war in Vietnam heated up, the number of Marines and Army troops deployed there by early 1967 surpassed 200,000. Chris decided he wanted to opt out of his training role. He was interested in becoming a fighter pilot and spoke with his detailer about his chances of being accepted for pilot training. He also contacted his father-in-law about his plans.

Unfortunately, before he was selected for pilot training, he received word that Camille was severely injured in an automobile accident. Chris was granted emergency leave and flew to San Diego. Camille was in an induced coma having broken her leg, pelvis and jaw. She was scheduled for several rounds of surgery and remained in intensive care.

Camille's father was expected home within 24 hours. What Chris was able to piece together was that Camille received a phone call from a former high school friend, a Marine private on his way to Hawaii. Apparently, as they left for the airport, they were struck by a speeding semi-trailer truck. The Marine was killed instantly. Mrs. Iverson confided to Chris that her daughter was not taking her meds on a regular basis. Camille was depressed over Chris's absence like she had been for years with her father's long absences from home.

When the general arrived, he asked a lot of questions and took his anger out on his wife for letting Camille drive to the airport when she was off her meds. Chris never saw his in-laws as he did that day in the hospital.

Two days after arriving in San Diego, Chris was notified he had been accepted into the pilot training program and had to report in two weeks. The general told him not to cancel his opportunity to become a pilot; he'd extend his leave to be with Camille after Chris had to report to Pensacola.

A few days before Chris departed, Camille was awake and on heavy pain medication. Her injuries were surgically repaired but she faced a long regime of physical therapy. Her jaw was wired shut to allow it to heal so she couldn't speak. Everyone was worried about her mental state because to recuperate she had to be positive and remain strong. If she wasn't motivated to return to normal, her chances of a full recovery weren't good. Her medical team was made aware of her psychological condition which led to extensive mental therapy as part of her regime.

Chris was torn between delaying his pilot training to remain with his wife and doing what his father-in-law recommended. The medical team told Chris it would be better to return in a few months when his wife was stabilized and able to walk.

In February, 1967, Chris received orders to proceed to Pensacola, Florida for primary pilot training. He left with a heavy heart and a lot of guilt. He was assured his mother-in-law and his mother would take care of Andy and Camille.

During his training, he made it known he wanted to fly fixed wing jet fighters. To insure he got his preferred choice, he finished first in his class. Upon completion of undergraduate pilot training, he was trained to fly the F-8 Crusader, utilized by the Marine Corps to support ground troops. As noted, the Navy employed the Crusader to bomb targets in North Vietnam.

Chris returned to San Diego on his way to Southeast Asia where he found a despondent Camille, who had to use a walker to get around. Her jaw healed but she had a noticeable scar along her jaw line. She was not very communicative at first but brightened up a bit after a few hours alone with Chris and Andy.

Camille's mom was concerned about her daughter's will to return to normal, whatever normal was for someone with a bi-polar disorder. Camille was undergoing intensive psychological therapy three times a week to overcome depression. Chris was sick to his stomach about his inability to play a larger role in Camille's recovery. Her doctor informed him there was no guarantee that his continued presence would have a lasting impact on her mental state.

With mixed emotions Chris deployed to Da Nang air base in early 1968, as the military reached its highest number of in-country troops of about 400,000. The TET offensive in late January, early February was a major turning point in the war. Though American forces defeated the Viet Cong and North Vietnamese armies in every major city in South Vietnam, the media claimed the 1968 TET offensive was a colossal failure for the United States.

Chris's father-in-law received his second star and returned to San Diego for about a month before being assigned as the deputy division commander of the 1st Marine Division with headquarters in Chu Lai, Vietnam. Soon after the general arrived in Chu Lai, he visited Chris in Da Nang to tell him about Camille. Fortunately, she decided to return to school to complete her degree. Her father attributed her turnaround to the great psychological and physical therapy she received. She walked without assistance and faithfully stayed on her meds. Chris was buoyed by the news. In her recent letters, Camille didn't tell Chris she returned to school. The general promised to keep Chris in the loop since he spoke to his wife a few times a week.

4

THE WAR

The North Vietnamese Army, a far superior force than the Viet Cong cadres in the south, played an ever-increasing role in the war against the Republic of Vietnam. Chris's squadron flew combat missions almost every day. Though Chris's role was limited to supporting Marine forces engaged in combat, Chris had a unique experience.

In June, 1968, a fellow Marine pilot was engaged in a ground support role near the demilitarized zone just south of the North Vietnamese border. The pilot became disoriented and crossed over the border heading in the wrong direction. Two MiG-17 fighters were alerted to the intruder's location and made a few passes to identify the aircraft. Once identified it as an enemy fighter, they attacked the F-8 Crusader. Chris heard the distress call and without getting permission, headed toward the F-8 for support.

Chris had no training in air-to-air combat so what he did to save his fellow Marine was based on his gut instinct. He attacked one MiG-17 from the rear at a higher altitude and bore down on it with his guns blazing away. The MiG-17 pilot never saw Chris but felt the sting of his 20mm guns. Chris contacted his fellow Marine pilot and reoriented him toward his base at Chu Lai. Apparently, the disoriented pilot's navigation system wasn't operational. For his actions, Chris earned a bronze star for valor.

During the Vietnam War, the Navy's F-8 was very successful in aerial combat having been responsible for nearly 20 downed enemy aircraft. Most of those kills were attributed to air-to-air missiles, known as the AIM-9

Sidewinder, and only a few were attributed to its 20mm guns. Chris's squadron wasn't equipped with the AIM-9 at the time of his MiG-17 kill.

Marine Corps Crusaders flew only in the south from land bases, while Navy carrier-based Navy F-8 Crusaders flew to targets in North Vietnam where they encountered enemy fighter interceptors.

As Chris neared the end of his tour of duty, he had another opportunity to stick his neck out and save another pilot. On his return from dropping bombs on enemy fortifications, Chris heard a distress call from an Air Force F-4 Phantom jet. The aircraft was seriously damaged after it was hit by its exploding wingman's aircraft as a result a surface-to-air missile strike. The pilot's weapon's officer was badly wounded; the pilot was nearly blinded and couldn't sustain his flight path.

Chris reached the stricken aircraft and assured the pilot he would guide him to the nearest airfield. He gave the pilot verbal instructions on changing course and maintaining altitude until they reached Da Nang air base. Chris alerted the air base regarding the situation. He flew parallel to the sightless pilot and guided him to a safe landing and then pulled up to land a few minutes later.

Chris's actions earned him a silver star which the Marine Corps and the Air Force jointly submitted. His last month in combat operations went by without further heroics.

He was sent to Pensacola in early 1969 to retrain in the F-4 Phantom fighter/bomber. Chris didn't quite understand why, but had a hunch he would be assigned to a Navy carrier-based squadron to fly missions over North Vietnam.

On his way to Pensacola, he spent three weeks in San Diego with his family. Camille appeared to be doing well and was taking her meds routinely according to her mom. Andy was doing great and behaving like a typical two-year-old. Unfortunately, he didn't really recognize Chris, a price he paid with much regret.

Unbeknownst to Chris, his departure affected Camille more than anyone suspected. It left her despondent beyond anything she experienced before.

5

A TRAGEDY

Two weeks into his training, Chris received a call from Mrs. Iverson; Camille died from an overdose of heroin. Preliminary reports were that it was a deliberate attempt to kill herself. Chris returned home 20 hours after receiving the call.

Mrs. Iverson was inconsolable. Chris blamed himself for the tragedy. He should never have enlisted in the Marine Corps knowing how fragile his wife was. He knew her mother and his mother believed it as well. The only one who was on his side was the general. He grieved along with Chris. He had to feel some responsibility for his daughter's death because he had so little time with her during her life.

After a few days, Chris thought of applying for a compassionate discharge so he could take care of his son. Though the general believed it would be granted, he urged Chris to reconsider.

Camille's mom assured Chris she would take care of Andy until he left the Marine Corps. Chris believed it was the best thing for both of them. The general was away, Camille was gone, all she had left was little Andy. Chris wept the day he left. He wept for Andy, for Camille and for her mother.

6

A TOUGH DECISION

A return to Pensacola was not something Chris wanted but he felt an obligation to complete his tour of duty. He breezed through F-4 training earning top of the class honors. His Navy classmates received their orders to various aircraft carriers in the fleet, mostly in the Pacific but some in the Mediterranean. Chris didn't receive an assignment. He was given two weeks leave and returned to San Diego. The reunion with his three-year-old son was unexpected. Chris cherished it.

Chris received notice to report to Naval Air Station Miramar, just north of San Diego. Again, he was puzzled as to why he wasn't being assigned to a carrier. As soon as he arrived at Miramar, he was certain the Navy made a mistake. He was assigned as a student to the United States Navy Fighter Weapons School, later known as 'Top Gun', a school that trained the best Navy fighter pilots to be even better. The school was established on March 3, 1969. Chris was in the second class. Though a Marine Corps pilot, Chris was still a naval resource so someone, somewhere believed he earned a shot at the school.

His classmates were all Navy pilots; some had MiG kills to their credit, as did Chris, but not as dangerous an environment as what Navy pilots experienced over North Vietnam. His downing of a MiG-17 was a chance opportunity, as some of his classmates said, a walk in the park, but it counted.

During the training which was highly competitive, Chris learned what the F-4 could do and couldn't do against MiG aircraft. He scored well enough to be near the top of his class. He was paired with a Cuban-American weapons officer named Javier Maria Cruz, a Marine lieutenant. Javi had more than 50 missions over North Vietnam with the Navy so he was an invaluable teammate for Chris.

Javi pushed Chris to the number one spot, an honor that would last his entire career. Chris's stiffest competitor was Navy Lt. Kenneth Walsh, Jr., a Naval Academy graduate and the son of an active-duty vice admiral. The school commander was under subtle pressure to see to it that Lt. Walsh finished top of his class like he did at the academy.

When the final competition was completed but before the class standings were announced, the school commander asked to speak with Chris.

"Captain Harrington, you are one helluva fighter pilot. I have a small, no, a big problem. Lt. Walsh is also a great pilot; you and he finished one, two in your class. I have to determine whether a Marine Corps pilot will get the nod over an admiral's son, and a top naval academy graduate. Do you see the predicament I face?"

"I never liked politics, sir. You have a tough decision. I don't envy you. Make the honorable one based on the numbers. If I'm number two, so be it," Chris responded.

The commander paused as if in thought, then stood up and shook Chris's hand. He smiled as he left the office, either way he was pleased with the outcome.

The class standing was posted for all to see. Chris and Kenneth were both named number one in their class. The commander did the honorable thing.

7

RETURN TO COMBAT

Chris and Ken Walsh were given orders to the same carrier. Though staunch competitors in school, they became friends. Surprisingly, they had to report to Japan to pick up their aircraft. No reason was given but it appeared to be an unusual order. Since Chris finished atop his class, he requested that Javi remain as his weapons officer on his deployment to the fleet.

During his time at Miramar, Chris got to see his son on numerous occasions. Andy finally recognized Chris as his daddy. After graduation, Chris had to leave after only a week at home. He met Javi and Ken in Hawaii where they flew to Yokota Air Base, Japan. They traveled to Marine Corps Air Station, Iwakuni, Japan to pick up their aircraft. They were met by a Marine Corps officer who informed them their aircraft would be ready to depart in the morning. He took them to the officer's club to meet two other Navy pilots who graduated from the first Top Gun class at Miramar. They finished second and fourth. They also met the three other weapons officers whom the Navy pilots knew from previous deployments.

None of them knew why they had to pick up their aircraft in Japan. Chris asked where they would meet the carrier. None of them had that information. When Chris mentioned he never landed on a carrier before, they all choked on their drinks and broke out laughing.

"You've got to be kidding us, Chris. Didn't anyone check your flight records? We all trained for weeks making dozens of landings on carriers in all types of weather. You sure are fucked," one of them said.

"Is it really that difficult?" Chris asked.

"When that deck is bouncing around in a rough sea and you are bouncing as well, you have only one chance to get your butt down, my asshole tightens up each time I approach the carrier's deck and I've made nearly 100 carrier landings," Ken said.

"I'll just pray for a calm sea," Chris laughed.

They explained to Chris what to expect on his approach and who was responsible for bringing him down for a safe landing. He was told if he was waived off, he had to go around again

"When you land on the deck you will be snared by an arresting wire but you can't decrease you speed until you are jerked to a stop. If something happens and you don't catch the wire you have to full throttle off the carrier or you'll end up in the sea," they said.

They also talked about take-off experience and how the catapult worked.

"Someone sure fucked up when they forgot to send me to that training program," Chris said laughing.

No one else laughed, including Javi.

The next morning, they met for breakfast and then drove to the airfield. They spotted four F-4 Phantoms painted Navy blue instead of the customary gray color.

The airfield's operations' officer met them and took them inside a hangar for a briefing.

"You will be flying an upgraded aircraft with an enhanced capability to seek and destroy enemy air targets. The aircraft are configured with AIM-9 Sidewinders with both radar and heat seeking capabilities. Since the Navy has been using these missiles for some time, I'm sure you are familiar with them. The four aircraft were transferred to us from the Air Force and upgraded to Navy specifications. These aircraft aren't configured to carry bombs. That's all I can discuss with you now. Are there any questions?" He asked.

"Why are they painted blue instead of Navy gray?" One of the pilots asked.

"You will be briefed on that and on your mission when you land on the carrier," he responded.

Their first destination was Clark Air Force Base in the Philippines to refuel and then were to meet an Air Force tanker over the South China Sea to take on enough fuel to make it to the carrier. Thankfully Chris had two refueling exercises during pilot training; he never had to do it during his ground support missions in Vietnam.

It was late afternoon before Chris got a glimpse of the carrier; it seemed so small. Chris had to land last since it would be his first landing and if anything went wrong, the rest of the guys wouldn't be able to land.

Chris was extremely nervous as he approached the end of the short runway. He saw the signal man with the paddles, lined up on center and kept his aircraft level. The carrier undulated as the sea had a small chop. He hit the carrier deck at full throttle and when his aircraft jerked to a stop he throttled back. Javi, who was tight as a drum, congratulated him on a great first attempt. They both needed a drink but none would be offered aboard ship.

When Chris climbed down from his aircraft the other three F-4 crews applauded him. The carrier air boss beckoned them to follow him to the briefing room where a group of F-8 Crusader pilots waited to be told about the four new Phantoms on board.

The air boss introduced Lt. Walsh's crew members. There was a lot of booing when Chris was introduced as a Marine Corps pilot. The air boss explained that the four F-4s would fly combat air patrol, or MiGCAP cover for the squadron while on their missions over North Vietnam. This would alleviate a problem of an F-8 having to ward off MiG fighters during a bombing run. The entire squadron could concentrate on its targets while the F-4s protected them.

A pilot asked why the new guys would be any better to defend their squadron than any one of them.

"All of these pilots attended the Navy Fighter Weapons School at Miramar. Warren was fourth in his class; Davis was second in the same class, and Walsh and Harrington tied for first in their class. They've all had prior combat tours before going to the Top Gun school. By the way, Harrington made his first carrier landing today, a terrible omission in his training prior to this tour. Let's hope his luck continues."

They all laughed. Javi said he didn't think it was so funny. Another pilot asked why the Phantoms were painted blue.

"We want the enemy pilots to know they are facing the best of the best. Remember the Red Baron from WWI? It's really a psychological thing," he replied.

After their meeting, the pilots introduced themselves to the new guys. They were taken to their tight living quarters that Navy pilots were used to, but not Chris. He didn't complain about it

The first bombing mission was scrubbed due to bad weather over the targets. On the second day, Chris had his first experience taking off from the carrier's deck. He thought it quite exhilarating. Walsh's four aircraft flight was about 30 minutes behind the main force of F-8's flying to targets south of Hanoi. It would be Chris's first planned flight over North Vietnam.

There was low cloud cover, a residual of the recent bad weather. The bombing raid had to be conducted at a lower altitude than normal exposing the aircraft to heavy anti-aircraft fire. The only benefit to the low clouds was the cover they provided from MiG fighters. Walsh's flight remained above the clouds waiting for the Crusaders to break through on their return to the carrier. Walsh led his flight to cover the Crusaders as they headed out to sea. It was an uneventful first mission for Chris.

After the Crusaders landed, Walsh led his flight to the carrier. Chris was a bit tense as he made his second carrier landing. He managed to hit the first wire just like he was a veteran carrier pilot.

The one thing Chris liked about being aboard a carrier was the food. It was very good, better than at Da Nang. Between missions, Chris had a lot of time to think about Andy and Camille. He missed them both very much. He was bothered by the fact he had become an absentee father, like Camille's situation. He hoped Andy would forgive him one day.

At the next day's pre-mission briefing, the operations officer stated the carrier would be very proud to record any MiG kills by painting red stars below the carrier's bridge. The carrier had two of them from a previous deployment.

The second mission was a bit more eventful. The weather was good and the target was well defended. The intelligence officer said they'd see enemy missiles on the way in and MiG interceptors on the way out. Due to the location of the target, the Crusaders had to approach from altitude and then rapidly come in low; a perfect target for missiles.

The F-4s took off 20 minutes after the Crusaders. They would wait for the bombers to return and then take on any MiG interceptors. Apparently, intelligence on the target wasn't perfect. The Crusaders were attacked by MiG's before Walsh and his flight arrived. They engaged the MiG's as soon they arrived. The MiG's finally broke off and the Crusaders continued to their targets while Walsh chased the MiG's. Chris noted they wouldn't be in position to help the Crusaders on their way back and mentioned it to Walsh.

He made the decision to split his team, sending Davis and Warren back to the F-8's while he and Chris continued after the MiG's. After a few minutes of maneuvering to take a shot, Chris launched a Sidewinder and scored a hit. The other interceptors disengaged and headed north. Chris and Ken departed the area to meet the rest of the returning aircraft. Ken praised Chris on his kill and said he'd get one the next time.

Chris's third carrier landing was uneventful. No one aboard the carrier knew about the downing of the MiG yet since it had to be confirmed through intelligence. It took about 12 hours for confirmation. A ship's crew member painted a third star near the bridge and Chris's F-4 got its second red star painted on its fuselage. After that event, Chris changed his call sign to Cisco because he and Javi were called the Cisco Kid and his pal Poncho by fellow pilots, in fact, everyone on the ship called them the Cisco Kid and Poncho.

Over the next three months, Chris flew 43 missions over North Vietnam, which meant 43 landings most of which were in calm seas. On his 44h mission, Chris had the opportunity to get his third MiG, but instead he helped Walsh get his second one. It was an unselfish act because Ken wanted to please his father. The carrier notched its fourth star.

Six months into his tour, Chris experienced a few tricky landings in rough seas and one, a night landing, freaked him out. During his approach, he was forced to go around two times before he made it down onto a pitching deck.

Two months before the carrier was pulled off station, Chris's flight had a nasty encounter with four MiG-19's. Davis got his first kill, Walsh got his third as did Chris. However, Chris ran into aircraft debris from Ken's kill. The bottom of Chris's fuselage was pierced by shrapnel. His wing was also hit which caused a fuel leak. Chris couldn't make it back to the carrier so he headed for Da Nang air base. Though it was much closer than the carrier, it became a difficult situation to handle. The F-4 became very unstable as he continued toward the air base. He contacted Ken to let him know why he was diverting to Da Nang. He refused to bail out at first but considered it once he was over South Vietnam.

After a tense 30 minutes, he had the familiar runway in sight and landed on fumes. He had to be towed off the runway. After a preliminary inspection, the ground crew said they'd have it repaired in about three days.

He hitched a ride to the bachelor officer's quarters while Javi left with a friend. Since Chris was alone, he headed for his favorite hangout, the officer's club. Most of the Marine aviators stationed at Da Nang didn't know him since he was last stationed there in 1968. Fortunately, two of his former squadron mates on their second tours waived at him.

"Hey Chris, over here, sit with us," Major Boyd Ferris yelled.

As Chris walked toward their table, he passed by a group of air force nurses having dinner together. He spotted someone who took his breath away. She was a raven-haired beauty with midnight blue eyes. He stopped by her side and spoke to her.

"Hello, my name is Chris. I'd like to have dinner with you tomorrow night. I'm only here for three days so you have to say yes."

The other nurses laughed at his invitation as if they hadn't heard a Marine come on to a nurse before. She turned to face him.

"Chris, aren't you one of them?" She said pointing to the other Marine pilots.

"No, I'm stationed on a carrier and was forced to land here this afternoon. You are the most beautiful woman I've ever seen."

Chris knew he was pushing it, but what the hell, it worked before.

"Why don't you come to the hospital tomorrow and we'll have lunch together? My name is Katherine but everyone calls me Katie." She said with a smile.

"I'll be there Katie," he said as his heart started pounding.

Chris took the initiative with only one other woman, his late wife, Camille. He remembered how that first encounter occurred. He smiled thinking perhaps lightning could strike twice. As he walked away from Katie's table, he heard the other nurses whispering things like how could you say yes, and wow, he is quite good looking.

The following day, Chris walked into a few hospital wards looking for Katie. He stopped to chat with some of the wounded Marines until he caught a glimpse of her. When she turned around and saw him, she smiled. She pointed to her watch and held up five fingers.

Five minutes later she approached him.

"Hello, Chris, I knew you'd come. Let's have lunch," she said with a beautiful smile.

They went through the cafeteria serving line and then led him to a table that was fairly isolated.

"I think every nurse here is staring at me," she said.

"What makes you think that, perhaps they are staring at me," Chris quipped.

She laughed. Chris didn't touch his food. He just stared at her while they conversed. She told him she was returning to the States in three months but didn't have an assignment yet. She acknowledged she had a three-year old daughter who lived with her sister-in-law. Her brother was a B-52 pilot stationed in Guam.

Chris had a similar story. He began with his chance meeting of his belated wife and how her father, now a Marine general, encouraged him to join the Marines. He mentioned his wife's severe depression and bi-polar disorder that resulted in her taking her life. He too, had a child, a four-year old boy who lived with his grandmother.

"This war is certainly tough on families," Chris said.

"I miss my daughter but I know she is in good hands and I will see her soon," Katie replied.

As they talked, Chris realized they had much in common. He was from rural California; she was from a small town near Reno, Nevada. He felt very comfortable with her and he sensed she was at ease as well. She agreed to have dinner with him. They made arrangements to meet. When he walked her back to her ward, he touched her hand and she held on to it.

Chris hitched a ride to the flight line to check on his aircraft. He found it inside a hangar but no one was working on it. He approached the maintenance officer who explained they had to get approval from McDonnell Douglas to repair the fuselage and wing since they could only patch the damage with what material they had on hand. They needed approval to move forward without the manufacturer's required fix. He mentioned it might take another 24 hours to get a response.

Chris walked over to wing headquarters to send a message to the carrier with an update on the status of his aircraft. While there, he was informed Maj. Gen. Iverson was on base visiting the Marine units at Da Nang. Chris was informed the general just left the hospital and was headed to the Marine fighter squadron to chat with the crews.

Chris decided to see his father-in-law once he finished his tour of the Marine facilities. However, he soon dismissed the idea because the general might want to have dinner with him and Chris didn't want to cancel his last time with Katie.

Chris asked the officer of the day how long the general would be on the base. He was told he would be leaving in the morning after breakfast.

He met Katie in front of her barracks. She took him to a bar near China Beach which was a great in-country rest and recuperation location for troops in the field.

The bar served a rather good hamburger and a few side orders. The beer was cold and the music was loud. Chris couldn't keep his eyes off Katie. If she could only read his mind, he'd be in trouble. She suggested they take a walk along the beach. As they were about to leave, an air force major approached their table.

"Hello, Katie, can I see you tonight?" He asked.

"Not tonight, I am with someone," she said defensively.

"Do you think he's a better man than me? Are you sleeping with him too?" he yelled.

The major was obviously drunk. The Marines that heard his remarks started moving toward him. Chris stood up and told him to apologize to her.

"Don't you know all these nurses are just whores?" He yelled.

At that point two burly Marines grabbed the major and escorted him out the door. He tried to fight them off but it wasn't a fair fight. Security forces arrived to take the major into custody. Chris gave them a full account of what happened. When he returned to the table, Katie was crying.

"I'm so embarrassed, I'm sorry for what happened," she whispered.

"Let's get out of here," Chris said.

They walked along the beach. Chris took Katie by the shoulders, turned her toward him.

"I don't care what you did before I met you. I like you a lot and if you have any feelings for me, we can move on," Chris said.

She didn't say anything for a second and then kissed him. As they stood there in the dark moonless night, listening to the waves roll onto the beach, it seemed like the opportunity was perfect for the next step. Chris refrained from anything more than to respond to her kiss. He assumed she expected more.

He took her by the hand and continued to walk closer to the water.

"I waited more than a year to make love after I met my wife. I don't want to take advantage of this fantastic evening with you. I didn't ask you to be with me to have sex. I want to preserve my memory of you at this moment to make sure I have a damn good reason for seeing you back home," Chris said.

"I don't know what to say. You are certainly different than anyone else around here. I could certainly fall in love with someone like you. In fact, I am falling for you," she said with tears in her eyes.

Chris kissed her gently on her face and lips. How could he resist making love to her? Would he then be no different than any other Marine or airman based at Da Nang? It was a difficult moment for both of them. His abstention had to be a sign of his true feelings; at least that's what he hoped she understood.

He put his arm around her waist as they walked back to her barracks area. They kissed for what would be their last time in a long while.

Chris found a note slipped under his door. His aircraft would be ready by noon. He had time for one last lunch with Katie.

He walked through the hospital wards searching for her. The charge nurse said she called in sick. He wanted to see her but he wouldn't be allowed to go to her room. He spotted one of Katie's friends and asked if she would deliver a note to her because he had to leave in about an hour.

"Is she very ill?" He asked.

"If you ask me, Chris, I'd say she's love sick. I hope you don't hurt her. Please find her when you return to the States," she pleaded.

After he handed the nurse the note, he realized he'd completely forgotten about the general. Chris was certain he left hours before.

His aircraft was on the tarmac ready to go. Off to his left he saw the general walking toward him.

"I'm glad my flight was delayed, Chris. I wanted to tell you how proud I am of your achievements. My son-in-law is a Top Gun, one of the best Navy fighter pilots, not too shabby for a Marine."

He extended his hand though it appeared for a moment he wanted to embrace Chris.

"Have you heard from my wife, Chris?"

"I received a letter about a week ago. Andy sure is growing up fast. He keeps asking for dada. I think I'll have to change my career if I want to be a great father. I never had one growing up, as you know, sir," Chris replied.

"At least you have the opportunity to make that decision, I sometimes regret I didn't so the same. I have to get back to Chu Lai in a few minutes. When does you tour end?"

"Sometime in December, I understand."

"Where do you want to go? I think I can help with that," the general offered.

"San Diego would be great. I could probably use a year or two back in a Marine fighter squadron," he replied.

They shook hands again. The general walked over to his helicopter while Chris conferred with his ground crew prior to take off. Javi Cruz showed up with a hangover. He had been partying for two days.

"Welcome back Poncho," Chris said.

"Ola, Cisco," he replied.

They told base operations they were headed for their carrier and needed its position. During the flight, Javi sang a few Cuban songs; it must have been the remaining alcohol in his system.

The flight was uneventful. Chris spotted seven red stars under the bridge of the carrier signifying all of his flight's kills had been confirmed.

Back on the carrier, they had a quick meal and then reported to the air boss. They underwent an extensive debriefing regarding the incident that resulted in having to remain at Da Nang for nearly three days. The air boss seemed satisfied.

Over the next month, Chris and Katie exchanged letters. Their words of love were expressed very often and they were very anxious to meet again in the States.

In September, the month Katie was to finish her tour of duty, the letters stopped coming. Chris thought it was due to her departure from Vietnam. One of Chris's friends at Da Nang sent him a message that Katie was in the hospital at Clark Air Force Base in the Philippines. There was no further explanation. Chris was beside himself but he had no way of getting more information.

8

REUNION

By the time Chris completed his tour of duty in mid-December, he hadn't heard a word from or about Katie. He flew home confused and worried. The only thing that gave him joy was seeing his son, Andy, who greeted him with open loving arms.

A week after he arrived in San Diego, Chris received a call from the Marine Corps assignment's office offering him a unique opportunity. After serving a tour aboard a carrier, he was anxious to return to the Marine Corps. Unfortunately, the offer was to become part of a new air force Aggressor Squadron to train air force fighter pilots in air-to-air combat skills.

"Is this similar to the Navy's Top Gun program?" Chris asked.

"I understand it will be much broader and less competitive. In case you turn it down, you should know the air force has specifically requested you by name."

"Why me, the air force has many experienced combat pilots?"

"They want pilots who have been credited with kills while in Vietnam. They have reached out to the navy as well."

"I'd really like to be close to home. Where is this assignment?" Chris asked.

"That's the good news. It's at Nellis Air Force Base, near Las Vegas."

"Is there anything else in the pipeline for me?" Chris asked.

"Do you want to train pilots at the primary flight school in Pensacola?"

"You haven't given me much of a choice. Is there anything for me at Miramar?"

"Not at this time. We are getting the new F-14 Tomcat next year and Miramar will be where Marine pilots will train to fly it. You can do that after your tour with the air force."

"Okay, I'll fly with the air force and just suck it up for a year or so."

Chris flew to Las Vegas at the end of January, 1971. He was anxious to get settled so he could send for his son. He wanted to be a full-time father and the assignment to Nellis would be the best place to do it.

He checked into the BOQ and then went to the officer's club to get something to eat. As he walked through the bar area, he heard some sort of celebration taking place so he stopped to see what the commotion was about.

Apparently one of the F-111 squadrons was welcoming its new operations officer. Chris was handed a beer and told he was welcome to join them. The new operations officer was Maj. Dan Ryan. It couldn't be, he thought. Katie had a brother in the air force but he was a B-52 bomber pilot stationed in Guam.

Chris stayed at the club until he had the opportunity to speak with the major.

"Hello major, do you have a sister who is an air force nurse?" Chris asked.

"Yes, I do. Do you know her?" the major replied.

"Is she okay? The last word I received was that she was in the hospital at Clark Air Base."

"How well do you know her, Chris?"

"I met her at Da Nang last year and we sort of hit it off. She and I exchanged letters until September and then I never heard from her again," Chris replied.

"Do you know Maj. Roger Brown?" the major asked.

"That son of a bitch, I met him once. He was drunk and verbally abused your sister. Why do you ask?"

"Let's find a quiet spot. I have to tell you something that might upset you."

They found a secluded table in the bar.

"Brown stalked Katie for a few months. He was obsessed with her. She liked him at first but found out he was married. In a jealous rage one night he attacked her and sexually assaulted her in a horrific way. He beat her face and broke her cheek bone and her nose."

"That mother fucker, I hope they put him behind bars," Chris said.

"Yes, they did, he got 20 years at Leavenworth. However, before Katie fully recovered, she had to return to Da Nang to testify at his court martial. She had to relive the assault again. As a result, she isn't the Katie you knew."

"How has she changed, major?" Chris said sadly.

"She is withdrawn, won't allow any man, not even me, to touch her, she is depressed and is seeing a therapist. The air force put her on limited duty at first and now she works with expectant mothers at the base hospital. Hey, call me Dan,"

"I assume she won't be happy to see me since I'll remind her of Da Nang," Chris offered.

"I can't say, Chris. But she has spoken of you. She told my wife you were the nicest person she ever met and she loved you."

That comment made Chris feel a little better.

"So how did a B-52 pilot wind up here at the home of air force fighter pilots?"

"I told my commander about my sister and that I had to be stationed with her. After a lot of hand wringing, SAC let me go and I transitioned to the F-111. Katie is living with us now."

"Is there any chance I could see her soon?" Chris asked.

"My wife takes care of her daughter and our kids when Katie is on duty. I have to pick Annie up and take her over to Katie. Come with me and meet my family."

Dan introduced Chris to his wife and daughters. Annie looked like Katie, quite beautlful.

"So, you're the guy Katie fell in love with. If anyone can help her out of her traumatic experience and deep depression, you could be the right person," Shelly Ryan said.

"I want to be there for her, Shelly. I just don't want to freak her out since I met the creep who attacked her."

"Why don't we all visit with Katie. Chris, you wait until I tell Katie you are here before you present yourself. Let's see how she takes the news," Dan said.

Chris remained near the front door of Dan's house. Katie was in the kitchen and knelt down to greet her daughter. Dan told her he ran into Chris at the club and he's here to see her.

As soon as she spotted Chris, she put her hand to her mouth, started crying and said it wasn't her fault over and over again. Shelly tried to console her. Chris felt helpless but didn't approach Katie.

"I'm so sorry, Chris. It wasn't my fault. I feel so ashamed of what happened. How could you possibly want to be with me?" Katie said.

Chris's mouth was so dry he had trouble speaking.

"I love you Katie, I'm here now so we can be together as we wanted it to be," Chris whispered.

Katie continued to cry. Shelly took her to her bedroom. Dan took the girls into the living room and turned on the TV.

"I feel so inadequate, Dan. What can I possibly do for her?"

"Try to be patient. Perhaps seeing you will do some good. She's convinced herself that she did something wrong. Her therapist is working on that problem," Dan replied.

Dan told him they usually go to the club on Sunday for brunch. If Chris showed up around 10:30 in the morning, he'd invite him to their table He said they had to have reservations because the brunch was so popular with families.

Chris spent the evening at the club putting a few away. He was devastated by Katie's condition. Chris had to make her look to the future and not the past. However, he was certain she'd never forget the attack. Nevertheless, he felt it shouldn't control her life for the long term. Chris wasn't sure if he should be part of Katie's life until she fully recuperated. He had a restless night.

Dan spotted Chris on the buffet line and waved him over to his table.

Chris sat next to Shelly, out of view of Katie. He didn't talk much to anyone. In fact, he regretted showing up. He was uncomfortable.

After brunch the whole family walked back to Dan's house, a short distance from the club. Chris sidled up to Katie and bid her good morning.

"I think we should talk," Chris offered.

"What's there to talk about?" She countered.

"I suppose I'd like to talk about us," he replied.

"Chris, there is no us," she answered.

The conversation was going nowhere fast. He wasn't going to force himself into her life. He said good-bye to Katie and left. Perhaps it wasn't the best thing to do. Maybe she was testing him but he didn't want to be played. He couldn't afford any complications in his life since he was beginning a new assignment and needed a clear head.

9

MIG KILLERS

After eating a light breakfast, Chris walked into the Aggressor Squadron's operations building. He joined about a dozen air force pilots seated in the briefing room. People stared at him because he wore a Marine flight suit. Some of the pilots sitting in close proximity to him introduced themselves. Though no one asked, Chris knew they wondered why he was there.

The wing and squadron commanders entered the room. Everyone stood at attention. The wing commander began the presentation by welcoming the new pilots and telling them what the unit's mission was. As Chris listened, he noted a flaw in the purpose of the unit. It was supposed to train air force pilots in air combat tactics to fight enemy aircraft. Every adversary and potential adversary utilized various versions of the Soviet MiG fighter.

Chris was puzzled because training F-4 pilots to shoot down F-4 pilots was no different than the Navy's Top Gun school. The MiG aircraft had certain advantages over the F-4, as well as disadvantages.

Part way through the presentation, the Air Force Fighter Weapons Center's commanding officer entered the room. He reiterated what had previously been mentioned and summed up his comments by telling everyone they were handpicked for the squadron. Apparently. every pilot in the room had at least one kill in Vietnam. Some had more than one, and one pilot was an ace with five kills.

When the speakers completed their remarks, the general asked for questions. Only one hand was raised, it was a simple question that was easily answered. No one else had a question so Chris raised his hand.

"I understand we are training pilots in combat tactics to down enemy aircraft. How can we accomplish that by flying F-4s against F-4s? The mission seems more like the Navy's Top Gun school. Are we really training pilots to shoot down F-4s?"

Chris could see that the general was taken aback. Instead of answering Chris's question he asked what he would suggest. Everyone turned to Chris who was on the spot for an answer.

"The MiG is smaller, more maneuverable and can turn tighter than the F-4. Perhaps the aggressor aircraft should be smaller and more comparable to the MiG."

"Well captain, if we could procure a squadron of MiG fighters we would have done so, don't you agree?"

"Yes sir, but why not use what we have? We could use the smaller more agile F-5 to simulate a MiG," Chris replied.

The general didn't reply. Instead, he turned to the wing commander and spoke with him in hushed tones. A few pilots gave Chris the thumbs up.

"Are there any other questions or observations?" The wing commander asked as the general departed the room.

A few pilots voiced their support for Chris's recommendation.

"Over the next two weeks you will work on tactics to be employed by aggressor F-4 combat aircraft. You will be divided into two groups; one will work on aggressor tactics and the other on F-4 tactics. Let's assume for the moment that F-4s will be on both sides."

"I will post the two group lists in the morning. You were selected for each group based on you records, performance reports and recommendation by your respective wing commanders. This is a two-year assignment unless there is a compelling need for you to return to Vietnam," the squadron commander related.

"In about two weeks, the air force will announce the squadron's new mission. The following day we will host the media for a briefing and pilot interviews. Public affairs will provide guidance on what we can and can't discuss. Since you all have recorded at least on kill, be prepared to talk about it," the wing commander said.

"We are arranging a visit with the civilian-military community relations committee which has been a longtime supporter of the men and women here at Nellis. I'm sure you will be offered some opportunities to avail yourselves of the many attractions in Las Vegas. You can accept complimentary tickets for shows and dinners but you can't accept any tangible gift valued at more than $25," the squadron commander related.

"There are a lot of temptations in this city. I expect there will be no incidents involving any of you. It's easy to get into trouble especially with free drinks being served in the casinos. Did you I make myself clear?"

Everyone applied in the affirmative.

"One last thing, this evening there will be a no host bar reception for you and your wives followed by dinner at the club. This will be an opportunity for you to meet each other as well as some of the senior officers from the other squadrons. The Thunderbirds will also be there. Some of you have crossed paths over the years but many have not. Our Marine pilot doesn't know anyone, so be especially kind to him. By the way he is a Navy Top Gun graduate and was number one in his class, so watch your six o'clock. Are there any questions?"

"Sir, what's the dress code for this evening?"

"You should wear civilian clothes. Each one of you will be given a name tag to wear to facilitate introductions. We are one big team. The only competition will be between you and our students. This assignment is a great opportunity to assume a leadership role and to transfer the knowledge and skills you've acquired to other pilots who will leave this school for Southeast Asia."

As they were leaving the building, the air force's only pilot ace introduced himself to Chris. Maj. Richie Stevens thanked Chris for saving the life of one of his close friends in Vietnam.

"You helped him land at Da Nang when he was blinded after being hit by SAM fragments," Stevens said.

"I remember that very well. He did a great job landing his aircraft blind. How is he?" Chris asked.

"He regained his sight but not good enough to fly any longer. His weapons officer died of his wounds," Stevens added.

"What did you think of my comments? Was I out of order?" Chris asked.

"I agree with you. You can't train an F-4 pilot to kill MiG's by trying to kill an F-4. I was surprised the brass never thought of that. You were right by saying it wouldn't be anything different than the Navy's Top Gun School."

"I've been there, done that, no need to go through it again," Chris.

"I didn't know Marine pilots went to that school. The Marine pilots I knew in 'Nam flew ground support missions. How did you luck out?" Stevens asked.

"I'm still trying to figure that out. I had one kill while on a ground support sortie. One of our pilots lost his navigation system and flew into North Vietnam. I heard his distress call and went after him. By the time I reached him he had a MiG on his tail. I came up behind him and took him out with my cannons. We didn't have Sidewinders."

"I assume you weren't trained in air-to-air tactics," Stevens postured.

"We played around chasing each other but nothing serious. When I rotated back to the States, I was sent to Pensacola to qualify in F-4s. We had some combat air training and learned to fire Sidewinders. The rest of my class deployed to Southeast Asia but I was sent to Miramar to the Top Gun school. I certainly didn't have the experience the rest of the pilots had. Some pilots had several confirmed kills," Chris said.

"Is that why you were selected to come here?" Stevens asked.

"I'm not sure. My next assignment was to fly MiGCAP for a carrier group. I was lucky to get two more MiG's. I had 103 missions over the north. The only time I was nervous was when I had to land on the carrier. Someone forgot to check my records before I deployed to the fleet; I never had any carrier training. I made my first landing at sea, almost shit my pants."

Richie slapped him on the back and said he'd make sure they were in the same group.

"Do you want to be the instructor or the aggressor?" Stevens asked.

"I don't know, perhaps an aggressor as long as I'm not told to lose."

They both had a laugh as they entered the club for lunch.

"You will probably be the center of attention during tomorrow's press briefing. Do you think they want us to answer questions or will the commander handle it all?" Chris asked.

"I've been interviewed a few times since I came back. I think, if asked, we should focus on our role as instructors and not on our accomplishments," Richie offered.

"I'll probably get questions on why there is a Marine pilot in the squadron? I'll have to come up with something good," Chris said.

"If they expect us to show up tonight in a suit and tie, they will be disappointed," Richie said.

"I don't even own a suit," Chris said with a chuckle.

Chris returned to his quarters after lunch. He phoned Shelly Ryan to inquire about Katie. She told him what Katie said after they parted company on Sunday. Apparently, Katie doesn't want him to think things could return to normal in the near future. Katie hoped Chris would understand and if he wanted to find someone else, he should.

"Did she mention how she felt about me?" Chris asked.

No, but I asked her anyway. She said she can't think about it now," Shelly responded.

"Have you or Dan talked with her therapist?" Chris inquired.

"Dan had a meeting with her to give some background information on Katie, mostly family stuff. Dan was told Katie has a long way to go. She mistrusts men and is quite devoid of any emotions or feelings regarding sexual relationships. I'm sorry Chris, perhaps you should give up on her, besides you've only known her for a few days and that was months ago," Shelly offered.

"You are probably right, Shelly. Thank you and if anything changes, please let me know."

Chris called Mrs. Iverson to speak with Andy. She told him how well Andy was progressing in pre-school. Chris wanted to know when it would be best to take him to Las Vegas. Mrs. Iverson was hesitant and chose her words carefully.

"I think you should wait until you get your own place to live and then check on what schools would be nearby. Andy starts Kindergarten in the fall. Will you put him in day care when he's not in school?" She asked.

"I'd hate to do that. If I could find a nanny whom I could trust, I'd prefer that. I'll check it out. I won't take Andy until everything here is set for him. He should finish his pre-school before he comes here," Chris replied.

Mrs. Iverson seemed satisfied with those arrangements and didn't offer any resistance. Chris knew she would be heartbroken to let Andy go. Before she hung up, she mentioned the general was back and stationed at Quantico. She expected him to retire within a year.

The reception at the officer's club was a bit boring. Chris was only one of two pilots in the squadron who was single. At least three of the wives wanted to fix him up with friends or relatives. He told them he'd be interested but he probably didn't have the time unless they came to Las Vegas. He also mentioned he had a four-year-old son who would be living with him in a few months.

The following day there was a press briefing regarding the new squadron and its mission to train pilots for combat using instructors who had served in Southeast Asia and were credited with at least one confirmed kill. Each pilot was introduced to the press after the senior leaders gave their speeches. The public affairs officer moderated the question-and-answer part of the event. Most questions were directed to Major Richie Stevens, the only pilot ace in the group. Surprisingly no questions were directed to Chris who was thankful to dodge a bullet.

Lunch at the club for the squadron was hosted by the civilian-military affairs committee. The civilian co-chairman was a big real estate mogul who passed out business cards. He promised everyone a fair deal.

A sixtyish year-old woman approached Chris and took him aside to speak with him.

"Captain Harrington, I am Grace Abbot and I'm very pleased to meet you. I'm in the insurance business but I'm not trying to sell you anything, trust me. I noticed you aren't married or am I wrong?" She said.

Chris thought this was another matchmaker who wanted him to meet her daughter or granddaughter.

"You are correct, Grace, my wife passed away a few years ago," Chris replied.

"I'm sorry to hear that. I want to be quite delicate at the moment. Here is my sister's business card. I will call her and let her know to expect a visit from you."

"What line of business is she in?" He asked.

"She owns Polly's Ranch about 30 minutes north of here."

"I don't ride horses, Grace."

"It's not that kind of ranch young man. It's a legitimate brothel and it's very high class. It's better than what you will be introduced to in Las Vegas," she said with a wink.

Chris thought about it for a second and then told her to let Polly know he'd see her on the following weekend. Why he said that? He didn't have a clue but one visit might be fun. During the luncheon, Chris collected about a dozen business cards from car dealers, furniture stores, investment bankers and a few from Casino public relations folks.

The squadron was divided into two groups; instructors and aggressors. Richie was the team leader for the aggressors, the team Chris was assigned to. Each team spent the rest of the week planning the details of their respective roles. Richie said he heard the squadron would get four F-5 aircraft as soon as they were painted with specific markings as aggressors.

On Friday night, Chris went to a few casinos to play blackjack. He started with $100 and lost all but $30 in less than an hour. He took his lumps, then hit the slots and won a $2,000 jackpot. He returned to the blackjack table and eventually won $11,000.

On Saturday, he looked for a two-bedroom apartment near the base. He also made a down payment on a new truck.

He called Polly to get directions. She was pleased he decided to visit. She told him his drinks would be on the house but he'd have to pay for any other treats. He arrived around six in the evening. The building didn't look like much from the outside. There were a few trailers parked at the rear of the building. Once inside, he was surprised at the opulence of the place. There were lots of gold fixtures, crystal chandeliers, leather furniture and beautiful women. The women weren't allowed to approach anyone entering the building. After he walked inside, a hostess gave him a 'menu' with the picture of each girl and their particular specialties.

Chris asked to speak with Polly. The hostess escorted him to her office where she was seated behind an oversized desk smoking a cigar.

"You must be Chris. My sister said you were very handsome and she was damn right. Please sit down, I'd like to discuss something with you."

Chris sat in an overstuffed velvet chair. She offered him a cigar which he declined.

"You don't look like someone who needs to come here to find a partner. I'm sure you could find many nice girls in Vegas. My sister said she didn't think you'd be looking for working girls, but here you are."

"I was just curious, Polly. I love women and I'm not the shy type. What do you want to discuss?" Chris asked.

"Many women show up here looking for work. I am very particular about who works here. I am good at picking the right ones. From time to time I get young girls, some underage who think this is the life for them. I know it's not the right place for young inexperienced girls. A month ago, a 19-year-old beauty showed up for a job. I liked her very much. She was abused as a young girl and had problems in relationships with men. She thought this environment would help her in some way. So, I gave her a job as a cocktail waitress to help her with her ability to communicate with our customers. She received numerous offers but I wouldn't allow it. She's not on the menu."

Chris had a hunch Polly was a matchmaker and he was one side of the match.

"I'd like you to meet with Chelsea and speak with her. You seem like a compassionate guy who might be able to talk sense to her. She doesn't belong here, Chris," Polly asserted.

"How should I introduce myself and would she speak with me?" Chris asked.

"Tell her you are a friend of mine and that I wanted her to speak with you about her future. That might work, after all she works for me," Polly replied.

"Can I sit at the bar and have a drink before I meet her?"

"Of course, and I'll arrange a quiet place for you two to talk. I have an empty room this evening."

Chris sat at the bar and watched a football game. Most of the men in the room were either at the bar or sitting in the 'parlor' waiting for their menu selection to appear. Not a very busy place for a Saturday night. The women who had not been selected yet were seated in various places talking to each other. He spotted a real good-looking dark-haired girl; she was young and reminded him of Katie. He didn't mean to stare at her but he did and she returned his stare. Unfortunately, the house rules stated she wasn't allowed to approach the customers.

Twenty minutes later, Polly came by with Chelsea in tow. She introduced Chris as a good friend who wanted to chat with her. She told her to take Chris to her trailer. That didn't sound right to Chris.

Chelsea opened the door to her trailer, sat on the bed, and started to undress. Chris told her to wait until they got to know each other better.

"Apparently you are new to this type of entertainment," Chris said.

"You are my first client, I'm a bit nervous," she said.

"You don't have to rush into anything. Sometimes your client can be nervous as well, so take it slow," he said.

"Are you nervous, Chris?" She asked.

"I'm not a client. I just want to speak with you," he responded.

"I'm not sure about this," Chelsea said a bit unnerved.

Chris was beginning to lose the initiative to gain her confidence.

"Chelsea, Polly likes you a lot. She doesn't believe you belong in a place like this. I understand you want to make a lot of money and you may think this is the best way to do it. Do you really want to prostitute yourself at such a young age?"

"I want to go to college to become a nurse, that's why I'm here," she replied.

"Where are you from?" He asked.

"I'm from Utah. I left last year because my father wanted me to marry his cousin. I was sexually abused by my older brother and I had to get away," she said.

"Why come to Nevada and why to this place?"

"My girlfriend moved here with her family and offered me a place to stay for a while. I told her my plans for college and we decided this might be the best way to earn a lot of money in a short period of time."

"Do you have any younger brothers or sisters?"

"Yes, I have one younger brother and two sisters."

"Did you care for them at all, other than babysit? Do you like little kids?"

"Yes of course I do, what are you getting at?" She asked.

"If you could go to college without doing this, would you be open to another solution?"

"I don't know. What do you have in mind? Why should I trust you, I don't even know you, Chris?" She said looking a bit scared.

"Okay. Hear me out please before you answer. I am a fighter pilot based in Las Vegas. I am a single father of a four-year-old boy. I need a full-time live-in nanny. If you would consider my offer, I will pay for your college tuition as long as you are taking care of my son. There are no strings attached. You would have your own bedroom and privacy," Chris offered.

He never planned on doing this. It came to him as he was trying to win her confidence.

"I don't know what to say. No man has ever been kind to me. I don't know if I could live up to your expectations," she said as she began to cry.

"You don't have to give me an answer now. Talk it over with Polly. I'll call her in a few days and if you accept my offer, I'll pick you up next weekend."

Chris thought it was a fair offer. He didn't know if they could live under the same roof but he needed someone for Andy. He also thought it was a way to save her from a terrible life. He hoped she'd see it that way.

"Thank you, Chris. I have a lot of thinking to do. I know you and Polly mean well. I'm just not sure what to do."

"Well look at it this way, and I hate to be so blunt, but would you rather take care of a sweet little boy, or sleep with several gross men every day that may or may not be kind to you?"

She stared at him without saying anything. She probably visualized his graphic comments.

10

NEXT PHASE

The second week with the Aggressor Squadron was more interesting. The two groups of pilots were told to develop their own scenarios for training based on certain specific requirements. The F-4 pilots had a tougher assignment since they would train less experienced pilots in air-to-air combat, whereas Chris's group just had to keep out of their crosshairs.

On Wednesday, Chris and four other aggressor pilots flew to California to pick up five new F-5 fighters that would become part of the Aggressor Squadron. Once the word got out, all of Chris's cohorts thought he had some influence on the decision to use the F-5 as the aggressor fighter which was comparable to the MiG-21. The truth was the air force had planned to use it, but not so soon, Chris's comments might have impacted the timeline.

The five pilots boarded a small air force passenger jet and flew to California. They were scheduled to spend three days for familiarization with the aircraft. Since they were given time off until the following morning, Chris rented a car and visited his son in San Diego.

Chris was pleased his son was growing up so fast and was a pretty smart kid. He discussed the possibility of hiring a nanny with Mrs. Iverson. She was concerned and professed he should look for another wife. Chris would have preferred that as well but Katie was no longer a viable candidate, at least for the foreseeable future.

Chris returned to the Northrup facility in time to attend a two-hour classroom session on the F-5. After lunch, each of the five pilots got a check ride in a two-seat trainer version of the aircraft. Chris really liked its maneuverability and believed no F-4 pilot could keep up with it. Each of the five single seat F-5s the pilots flew to Nellis AFB, were painted in camouflage but had distinct black tails with red stars on each side.

On Friday morning, they took off at eight and headed to Las Vegas. They decided to fly over the flight line at low altitude and then land. The flyover certainly got everyone's attention along the flight line. They landed and taxied past the Thunderbird squadron, opened their canopies and saluted the men and women who came out to see them. Once in place in front of the Aggressor Squadron's operations building, they were met by the rest of the squadron. Everyone commented on the paint job and how small the F-5 was compared to the F-4.

Chris remembered he never got back to Polly about Chelsea. He called her later that day and was informed Chelsea turned down his offer and was planning on living with her friend's family until she got a job. Chris had a mixed reaction but was pleased she decided to leave Polly's Ranch.

Chris called Dan to check up on Katie.

"She's doing much better, Chris. Her therapist has apparently had some success and told me she is putting the incident behind her as best she can. We are encouraged. Katie even mentioned this morning that she'd like to see you again."

"That's great news. I want to see her as well but I doubt she'd want to do it alone. Can we all get together?" Chris asked.

"I'll speak with my wife, perhaps we can have a barbeque at the house on Sunday," Dan replied.

"I've moved off base into my own apartment. I was thinking of hiring a nanny to take care of my son. I don't know how feasible that is but I want him to live with me."

"I understand, that's a good decision. Please don't give up on Katie. I think she needs you in her life. Take it slow and let her make up her mind without any pressure."

Chris agreed that it would be foolish to push Katie so soon.

11

TRY AGAIN

Chris was very nervous as he drove onto the base. He went over and over again how to behave with Katie. Regardless of her actions or words, he had to remain calm and smile. Whatever the original attraction to each other was, sex was no longer part of it.

Shelly met him at the door. He handed her a bouquet of flowers and kissed her on the cheek. He placed a bottle of wine on the kitchen counter and followed the conversations to the backyard of the house. Dan greeted him and introduced him to his neighbors. Everyone there was either married or with their significant other. Katie's daughter and Dan's two girls were off to the side playing with a few other children their age.

When Chris made eye contact with Katie, he smiled and approached her.

"It's so nice to see you again Katie. How are you?"

"I'm so happy you came. I missed you and I'm sorry for what I said to you the last time I saw you," she said.

Chris thought she really meant it. However, had she really turned the corner or was it just a temporary moment of contrition? She stood very close to him. If he moved his head forward three inches, he could have kissed her forehead. Chris wanted to take her in his arms but he stood there frozen in fear of spooking her.

"Would you like something to drink?" She asked.

"I suppose I could do with a cold beer. I'll get it, what about you?"

"I'm fine, Chris. Can we go inside and talk a while?" She asked.

He nodded. Perhaps things had changed for the better. Would a relationship with Katie always be overshadowed by the memories of her assault? Chris recalled that he was very tolerant over Camille's condition and accepted her illness. Could he muster up the same patience with Katie? He didn't like having to walk on eggshells in fear of stirring up a hornet's nest.

They sat on the couch. It was difficult for either one of them to begin the conversation. The words stuck in Chris's throat like a piece of popcorn. When she looked into his eyes, he felt compelled to say something.

"I'm not sure where to begin, Katie. I love you and I want you in my life. I've envisioned the two of us raising Annie and Andy together. I have a two-bedroom apartment near the base. I'm going to bring Andy to Las Vegas as soon as school is over in San Diego," Chris said.

"I had those same desires last summer when you returned to your ship. Even though we only knew each other for less than 48 hours, I fell in love with you. I want those dreams to return and I'm trying very hard, Chris," she said through tears.

"I'm a very patient man, Katie. When you are ready to take the next step, I'll be there for you. We have two wonderful children who need our love and attention and they must come first in any decisions we make," Chris responded.

"What is the next step for us, Chris?"

He wasn't prepared for that question. He took a deep breath and prayed he had an appropriate answer.

"I want to spend more time with you each week, if you'd like that."

"Yes, I would. I know it's old fashioned, but I'd like to go out on a date," she said laughing.

"What time do I have to bring you home?" He said with a smile.

He wanted to reach out to touch her hand but he kept to himself. He held his emotions in check. He hoped she knew he was on his best behavior. Annie came into the room and jumped into his lap.

"Hello, Chris, I missed you," she said.

Katie laughed and then cried. She probably realized her daughter needed a father and the sooner the better.

"I think Annie likes you. Chris. She has good instincts about you. I guess she got it from me," Katie teased.

"Unfortunately, Andy never really knew his mother. He's lived with his grandmother for nearly four years. I hope he makes the adjustment without complications," Chris replied.

Katie seemed more relaxed around him than before. They got along quite well considering they hardly knew each other. He didn't know when to tell her he liked to gamble and went to the casinos every Friday night. It was a vice, but he wasn't addicted to it. He decided to tell her another time.

"How long will you remain in the air force?" Chris asked.

"I haven't thought about it. I hope to stay here as long as possible. If I don't like my next assignment, I'll get out. I could make so much more as a civilian nurse. What about you? Are you a lifer?"

"Once my son is living with me, I don't want to move. I've had some ideas about my next adventure but I'm not ready to discuss it. To answer your question, I'm not a lifer," Chris replied.

They left the living room and joined the rest of the guests in the backyard. Shelly looked at Chris for some sign that things went well. He just smiled. The rest of the evening Chris and Katie were preoccupied with other folks, though they often looked at each other from afar. The magic was slowly creeping in again, at least Chris thought so.

The Aggressor Squadron's pilots remained in small working groups creating a syllabus that had to be approved by Tactical Air Command headquarters. In the meantime, no one flew the F-5s. Some of the pilots got a few hours in the F-4 since it was required to maintain proficiency. Later in the third week, Northrup Grumman employees delivered three addition F-5s, one of which was a two-seat trainer. By the end of the fourth week, all eight aggressor pilots qualified to fly the aircraft.

Chris's luck at black jack and at the craps table continued. After four trips to the casinos, Chris was ahead by over $17,000. That didn't include the money he won the first time he gambled. He made sure to gamble at different casinos so he wouldn't be on anyone's radar as a possible card counter. When it came to craps, he was just plain lucky.

Chris and Katie went out on 'dates' on two occasions since the party at Dan's house. They had dinner and went to the movies. They didn't do much more than hold hands. Chris was concerned that it was slowly becoming a platonic relationship. He really didn't know what to do about moving forward in a romantic relationship. He hoped she'd eventually take charge of the situation but Katie might be gun-shy. He just didn't want to blow it with a stupid or feeble effort to move to the next level.

The Aggressor Squadron commander approved the training syllabus but before he sent it to headquarters for approval, he wanted the pilots to test it. For two weeks, the F-4 and F-5 pilots engaged in mock combat scenarios over the vast desert area north of the air base. It was obvious the F-5 was a good match for the F-4. Most of the F-5 pilots won their air-to-air engagements, Chris never lost.

Tactical Air Command headquarters made some modifications to the syllabus by adding some complexity to each scenario. They fully realized the F-4 was not the best fighter for close air-to-air combat, but rather its advantage was its acceleration and ability to win with standoff weapons like the Aim-9 Sidewinder missile. Based on what Phantom pilots achieved in Vietnam, it was obvious how best to use the aircraft other than to drop bombs.

The changes to the original plan put the F-5 at a disadvantage since the F-4 wasn't allowed to engage it in close air-to-air combat. Chris thought it was a waste of training dollars to have F-4 pilots fire missiles at a standoff range. Besides, it would be the weapons officer in the backseat who would do the job. As he saw it, the F-5 was merely a moving target on a radar acquisition scope.

Chris was discouraged. He didn't accept the assignment just to become a target. He had to come up with a few ideas of his own on how to evade an air-to-air missile. However, the rules of engagement would probably not permit deviations from the script.

Chris and Katie were getting to know more about each other since most of their time together was spent talking about themselves. There were no references to what occurred in Vietnam and Chris refrained from discussing moving in together.

It was obvious to Dan and Shelly that Katie was a different person since Chris came back into her life. However, Chris still felt as though there was a barrier between them and he shouldn't try to climb over it. He was getting a little impatient especially since Andy would be living with him in three months. He wanted his ready-made family to live under one roof even if he and Katie slept in separate bedrooms.

Chris continued to gamble every Friday night. Though he lost money every once and a while, he was still ahead by about $25,000. He hadn't told Katie of his 'hobby' fearing she might disapprove.

While waiting for Katie to come to terms with their relationship, Chris felt a need to avail himself of some of the pleasures available in Las Vegas. Having his sexual desires satisfied by working girls was a lot safer than dating someone other than Katie; fewer complications.

Chris thought about his double life as a gambler and as an unfaithful companion with respect to what impact either or both would have on his relationship with Katie. He expected to give up gambling once he and Katie lived together. That day, he believed, was a long way off.

After a month of innocent dating, Katie took Chris's hand as they walked into a movie theater. It was the first time she had reached out to touch him since he last saw her in Vietnam the previous summer. Once seated in the theater, she did it again. This simple act could be the beginning of her healing process. Chris decided to follow her lead wherever it took them.

One day, during a telephone conversation, Katie asked who would take care of Andy when he came home from school. Chris was unprepared for the question. He said he thought of hiring a nanny but hadn't done anything about it yet. She didn't follow up after he replied. He really wanted to tell her he would like her to move in with him but that wouldn't solve the problem of child care.

"Did you ever think about leaving the air force next year?" Chris asked out of the blue.

Her response was startling.

"Is that what you want, Chris? Do you want me to be a full-time mom for two children?"

Chris didn't know which way to go with his answer. He sucked it up and merely said it was something he thought about.

"I've given it some thought as well. Does that surprise you?" She asked.

"As a matter of fact, it does. I really believe it could work but I won't push it until you are ready," he replied.

Katie didn't continue the discussion. She mentioned a show she'd like to see at the Riviera Hotel. Chris said he'd look into it and make reservations.

After the conversation, Chris thought they were making progress in their relationship. Perhaps he was being foolish to believe Katie would leave the air force to become a full-time mom but it would be something he'd like to happen.

Over the next several weeks, the Aggressor Squadron finalized its training syllabus. The selection of aggressor school attendees had begun. The first contingent of pilots had no combat experience; their results would become the benchmark for the following classes. The F-5 pilots had been instructed to take evasive action but not to turn the tables on the F-4 pilots, until later in the program. Chris was anxious for the day to come when he could go after an F-4 to demonstrate the air force needed a more capable fighter to be successful against the smaller, more agile MiG-21, and future MiG variations.

12

ADDICTED

Chris's once a week trek to the casinos became twice a week. He took added risks by betting more money on each turn of the card and roll of the dice. His losses went from a few hundred a night to several thousand. He also won large sums. He became addicted to gambling and to the charms of working girls.

Chris realized his downward spiral after he missed a few phone calls from Katie. She was concerned that he lost his patience with her. Unfortunately, she didn't know the truth until her brother mentioned something to her. He heard from mutual friends that Chris spent the early morning hours on the weekend at the casinos. Katie blamed herself for taking too much time during her recovery. She questioned herself, what was she afraid of? Chris certainly loved her and showed no signs of having interest in any other women. If he had, she wouldn't blame him.

The truth was that Chris was bored playing a rabbit for the Aggressor Squadron. If it weren't for Katie, he'd have asked the Marine Corps for a new assignment. His rationale was simple. Whatever he gained from his experience wouldn't help Marine pilots. It had been three years since he was assigned to a Marine aviation unit and he missed it.

His excuse for gambling was shrouded in feeling sorry for himself. He also thought of resigning and doing something else, though he loved the Corps as much as anything except for Andy. Military life wasn't the greatest career for a family man, especially for a single father.

It was no surprise that Chris seemed preoccupied with those thoughts even when he was with Katie. One evening when Chris fell silent, Katie decided to confront him.

"Chris, I know there is something bothering you. Perhaps I'm to blame but I have to know what's troubling you."

He realized it was time to tell her about his addiction and his frustration with his job, but he didn't want to say anything to hurt her.

"I have become addicted to gambling out of boredom and frustration. It used to be sort of a hobby and now it's a serious thing. I don't want to stop because I'm fairly good at it," he admitted.

"If your son were living with you, would you still gamble?" She asked.

"I thought about that, Katie. I'd hope I'd have the will to stop".

"What about me? Would you stop for me and Annie?"

Chris felt a pang in his chest. If he said yes, it might force her to move in with him but he didn't want to put her under that kind of pressure. If he said no, their relationship had no future. He chose his words carefully.

"I gamble to fill a void in my life. I have a son that I rarely see, I have a woman in my life I can barely touch, and I have a job that is frustrating. I don't want you to worry, I can handle my problem. I love you very much. I just want you to know that. Of course, I'd love to have all the people I cherish living under one roof someday. I pray for that all the time. As far as my job is concerned, it will end one day and I'll get to do something else."

She looked at him with sadness on her face, but didn't respond.

"I hope I've answered your question. I don't want to talk about it now," he said.

"You never really invited Annie and me to live with you. I know the subject came up but nothing came of it. Is that what you want, Chris?"

"Yes, more than anything else."

"I gave it a lot of thought and consideration the last few weeks. My decision has nothing to do with what you told me about your addiction. I'm ready to take the next step, not just for me but for Annie, Andy and you. I love you Chris, I really do and I'm sorry if my behavior has contributed to your need to gamble to fill the void in your life."

As they stood in front of Katie's house, Chris wanted to kiss her but held back. Surprisingly she leaned in to him and kissed him gently on the lips. He hesitantly put his arms around her. She didn't pull away.

"I feel safe with you," she whispered.

"I don't want to let go of you," he responded.

Since Chris didn't know when she wanted to move in with him, he suggested she visit his apartment to decide if she'd like to live there.

"Can we see it tomorrow after work?" She asked.

"Of course, but don't mention anything about my housekeeping."

"I'll bring Annie and see if she likes it."

Chris was pleased and held her in his arms until she took a step back, kissed him again and then went inside the house.

Chris was anxious to show Katie his apartment. He hoped she'd like it and if she didn't, they could look for a new one. It had two master bedrooms, with two double beds, each with its own master bath. The kitchen was large and modern. It was better than the room she lived in at her brother's house.

Katie was very talkative as they drove to the apartment. Chris thought she was nervous since she was usually quiet. When he opened the apartment door, she was very surprised and said it was great. Annie ran around looking for something to play with. Then she ran into Chris's bedroom.

"Is this where daddy sleeps?" She asked.

Katie, seemingly embarrassed, blushed and covered her eyes.

"I didn't say anything to her, honest, Chris. She just assumed you were her daddy."

"I'm good with that, Katie. I've been called a lot worse but I am honored to be called daddy. Maybe someday it will be true," he responded.

She snuggled up to him and he embraced her.

"Let's see your bedroom Annie," Katie said.

Annie ran into the other bedroom and jumped on one of the beds.

"This one is mine, mommy," she exclaimed.

Katie surmised that Chris would have Andy in his room and she would stay with Annie. Much to Chris's surprise she had another idea.

"Do you think we could make this a kid's room, Chris?"

Chris didn't expect to sleep with Katie for a few days or even weeks after she moved in. He was unprepared for the question. She must have put her devastating physical and mental assault behind her.

"Whatever will make you happy, Katie. I don't want to rush you."

"Are you saying you don't want me to rush you?" She teased.

"Just having you here with me is enough but if you insist, I think it would make a wonderful kid's room," Chris quipped.

They discussed finding an adequate school for Andy and Annie. Since Katie didn't have a car, Chris offered to buy one for her. Neither Chris nor Katie had a definitive nine-to-five schedule so they would have to keep in touch several times a day about picking up their children.

"It sounds like we are already a couple with kids and we haven't even slept together yet," Katie said laughing.

"I think we can remedy that enigma soon," Chris replied.

Katie called her sister-in-law to tell her that she and Chris were taking Annie out to dinner and would be back in a few hours. Shelly was full of questions about her decision to move in with Chris. While they were chatting, Chris spent time with Annie who kept referring to him as daddy.

Chris didn't fly many hours over the next two weeks. The new pilots were going through the early syllabus flying with instructors in the F-4s chasing each other over the Nevada desert.

Once they learned the basic combat air-to-air attack tactics, the next phase was to survive an enemy attack. The F-4 pilots, spent the next two weeks trying to shoot down the F-5. In close encounters, the F-5 was superior in its capability to maneuver and to maintain contact. However, in a situation where the AIM-9 was employed, the F-4 prevailed. It had greater speed and if it could get enough separation to turn back on its aggressor it could get a kill.

In Chris's opinion, some of the students were quite capable, somewhat comparable to the Navy's newer fleet pilots. Regardless of their individual skills, Chris was never shot down. The squadron commander offered any F-4 pilot an incentive to get Chris so it became their sole purpose every day. They even ganged up on him, two and three to one but Chris managed to elude them.

Katie and Annie moved in with Chris three weeks before he flew to

San Diego to pick up Andy. Chris was hesitant to tell Mrs. Iverson about Katie even though Camille had been gone for nearly four years. It would be stressful enough to see Andy leave so Chris decided not to mention Katie. He discussed his feelings with Katie who agreed with his decision not to tell her.

"You know, Andy will want to speak to his grandmother and will likely tell her about Annie and you," Chris said.

"If he doesn't tell her he's living with us, then it would be okay. I think you should be prepared to provide an explanation if he does mention it," Katie wisely said.

Katie didn't sleep in the same room with Chris. She was concerned Annie would be scared sleeping in a new room alone after being with her mother in the same room. Chris suggested she spend a few nights with Annie and perhaps when she fell asleep, she could join him.

The third night in the new apartment, Katie crawled in beside Chris. He turned and faced her. He was aroused before they even kissed. The both slipped out of what they were wearing. Chris began to kiss her gently.

"Let me know if you want me to stop," he said.

"Don't stop, I want you so much," she whispered.

Needless to say, their love making was the most fulfilling experience. It was a long-awaited consummation of their emotional feelings manifested in a long sensuous love making ritual. She cried with happiness and relief. Chris held Katie in his arms as they slept and never changed his position.

When daylight punched at Chris's eyes, he opened them to find Annie standing by his side of the bed.

"Where's mommy?" She asked.

Chris thought perhaps Annie never saw her mother in bed with a man before. He didn't know what her reaction would be. Before he answered, Katie raised her head.

"I'm over here sweetie, come to mommy."

Annie jumped on the bed, crawled over Chris and laid down beside her mother. Both Chris and Katie were stark naked, it was awkward for Chris. He carefully reached under the bed for his underwear and carefully slipped them on. He had to pee so much but he didn't want Annie to see him in his underwear. He mimed to Katie to cover Annie's eyes and then made a mad dash for the bathroom. After he relieved himself and brushed his teeth, he put on his robe and returned.

"Come with me, Annie and I'll make you breakfast. What do you want to eat, sweetheart"?

"Why is mommy in your bed?" She asked.

Chris and Katie were stumped for an answer.

"We were discussing what to do on the weekend. What would you like to do, sweetie?" Katie said, winking at Chris.

"I want to go to the circus," she exclaimed.

"The circus isn't in Las Vegas this weekend," Katie replied.

"Yes, it is. My friends go to the circus all the time," Annie replied.

"You are right, Annie, there is always a circus here at Circus-Circus hotel", Chris said.

"Is that true, Chris? I thought it was just the name of a hotel," Katie said.

"Yes, there are always great circus acts inside the hotel and it's free."

Chris took Annie by the hand and left for the kitchen. Katie popped out of bed and ran to the bathroom. Chris heard her yell to put the seat down next time; he was just like her brother, she thought.

Over the next few nights, Katie returned to Chris's bed after Annie fell asleep. Neither of them had a clue what to tell Annie about the new sleeping arrangement. They decided to wait until Andy arrived to announce who slept in which bed.

Chris was anxious to finally be able to have his son with him. He understood it would be a great adjustment for him. He was moving to a new home with two strangers who might become his new family. Chris was relieved he didn't have to fly very much and when he did it was for less than two hours each time.

In early June, Chris left for San Diego to bring his son to Las Vegas. He was nervous. He didn't know how to handle Andy if he became upset. However, since Andy was five years old, Chris thought he could reason with him. Mrs. Iverson had become the one constant in Andy's life so leaving her could be a problem.

Surprisingly, Andy seemed shy when Chris approached him. He was told his father was taking him to live in his home. Mrs. Iverson mentioned that Andy was a bit upset to leave her but she promised to visit him often. Chris spent the night so Andy could adjust to his father whom he hadn't seen for several months. The following day, Chris decided to take a taxi to the airport rather than have his mother-in-law drive. It would make it easier to say good-bye. Mrs. Iverson seemed determined not to show any emotions fearing she would upset Andy.

Chris's decision paid off. Andy cried at first but by the time they got to the airport, he was excited about flying for the first time. Andy behaved himself on the short flight. Chris drove to his apartment anticipating a big reception, but when he arrived, no one was there. He called Katie's brother's house hoping to find her. She answered the phone but wasn't very talkative. Chris was concerned. What went wrong?

Katie explained she thought it would be best if he and Andy spent a night or two alone in the apartment. She thought there could be too much confusion with two other people around. Chris didn't agree but he didn't argue with her. In a way Chris was relieved. So, Chris Harrington and son spent two days getting to know each other. The only problem Chris had was that Andy wanted to sleep in the bed next to his father. It was the same problem Katie had with Annie. It was something they had to figure out soon.

Chris was enjoying being a father to Andy. He didn't know much about being a father since his dad died when he was Andy's age. He decided to take it one day at a time. On Sunday, Dan invited Chris and Andy for dinner. He suggested it might be a good way for Andy to get to know Annie and his two girls. Chris thanked him and said his son needed to be around kids his own age.

On the way to Dan's house, Andy asked a lot of questions about the people he would meet. When Chris gave him the names of the three girls, he was disappointed there were no boys there.

When Dan greeted them at the door, Andy suddenly acted shy and clung to his father's trousers. Shelly introduced herself and her daughters. Andy tried to hide behind his father's leg. Katie came over and kissed

Chris on the check and spoke to Andy. She coaxed him out from behind his father and took him by the hand.

"Sorry Shelly, I didn't know he preferred dark haired girls."

"Wait until he grows up, he'll chase after all the blond girls," Shelly said with a laugh.

Chris noted that Katie was sitting on the floor with Annie and Andy. There was some interaction between the two children which made Chris feel a lot better. As Chris approached them, Annie pointed to him.

"That's my daddy," she screamed out.

Annie ran to Chris and gave him a big hug. He picked her up and kissed her. He looked out the corner of his eye to see Andy's reaction.

"He's my daddy, not your daddy", Andy exclaimed.

Chris picked him up and held both of them in his arms.

"You are right, Andy, I am your daddy but Annie wants me to be her daddy too. Is that okay with you?"

Andy looked down thinking of what to say. He looked at Annie and then to Chris and nodded yes.

Chris took a deep breath while contemplating his next comment.

"Katie wants to be your mommy. Do you want her to be your mommy?"

"I want to go home," Andy said.

"Let me handle this, Chris. You are moving too fast," Katie said.

She took Andy and Annie to the bedroom and closed the door. She must have been there at least 20 minutes. When they emerged, Andy ran to his father.

"Can Katie and Annie live with us, daddy?" He asked

Chris looked at Katie in bewilderment.

"Of course, they can, Andy. Do you like Annie and Katie?"

He nodded yes. The two of them ran to join Shelly's kids.

"What did you say to him? I'm amazed at how quickly you were able to do that," Chris asked.

"It's just a mother's instinct, besides I had child psychology courses in nursing school."

"Does this mean you are coming home with me tonight?"

"If you promise to spend time with the children and make sure they are asleep before we go to bed," she responded," Katie replied.

"It sounds as though that will be a nightly routine."

Katie left to pack the few things she brought for the weekend. The four of them left after dinner to begin a new life together.

When they arrived at the apartment, the phone rang. It was Mrs. Iverson asking about Andy. Chris never mentioned Katie or Annie and he knew Andy would spill the beans. He took the initiative to tell her about his new girlfriend and her daughter but didn't mention they were all living together.

Thankfully, Andy didn't mention it either, he probably didn't know or realize it would be a permanent situation. Chris got back on the phone to say goodbye. She mentioned that her husband was getting his third star and was assigned to Marine Corps headquarters. It would probably be his last assignment. She provided his phone number and suggested he call the general.

Katie and Chris spent nearly two hours getting the children ready for bed and another hour making sure they were asleep. Katie kept her fingers crossed they would stay put.

Unfortunately for the two lovers, Katie started her period. Though she offered to pleasure Chris, he declined so they fell asleep in each other's arms.

Over the next several months, life was great for the new family. Andy went to kindergarten, Annie to pre-school and Katie returned to her nursing duties with new motivation and enthusiasm. They married without fanfare at a small chapel in Las Vegas.

Thanksgiving was spent at Katie's brother's house where the two sisters-in-law prepared a sumptuous meal. Dan delivered solemn news when he announced one of the F-111 squadrons was being deployed to Vietnam and he was included in the group as the squadron commander because of his previous combat experience.

Chris was very upset by this news since the war was about to end, at least for American participation. The country had its fill of the nearly ten-year involvement in a war run by politicians and not generals. He wondered if he'd get the call to return as well.

Two weeks later, Chris was notified he was being sent TDY for 180 days to Da Nang AB. Apparently, the ground war had become untenable due to the large influx of North Vietnamese troops crossing into the south. They were accompanied by artillery and tanks as well as anti-aircraft weapons. The Marines needed constant air support to maintain their positions. The number of experienced pilots available to support the troops was down from several years earlier. Chris was an experienced combat close air support pilot and though he hated to serve as a bomb dropper rather than a MIG killer, he knew he was needed.

This was devastating news for Katie who was just beginning to put her past troubles behind her. She had to become both mom and dad to two young children. Before Chris deployed in January, 1972, he managed to move his family into base housing for convenience and to be supportive to Dan's wife and their two children. Chris left in mid-January, a week after Dan's squadron deployed.

When Chris arrived at Da Nang, he was greeted by a friend of his who was now the squadron commander. Eric Collins, a newly minted lieutenant colonel, was in Chris's F-8 squadron in Da Nang on his first Vietnam tour of duty.

"You are a sight for sore eyes, Chris. You are the most experienced combat pilot in this squadron. Most of our guys are experiencing combat for the first time," Collins reported.

"Where are the veterans these days?"

"A few are here but many left the Corps. You will be my wingman starting tomorrow. Our job is much tougher now than a few years ago. Our troops are not moving forward any longer and are having a tough time holding their positions. The NVA has flooded into I Corps with heavy armor and weapons. We see a lot of anti-aircraft activity," Collins said.

"Are we losing this damned war, sir?"

"I think we lost it a few months ago. Congress wants to defund the war so it looks like we may be going home before long," Collins added.

The commander further stated the new guys seemed eager but lacked the perspective of what transpired since 1968. He cautioned Chris to become a role model and not show his disdain for the war. He said they flew twice a day almost every day to support the ground troops.

Chris went to his quarters, a Quonset hut with air conditioning, took a shower, and fell asleep. He managed to get to the chow hall before it closed. The next morning, earlier than he expected, he strapped into the cockpit of an F-4 ready for his first of many support missions. He'd rather be chasing MiG-19's but none operated over South Vietnam.

The terrain below was pock marked with B-52 bomb craters from just north of the base to the DMZ. A Marine platoon was isolated on a hilltop and couldn't be pulled out until the enemy units were destroyed. Collins took his squadron over the target area to point out where the friendlies were dug in. He told his pilots everything around their position was fair game. The squadron split into two flights, one south and one north of the platoon's position. They dropped fragmentation bombs on the first run and napalm on the second as the enemy left their positions.

Once the bomb runs were completed, helicopters came in to pick up the Marines, some of whom were wounded. The squadron remained for a while to cover the helicopters during the evacuation.

"Scratch another hard-won piece of real estate," Collins told Chris.

"It's just a useless hilltop," Chris replied.

"Perhaps, but a lot of Marines died to take it; we won't be back."

Chris was discouraged. In 1968, he supported Marine units that were on the offensive and now he had to protect their withdrawal. The next two months were no different. No Marine units were moving forward, grabbing new real estate. Most were just hanging on to their forward operating bases under withering enemy attacks.

Chris's weapon's officer was a young Marine first lieutenant who was on his first tour. He looked up to Chris though he was only three years younger. Chris felt he was too nervous before each mission because he talked a lot before they took off. Chris preferred silence so he could focus on getting to and from the target area. He only wanted mission related chatter but never said anything to Tony.

In early May, 1972, after expending their bombs, the squadron was directed to return to base. As they were turning south, the ground commander said another wave of NVA were mounting an attack and they didn't know if they could repel it. Without getting permission, Chris turned back with only his 30mm guns to provide support. He came in low enough to see the helmeted NVA forces charging the forward operating base on two sides. Chris made several passes, strafing the enemy forces. On his third pass, he noted an anti-aircraft gun hidden by trees. It opened fire on Chris, peppering the fuselage and wings. Tony was silent. Chris couldn't see him from his position so he tried to raise him on the radio. There was no response. He kept overflying the enemy even after he ran out of ammunition.

Chris noted he was losing fuel and headed to the base about 15 minutes away. Collins had come back for Chris after hearing the ground commander thank Chris for the help. Collins came alongside and told Chris that Tony was covered in blood and not moving. Chris reported his fuel situation as they headed to the base.

Collins alerted the airfield officer on duty to be prepared for a dead stick landing. Collins reported that Chris's aircraft was damaged under the fuselage as well, as a result he couldn't get his landing gear down. Collins suggested he bail out but Chris wouldn't leave Tony behind since he could still be alive.

Collins landed first and alerted the crash crew that Chris would make a belly landing on the dirt strip alongside the runway. Chris lifted the Phantom's nose up and touched down behind the wings. The aircraft spun around as the nose settled down. It slammed into a drainage ditch and lost its tail assembly.

Chris was stunned but managed to open the canopy and climb on to the wing to check on Tony. He unbuckled his harness and tried to lift the heavier man out of his seat. Tony was semi-conscious so Chris asked him to push himself up, which he did and then slumped on Chris's shoulder. Both of them slid off the wing onto the ground as the aircraft's remaining fuel started to leak out on the ground.

Chris grabbed Tony by his arms and hoisted him on his shoulder to flee from the aircraft just in time. It exploded spitting shrapnel into Chris's legs and back and as he fell down he covered Tony with his body. The crash crew arrived to pull them away from the fire. Chris didn't feel any pain so he told the corpsmen to take care of Tony. Chris blacked out and didn't remember much until he woke up in the field hospital.

The first thing he saw when he opened his eyes was his squadron commander who told him he was as crazy as ever.

"You must have a lucky charm, Chris. How many aircraft have you destroyed so far?" Collins said with a laugh.

"Ours, or theirs?" Chris replied.

"Why didn't you tell me you returned to the target area? I could have helped," Collins said.

"I heard the company commander call for more support because there was a massive attack on two sides of his position. It was instinct, I suppose," Chris said.

"Your decision to land rather than punch out saved Tony's life. Did you know he was still alive when you made that decision?"

"No, but I didn't care. He would have been dead for sure if I bailed out."

Collins told him he was being sent to the naval hospital at Yokosuka, Japan for additional surgery since some shrapnel was close to his spinal cord. He also said Tony was in better shape than he was and was ready to leave the hospital.

Chris had a sleepless night due to severe pain in his legs and back. He shipped out to Japan on a C-9 air evacuation flight the following morning. Over the next two days he had several surgeries to remove the shrapnel.

One of Chris's greatest concerns was whether he could fly again. His doctor said he could, but not in Vietnam.

13

BETRAYED

Chris was eventually sent to the naval hospital in Balboa, California to recuperate. A week later he was able to walk without crutches but still couldn't bend or twist his back. He wore a brace to help maintain his posture.

He spoke to Katie a few times from Japan. She decided to come to the hospital after he called her from Balboa. Their reunion was a tearful one. Katie didn't have the details on the events leading up to the crash. Chris didn't want to talk about it yet. She told him that one of the aircraft in her brother's squadron was shot down and the crew was believed to have survived.

Since Chris was ambulatory, the hospital allowed him to spend a few days out of the hospital but he had to return for further treatment on his back. It was tough going for Chris during his long-awaited love making with his wife. He couldn't lie on his back and had to have Katie find the most comfortable position for both of them.

Several times, Katie said she wanted to become pregnant again, something they never discussed before. He was curious and suspected the worst. When he realized it was her time of the month and she didn't have a period, he suspected she might have been unfaithful and perhaps was pregnant. The thought of it nauseated him. He didn't want to interrogate her because he could've been wrong. She sensed he was concerned about something. Chris thought it best to deal with it as soon as possible.

"Katie, I noticed you don't have your period and it's about the right time for it."

"Oh, I'm not always regular, Chris especially when I'm stressed out," she replied.

"What kind of stress? Is there something you have to tell me?"

She looked at him for a few seconds. Suddenly tears flowed down her cheeks and she sobbed saying she was so sorry.

"You're pregnant, aren't you? He asked.

She nodded and begged his forgiveness. She said it was a spontaneous encounter with a doctor at the hospital.

"It only happened once, I swear," she said.

"I believe once is too often. I don't think I can deal with this now. Why don't you leave and I'll see you when I return to Nellis?" Chris said emphatically.

Though Chris was angry, she didn't want to go. She professed her love for him and begged him to forgive her. Chris stood his ground and called a cab to take her to the airport.

Chris spent another week in the hospital before being discharged. He hadn't heard from the Marine Corps so he assumed he had to return to Nellis and was still assigned to the Aggressor Squadron.

Katie was at work when he arrived so he went to Shelly's house to speak with her.

"Chris, it's so nice to see you after what you've been through. I'm so sorry about Katie. She told me what happened during her visit. I didn't know anything about her situation until the other day. Are you going to forgive her, Chris?"

"I thought about it, but I couldn't accept her 'love' child. I plan to move off base with Andy and request a transfer. I can't forgive her for what she did, I'm sorry," he said.

"I understand and I am so very sad for all of you. I hope someday you can forgive her," Shelly pleaded.

Chris left the base and located a two-bedroom apartment to rent by the month. He packed his and Andy's stuff and put it in his truck. He waited until school was out and picked his son up. On the ride to the apartment,

Chris tried to explain what had happened without mentioning details. Andy had a lot of questions, most of which Chris couldn't, or wouldn't answer.

Chris called his former father-in-law and requested another assignment as soon as possible. He explained what happened and why he wanted to leave. The general was very sympathetic and said he'd get on it right away.

Shelly contacted Chris at the squadron to tell him Katie resigned her commission and was going back to Reno to live with her parents. She said she would be leaving by the end of June. Upon hearing the news, Chris contacted the base housing office to find out if he could keep his base house until he received orders to leave. They agreed considering the circumstances.

When Chris found out Katie left for Reno, he moved back into his base house. Since Dan was still deployed, he and Shelly spent some time together. Andy was glad to see Shelly and her kids but missed Annie and Katie.

Shelly told Chris things about Katie he never knew before. Most of it came from Dan. It wasn't so bad but it shed light on why Katie did what she did. His opinion of her in Vietnam was a first impression that was based on emotion and very superficial. He knew everything about Camille and still married her. He knew nothing about Katie but married her anyway. What about next time?

Chris's squadron commander was happy to get him back in one piece though Chris wasn't medically cleared to fly yet. During their chat about his latest experiences in Vietnam, Chris alluded to his domestic situation but didn't mention he requested a transfer.

Chris visited the base legal office to obtain a referral to a civilian divorce lawyer. After explaining what had occurred while deployed, the lawyer said Chris should be able to get a quick divorce.

The next day, Chris filed divorce papers. The lawyer said it would be helpful to have the name of the person involved with his wife. Chris called Shelly to ask if Katie ever mentioned his name. She could only remember his first name and that he worked in the family practice clinic. Chris told the lawyer he'd have a name the next day.

He went to the base hospital to find out the full name of the person who had an affair with his wife. Dr. Ken Goldman was his name. Chris sought him out and when he approached him, the doctor spied his name on his flight suit and tried to avoid him. Chris grabbed his arm, held his temper and told him he was being named in his divorce papers. Chris also learned the doctor was married and informed him he would contact his wife about her new step child. The doctor begged Chris not to do that. He said he didn't know Katie was pregnant.

"It's a small price to pay for breaking up a family of four and ruining their lives," Chris yelled.

The doctor became pale and started to sweat. Chris had no pity for him. The encounter felt good but didn't make up for his pain.

14

GROUNDED

Chris's former father-in-law called him at home.

"Chris, how would you like to go to Quantico?" The general asked.

"I'd prefer to return to a flying unit, sir," Chris replied.

"I think you should know the Corps' general staff has you on a fast track. Next year you will be promoted early, very early. With you record of combat achievements, the best place for you now is the Command and Staff College where you can complete staff officer education and perhaps earn a master's degree if you work hard," the general continued.

"That's a year of stability for Andy and me. I'm in sir, when does the program start?"

"You have to report in about four weeks. Now I can see my grandson on weekends," he laughed.

Chris was a good student in college but since he was on an athletic scholarship, he never had to work hard. Now it would be all work and no play and Andy had to come along for the ride.

Dan's squadron returned to Nellis in early August. Shelly broke the news about Katie the second day he was home. He was very upset. He paid Chris a visit to tell him how sorry he was but said he wasn't surprised. Dan invited Chris for dinner the following weekend at which time Chris told him he was being reassigned to Quantico in two weeks.

Before Chris left, he was presented with his eighth air medal for his last tour of duty in Vietnam at a ceremony in the squadron briefing room. Every pilot in the squadron attended not only for the ceremony, but to say good bye to one hell of a fighter pilot.

After dinner at Dan's house, Chris thanked them both for their friendship and support. Chris and Andy left early Sunday morning for Quantico, Virginia.

Andy seemed to adjust to having one parent and when he learned he'd see his grandpa again; he was very excited. Chris had to find a place to live, a school for his first grader, and someone to take care of him after school. Fortunately, the base appointed a sponsor to help Chris get settled.

"I think you are one of the few single fathers to attend the school. I understand the requirements for your son, my wife and I will help any way we can," his sponsor said.

"Thank you, Major Romano, I appreciate that."

"Please call me Phil. Here's my base number and my home phone number. My wife knows several wives who would love to look after Andy. Oh, by the way, don't get upset if they attempt to introduce you to available women. They hate to see single Marines, especially if they are happy single Marines."

"I think I'll stay single for at least the rest of the school year. Are there any apartments near the base that are in nice neighborhoods?" Chris asked.

"My wife, Tina, has scouted the area in close proximity to Quantico and has a few to show you. She'll take you there tomorrow. Tonight, you will stay in the VOQ."

"You sure move fast, Phil."

"You don't know it yet, but you are quite a celebrity in the Corps, and having a three-star general in the family certainly helps."

"I was stationed with the air force before I left for my third tour to Vietnam and before that I was on an aircraft carrier, so I'm really a stranger to the Corps. Why the celebrity status?" Chris asked.

"Your combat achievements are quite a legend, besides each student has a bio that we all get to read. I can get you a copy of yours if you'd like," Phil said.

"Thanks, but my bio is up here in my head."

Chris and Andy checked into the VOQ and then went to the officers' club for dinner. He looked to see if he knew anyone but there were no familiar faces. Those in uniform weren't aviators. A young Marine in civilian attire approached Chris. He said he was in Chris's training unit during basic Marine officer training. Chris remembered his face but not his name. He invited them join him at dinner but he wanted to spend time with his son.

On Tuesday, Tina Romano picked up Chris and Andy for a tour of the apartments she selected. She was certainly an officer's wife by the way she dressed and spoke.

"Do you have any information about schools in the area for my son?" Chris asked.

"Three of the apartment complexes are served by the same primary school. It has a great reputation."

It took about an hour to tour the three apartment complexes. Chris only liked one of the apartments. She took him to a fourth one that was more expensive and a bit further from the base. She said she knew he'd like it. The primary school recently opened so she didn't have any information on it.

"Phil said you had a few friends who might look after Andy after school. Do they live near any of the apartment complexes?" Chris asked.

"Yes, two live near the first one you liked. They actually live in the complex and have children around Andy's age. Do you want to meet them?"

"Yes, of course. Are they home now?"

"They are expecting us."

"You are so organized. I appreciate everything you are doing for me," Chris said.

Chris and Andy spent the next few hours meeting two Marine wives who wanted to look after Andy. They both said they'd watch Andy and would take turns picking him up from school with their children. Chris thanked them for their care and support.

"Marine families have to stick together because our husbands are deployed so often. Thankfully they are students here so we have at least a year before we are reassigned. Perhaps the war will be over by then," one of them said.

Chris spent the weekend fixing up his apartment. He turned down several dinner invitations and asked for rain checks. On Monday, both he and Andy began the school year together.

Chris's class consisted of 20 Marine officers, all majors and captains. Most had served in Vietnam on at least one deployment. He was the only aviator in his class. During registration, the admissions officer explained that it was possible to earn a master's degree but it would be difficult. Chris was one of six to volunteer for the program.

In his third week of school, the general called and asked if he could visit them. Of course, Chris said yes, after all the general was responsible for the assignment, and was Andy's grandpa.

Chris looked forward to seeing the general again. The general's driver dropped him off at the apartment.

"How did you manage to get the weekend off, sir?" Chris asked.

"I have some business with the commander at Quantico so I came a few days early to see you guys."

Chris asked about his wife and whether retirement was in the wind. The general said he wouldn't retire until the war was over and all his Marines left Vietnam. He said his wife was well but preoccupied with her niece, Julia. Since Chris didn't know anything about her niece, he asked the general about her.

"Julia is her sister's daughter. She's 21 years old and resembles Camille a lot. She is attending San Diego State University as an exchange student for her junior year," he said.

The general showed a picture of Camille and Julia when they were teenagers. Chris remarked how much they looked alike.

"It's uncanny, isn't it?" The general said.

Chris couldn't help starring at the picture. Julia, was several years younger, and more beautiful than Camille.

"So, have the Marine wives been trying to match you up with their single relatives and friends?" He asked

"I told my sponsor I have to focus on school and Andy for the next year. As a result, the only thing I get is an invitation to dinner once in a while."

"I'm afraid my wife wants you to meet Julia before she returns to France. Would you be up for that, Chris?" the general asked.

"You know I'd do anything for you and Edith. We are family, Julia is related to Andy. So, when is Mrs. Iverson planning the wedding?"

The general laughed.

"My wife and Julia are coming to Washington during Thanksgiving week. You and Andy are joining us for dinner and I won't take no for an answer."

The general took them out to one of his favorite seafood restaurants in northern Virginia. Andy had lobster for the first time. The general spoke about his retirement after the Vietnam War ended, which he expected wouldn't be too much longer. He was quite saddened to think of all the fine Marines who died there when victory was never the real purpose of the war.

"I hope we never do it again. Korea was bad enough but Vietnam was really a waste of our treasure. Unfortunately, the world is full of evil, that's why we need men like you, Chris. You are an exceptional Marine and I am so proud of you."

"Thank you, sir, but after Vietnam I will probably resign my commission or at least after my commitment is over. I was trained to fly and fight. I don't know if I'll ever fly again. I just can't see myself sitting behind a desk and I'm too junior to command a squadron," Chris replied.

"I'm sorry to hear that, Chris. You are on a fast track to higher rank. Think of all the young men that will see you as a role model and consider those youngsters not yet in the Corps."

"General, it's really tough to juggle my career and being a single father. I don't want Andy to be jerked around the world every few years because of my assignments. What happens to him if I go TDY? You know the Corps rotates squadrons to various Pacific area bases for several months at a time. Dependents don't follow them on TDYs. After what Andy's been though so far, I think he and I need stability."

"What if I can arrange a stable three-year tour, would that dissuade you from pulling the plug?" The general offered.

"It would help, sir. But after you retire, I'll be on my own," Chris responded.

"Maybe by then you'll be married so Andy could have the stability he needs."

Chris changed the subject and asked the general about his retirement plans. He said he wasn't certain yet. He said his wife looked forward to travelling and taking it easy but he looked forward to a second career.

On Monday morning the general's driver picked him up early. Chris took Andy to school and he went to class. Just before the class broke for lunch, a young Marine corporal handed the instructor a note.

"Captain Harrington, this young Marine is here to take you to the installation commander's office," the instructor announced.

The students razzed him because no one was summoned to the installation commander's office unless they really screwed up. Chris followed the corporal to his car. When they arrived, the corporal led Chris to a large briefing room and then left.

Major Phil Romano met Chris and explained he was getting an award for his actions during his last Vietnam tour but offered no other information. They walked to the front of the room and sat down. He told Chris when he heard his name mentioned he should get up and stand next to the highest-ranking officer, and face the audience. In a few minutes, the room filled up with officers who worked at Quantico. The base photographer stood at the front of the room. Phil moved to the podium.

Phil called the room to attention as the door at the front of the room opened. Lt. Gen. Iverson walked in followed by the Secretary of the Navy and several other high-ranking officers. When Phil called out Chris's name he walked to the front of the room and stood beside Iverson.

Phil read the orders awarding Chris the Navy Cross for his actions that saved a Marine company from possible annihilation. Chris had no idea he earned the Navy Cross. The general didn't hint at why he really came to see him. The Navy Secretary pinned the medal on Chris and shook his hand. He told the audience the commander of the beleaguered company that was saved by Captain Harrington's actions was present and wanted to speak.

For the next five minutes, Maj. William Christopher, who won the bronze star for valor for his actions that day, related how Chris's heroic actions allowed the company to escape certain death at the hands of a much stronger NVA force. He said his company lost one man, sustained four wounded and evacuated 211 soldiers. Christopher walked over to Chris and shook his hand as the audience applauded.

Iverson stood and addressed the audience. He said saving the company wasn't the only heroic action performed by Capt. Harrington on that day. The general spoke about what occurred after he departed the forward operating base. He read the citation from Chris's second Navy Commendation Medal extolling his actions saving his weapons' officer from certain death after they crashed landed at Da Nang. The audience applauded again.

After the awards ceremony concluded, Chris was informed he would be having lunch with the Quantico base commander and the other dignitaries. The Navy Secretary was especially interested in speaking with Chris.

The secretary tried to persuade Chris from leaving the Corps. He said he was on a fast track for promotion and the Corps needed people like him. He predicted the Vietnam War would soon end and subsequently many officers would voluntarily leave the military. He said Chris's career opportunities would be unlimited if he stayed in.

Chris was candid in his response. He told the secretary he wanted to fly and someday command a squadron. He was concerned that his next assignment would be a staff billet since it was required for obtaining more senior rank. He was afraid the longer he remained out of the cockpit it would be easier to leave the Corps.

Iverson sat next to Chris and overheard the conversation. He affirmed that Chris's next assignment would be behind a desk but assured him he'd make it a good one and that he would be in close proximity to a Marine aviation unit so he could get his required flying hours. The general also projected that as soon as the Vietnam War ended, there would be many voluntary and involuntary separations in Marine aviation. He reiterated Chris would benefit from a reduction in force especially with many senior officers retiring.

Chris grasped the inference about his future, but when the general retired, what then? After he graduated Staff College and earned his master's degree, he would fly a desk for three years. At that point in time he'd have invested ten years in the Corps. Beyond that time he knew subsequent assignments wouldn't be ideal for a single father. He decided if he was still single at that time, he'd leave the Corps.

15

THE COUSIN

Chris was looking forward to the Thanksgiving break. The workload for his Master's degree and for the Staff College was a bit overwhelming. Being a single father was also a time-consuming activity. Andy couldn't wait to see grandma and grandpa again.

The general lived on Fort Myer in Arlington, VA, along with many general officers from all the services stationed in the Washington D.C. area. The large old houses had seen some of the most famous military leaders in residence over the years. However, on a holiday weekend, there was no sign of the powerful who lived along the tree-lined streets.

When Chris pulled up in front of the general's house, Edith ran out to great Andy with open arms and lots of hugs and kisses. The general remained at the door waiting for his beloved grandson, the only remembrance he had of his late daughter.

Edith proudly introduced Andy and Chris to her niece, Julia. When she stood to shake Chris's hand, he couldn't help notice the striking resemblance between Julia and her late cousin Camille. He might have held her hand and gazed too long, he thought it made her uncomfortable. She was much more reserved than Camille and perhaps a bit shy. She blushed but soon relaxed when Chris greeted her in French. Only God knows what Edith told Julia about him. He was a good husband to a troubled young woman who self-destructed in front of his eyes, but Julia probably knew that.

The general took Chris by the arm and dragged him to the kitchen where he offered him a drink.

"I know my wife would love to see you and Julia hit it off. However, she is French, and I know how difficult it was to take my French bride away from her home and insert her into not only American culture, but military culture as well. Edith was strong and at the time of our marriage France was still recovering from the war. Julia comes from a well-to-do prominent family. The chances of you having the same experience as I had will be quite remote," the general explained.

"That's a lot to swallow, general. Andy is my primary concern; the Corps is secondary and getting married again isn't even on my agenda. Julia seems quite lovely but as you said, she is French and probably would never accept my lifestyle, especially being away from home months at a time. I commend Edith for what she went through. You must be a very persuasive man," Chris replied.

"You know, being French isn't too bad. When we visited her family, we never had to pay for anything," the general said with a laugh.

"I married Edith before she completed her university studies. Julia, on the other hand, is majoring in art history and wants a career in that field. I doubt she'd give up her ambition to marry a fighter jock," he continued.

They returned to the living room where Andy was the center of attention. He seemed to get along well with Julia. Chris didn't think Andy would understand what a second cousin was; he only knew she was family.

Edith asked if they were spending the night with them. Chris hadn't thought of it since it was only a two-hour drive back to his apartment. The general insisted on them staying. After a slight protestation, Chris agreed but insisted he had to leave first thing in the morning to study.

After dinner, the general fell asleep on the couch. Edith said she'd put Andy to bed leaving Julia and Chris alone. He asked her if she wanted to take a walk. He was surprised when she said yes. It was brisk out but Chris was too focused on Julia to notice.

He got her to talk about herself. She wasn't shy at all much to his surprise. She told him her father was an American military officer who met her mother in Paris right after the war.

"So, your grandmother lost two daughters to the Americans," Chris said.

"Yes, she lost a son to the war, and I lost my father in a car accident. I was too young to remember him."

He loved her French accent.

"I'm sorry, my father was killed in Korea, but I still have some memories of him."

"Did your mother remarry?" He asked.

"Yes, to a wealthy French man, and your mother?"

"No, she didn't, but I never asked her why," Chris responded.

"I must tell you something, Chris. My aunt has spoken about you a lot and said you were a wonderful husband and father. I think she is trying to be a matchmaker. Is that the correct word?"

"Yes, it is. I assume that's her plan. However, my life is quite complicated and we'll probably never see each other again. I don't know how we could, you know, become friends living two separate lives. I don't know where I will be next year and you will probably be living in France. However, if you want, we could correspond from time to time."

"I think I'd like that. I am studying art history and believe it or not my interest isn't in French or European art for that matter. I am fascinated with Oriental art. I plan on studying in Japan after I obtain my degree in France."

Chris realized if true, they might see each other again since he'd probably spend some time in the Pacific area. Nevertheless, he didn't mention it to her. She'd marry someone with money since she was accustomed to it. What could he offer her? He noticed she was shivering so they returned to the house.

By the time they reached the front door, the general was leaving. He said his boss invited him stop by to have a drink. He asked Chris if he wanted to join him but he declined.

Edith noticed Julia was cold and offered her hot chocolate. Chris asked for one as well.

"You are a very nice man, Chris. Aunt Edith was right about you," Julia whispered.

Chris smiled and thought about his response.

"The general told me you were beautiful and reminded him of Camille. I have to agree with him and I think you are very nice too," he whispered back.

Edith brought them two cups of hot chocolate and asked what they were whispering about?

"We can't decide on whether we should get married in France or here," Chris quipped.

"You promised you wouldn't say anything yet until you met my family," Julia said teasing.

Edith looked at the two of them wide-eyed. She smiled.

"Chris, you sure don't waste any time."

"Actually, it was Julia who pushed me into it," he said laughing.

Edith left the two of them alone.

Chris felt compelled to tell Julia about his recent divorce. He explained everything from the time he met Katie until he decided to divorce her. She listened intently and reached for his hand.

"That was a terrible thing for her to do to you. Perhaps it was meant to be, you know, kismet," she offered while blushing.

"Is this kismet, Julia? If so, I look forward to reading your letters," Chris replied.

"I have something to tell you as well. About two years ago my family introduced me to the son of a family acquaintance, who is very wealthy and lives in Monaco. He is two years older, quite arrogant and too much of a playboy. I think he had other girlfriends. My parents were too focused on becoming part of the other family and not on my happiness. That is one reason I came to study in California. As far as I am concerned, it's over," she said.

"That's good to hear. So, we are both available," he said with a chuckle.

"Do you think we could see each other again before I return to France, Chris?" she asked.

He wanted to kiss her so much at that moment.

"When do you return?"

"I leave in June but I could visit here before I go home," she replied.

"I'll still be here. In fact, I don't leave until the following month. When do you have to return to school?"

"In August, late August," she replied.

The wheels in Chris's now mushy head spun fast. He couldn't come up with anything significant to say since he didn't know his next destination yet.

"Perhaps you could visit your uncle after you finish school until I have to leave, if that's okay with you," he offered.

She stared at him with her big beautiful blue eyes and without hesitation she said, "Or I could stay with you, if that's okay, Chris."

"No problem, we'd love to have you as our guest," he said without hesitation.

Chris gave Julia a European kiss on both checks though he thought of kissing her on the lips. He decided to change his plan and head for Quantico. The general was surprised he left when he returned home later that night.

As Chris and Andy drove home, he thought about his conversation with Julia. Was she just being flirtatious or was there something really there? Andy fell asleep so Chris had time to think. He really didn't expect to hear from her again. As soon as she returned to school, she'd probably forget about him. Besides, they lived two different lives and would probably live a half a world away from each other. She was nice, more than nice, but she wasn't cut out to be a Marine's wife.

Chris returned to his studies while Andy watched TV. Every once in a while, Julia's face flashed across Chris's mind causing him to stop and reflect. He married Camille because he was a positive force in her life and when she took her medicine, she led a normal life. Unfortunately, he left her too often due to his military commitments. He admitted to himself that his relationship with Katie was basically a sexual one, a very powerful impact on his decision making. When she admitted her infidelity, he snapped and divorced her with no forgiveness or remorse.

What about Julia? She seemed like a normal young woman with a great sense of humor and an idea of what she wanted to do in life. Though he found her attractive, he didn't lust after her like he did with Katie. So, what attracted him to her? He had a difficult time making sense of it. What if she really came to Virginia on her way to France and stayed in his apartment for a week or two? Would a loving relationship develop? Would it cause either of them to change their lives, one giving up his or her career goals for the other? Chris didn't see that happening though he thought about leaving the Corps if he couldn't fly again.

Chris took Andy to a matinee featuring the latest Disney film and some cartoons. They went out for dinner during which time Andy asked his father what he thought of Julia. Chris nearly choked on his food, never expecting Julia had made such an impression on his son.

"I think she is nice, but you know she lives far away and we won't see her too often," Chris finally said.

"Isn't she my cousin?" Andy asked.

"Yes, she is. Her mother and your grandmother are sisters. She was your mother's cousin, Chris said knowing his son didn't quite understand.

"Okay, so can she still be my mommy?"

"This time Chris needed to drink some water to swallow his food. Where did that question come?

"Do you want her to be your mommy, Andy?" He asked.

"I like her a lot and she is very pretty and she said she likes me very much," he replied.

"When did you two have the time to talk?" Chris asked.

"When you went to the bathroom after dinner," Andy replied.

Chris was at a loss for words. He didn't want to disappoint his son by telling him how difficult it would be for Julia to become part of their lives. He also didn't want to give him any false hopes. What he knew for sure was that his son desperately wanted a mother in his life. Sadly, that wasn't a good enough reason to marry the first woman who hit it off with his son.

Andy didn't mention Julia again until late one Sunday evening when Chris received a call from Edith who wanted to speak with Andy. What Chris didn't know was that Julia got on the phone afterwards and spoke with Andy. Chris left the room when he handed the phone to his son. After ten minutes, Andy yelled out that someone wanted to speak with him. It was Julia.

"Hello, Chris. I thought this would be a good time to talk to you since it is Sunday. I just wanted to say I enjoyed being with you on Thanksgiving and to tell Andy he is my favorite cousin," she said.

"I'm glad you called, Julia. I enjoyed spending time with you as well. I know it is seven months off but if you really want to visit us, we'll be happy to see you," Chris said.

"I hope to do that but my aunt will probably know something is up when I don't show up at my uncle's house. I really don't want my mother to find out I'm staying with an American Marine. My family has invested a considerable amount in my education and they'd like to see me finish school and have a career," Julia explained.

"I can understand that. I don't want you to change your life because of me. Isn't it possible we could just become good friends?"

"Do you think that's what will happen, Chris, just good friends?"

Chris was searching for the right response. He didn't want to nip this undeveloped relationship in the bud.

"Anything is possible, Julia. We are both adults looking for the next chapter in our lives. So, whatever happens, call it kismet," he stammered.

She laughed.

"Yes kismet, for sure. I have to go now. May I call you next Sunday?"

"Call me every Sunday, if you want," he replied.

Chris wondered how much Edith knew about the situation. Was she privy to the telephone conversation? He decided to approach his son to find out what he and Julia talked about.

"Andy, what did grandma talk to you about?"

"Nothing much, she said she missed me and loved me and then I spoke to Cousin Julia," Andy replied.

"Did you enjoy speaking with her?" He asked hoping to get some information.

"Yes, I did. She told me she might see me again and that she really liked me. She also said she'd like to have a son just like me."

"I hope she does too, but you are one of a kind, Andy."

"What does that mean, daddy?"

"It means there is no one else like you in the whole world, you are special," Chris replied.

"Grandma always tells me I'm special, so I must be very special," Andy said.

Chris had a lot of papers due before the Christmas break for both Staff College and his graduate degree. He tried to spend more time with Andy especially since he was off from school at the same time. The day he turned in his final paper he drove to New York to show Andy the Christmas decorations. It was the first visit to New York for both of them. They stayed at a midtown hotel at about the same time President Nixon renewed the bombing of North Vietnam. His goal was to bring them to the peace table.

Andy loved everything he saw including the Empire State Building, Macy's, Radio City Music Hall and the few flurries of snow that greeted them. It was a great father-son experience for both of them. They returned to Virginia the day after Christmas. The car was packed with Andy's Christmas gifts that remained unopened until they arrived home.

There was nothing else for them to do before New Year's Eve. The general returned to San Diego for the holiday. Most of the students at Quantico headed home so Chris decided to get a jump on his work for the rest of the school year. Andy was busy with his presents. He wanted to call his grandmother and of course Julia would want to speak with him, and probably Chris as well.

When Chris finally got the opportunity to speak, the first thing Julia asked was why he didn't spend the holidays in San Diego. He offered his excuse but he could tell she was very disappointed. Nevertheless, he was happy with his decision to spend a few days in New York with his son.

Toward the end of the conversation, Julia whispered in French that she missed him. Chris was taken aback since there was no indication, she had any strong feelings for him. She hardly knew him, but Edith probably told Julia a lot of positive things about him in her effort to be a matchmaker. Chris was concerned her expectations were set too high. He decided to respond in French that he missed her as well.

As the New Year celebrations ebbed, it became apparent the peace accords would soon be signed ending the U.S. role in Vietnam. The general called Chris and asked him to visit with him the following weekend. Andy was happy to visit his grandpa but disappointed Julia wasn't there. The general had a visitor who worked with him. Once Andy was settled in front of the TV, the two generals and Chris began a discussion about Chris's future.

The visiting general wanted to know what the Corps could do to keep him. Chris said he wanted to fly and eventually command an operational unit. General Iverson reiterated that Chris had to serve in a staff billet to attain senior rank. Chris knew that but insisted he didn't want to spend the rest of his career behind a desk.

"There are no more wars to fight, Chris. Marine Aviation will probably shrink in size and will be transitioning to a new fighter aircraft, the F-14 Tomcat," Iverson said.

"It may take two or three years for the transition during which time you could serve in a staff billet at one or two major geographic commands," the other general said.

Chris realized the Corps wanted him more than he wanted them.

"What are you proposing, general?" He asked.

"There is an opportunity for a field grade aviation officer with Marine Forces Pacific Command in Hawaii. From time to time we would send you TDY to Kaneohe MCAS to maintain your currency in the F-4. We wouldn't normally do that for any pilot but you are special," the visiting general said.

Chris realized his father-in-law was trying his best to do what was right for him and he appreciated it. He excused himself to use the bathroom which gave him time to think about it. He was concerned about Andy's future and the potential of having Julia in his life. A career in the Corps wouldn't be in their best interest. However, three years at one location would be good for Andy. As far as Julia was concerned, she had another year in school that he was certain she wouldn't forgo. Besides, she had her career goals established and his military career couldn't accommodate her.

"I accept your offer, gentlemen but under one condition though I know I'm asking too much of you. I want a guaranteed follow-on assignment to a squadron in the Pacific, if at all possible," Chris proffered.

"That will be difficult to arrange. You'll probably be assigned to a squadron, but the location cannot be guaranteed at this time. We foresee a lot of changes in various organizations due to downsizing in manpower and funding. In addition, we'll both be retiring in a year or two," the other general replied.

Chris realized after his former father-in-law retired, he'd be on his own taking chances on whatever he could do for himself. In three years, he would evaluate his career goals, and at that time after ten years in the Corps, he might opt out for something else.

Chris returned home unfazed by the meeting with the generals. He focused on his academic work with weekly breaks to speak with Julia on the phone. She too was mired in her studies so their conversations covered many subjects other than their nascent relationship.

On January 27th 1973, the Vietnam War Peace Accords were signed. This allowed the United States to withdraw its military support for the South Vietnamese government in a face-saving way. It temporarily halted hostilities between the north and south and it called for the release of all the American prisoners of war held by North Vietnam. It didn't address any prisoners that might be held in South Vietnam, Laos or in Cambodia.

While most of the nation was overjoyed with the news, the families of the more than 58,000 men and women who died over the 10-year war had to deal with a 'non-victory' and waste of lives for political reasons. Those same feelings were felt by the families of the Korean War's service members who died 20 years earlier for an 'opportune' truce. Chris had become somewhat cynical at the ripe old age of 28 years old.

Chris was a doting father who was very proud of how young Andy had grown up without a mother, living with his grandmother, and then a father who couldn't devote enough time to him. Chris was very grateful for the support of the military wives in his apartment complex that cared for Andy whenever needed. Chris began to feel guilty about not providing the mother Andy wanted, and, truthfully, the wife he needed.

Over the next three months, Julia and Chris spoke only a few times due to their respective heavy academic loads. There wasn't any mention of her visiting Virginia in June since before Christmas. It wasn't something

Chris wanted since any further relationship with Andy would be unfair to him. So, Chris relegated that thought behind the many other priorities in his life.

Chris managed to find time to attend his graduation ceremony from George Washington University in mid-May. Shortly before completing Marine Corps Staff College, General Iverson called to let Chris know he was on the major's promotion list, two years below the zone. The general congratulated Chris and told him he would attend his Staff College graduation ceremony.

Chris was more than pleased to learn of his early selection, though he would have traded it for an assignment to a flying squadron. His thoughts turned to his son and the obstacles they'd face in Hawaii which, as a single father, seemed daunting. They had to find a place to live, an elementary school, childcare and babysitters when needed. Chris didn't expect to have the support system he found at Quantico. He'd probably live close to Kaneohe and commute to Camp Smith.

Gen. Iverson was one of the guest speakers at graduation. During the ceremony, Chris realized it was the first time since he joined the Corps, he didn't finish first in his class. The workload at both schools was quite severe and the time he devoted to Andy, contributed to this fact. In hindsight, finishing in the top five was an achievement he could be proud of.

With time on his hands, Chris traveled around the area with his son touring all the museums and monuments. He took Andy to a library to read some books on Hawaii. Andy was excited to live near a beach after a tough winter in Virginia.

A week after graduation, Gen. Iverson called to tell him he was selected to chair a task force regarding future Marine tactics in guerilla warfare and in any asymmetrical battle environment. It was the result of a comprehensive lessons learned report on why the United States, with overwhelming firepower both in the air and on the ground, couldn't defeat a less equipped enemy force in Vietnam. The task force would eventually determine the shape of the Marine Corps in the future, or very near future. The general said the report could change the size and structure of the Corps.

After Julia finished school, she called Chris to discuss whether he really wanted her to visit him.

"Have you changed your mind, Julia," he asked.

"No, but we haven't discussed it much and I didn't know how long you'd still be there," she replied.

"Andy and I are both looking forward to seeing you again. I'll be here for a few weeks so make arrangements and let me know when you expect to be here."

"I want to see both of you again, I missed you guys. I haven't said anything about this to anyone so don't tell on me," she pleaded.

"Won't your parents know when you left school and when you are to be expected?"

"I told them I'd spend a few days with my classmates."

"That's very clever of you, Julia. We missed you as well and we would like to spend a lot of time together before we go our separate ways," Chris said.

She was quiet for a moment probably thinking about his last comment.

"Are you saying that when I return home, we'll never see each other again?" She asked.

"You still have another year of school and then you'll begin your career somewhere, if not in France. We'll be living in Hawaii for three years. Is it possible for us to see each other again? Yes, if you visit us in Hawaii," Chris said giving her something to think about.

"I'd love to visit Hawaii though it might not be possible for a while. In the meantime, I am excited about coming to Virginia. I'll let you know my travel plans as soon as possible."

Chris dismissed any notion there was a romantic interest on her part, certainly not on his. He surmised she wanted to get to know Andy better and keep that relationship fresh. As for Chris, he believed there was no future for them outside of family ties since their lives were incompatible.

The following day, Gen. Iverson called and asked if he could visit with them. Of course, Chris told him he was always welcome. That afternoon he showed up at the apartment. He was anxious to see Andy. The general told Chris he was transferred to Quantico and was moving into his new quarters in a few days. He invited Chris to move in with him while waiting his orders to Hawaii.

Chris realized the general's move to Quantico and the invitation to give up his apartment would screw up Julia's visit. He had to come up with an excuse to remain in his apartment. He thanked the general for his kind offer but made no commitment.

"Will your wife join you, sir?" Chris asked.

"She said she'd come to help me get settled and spend time with Andy until you leave for Hawaii. After that, I don't know how long she'll stay. She wants me to retire after this assignment which I promised to do. However, as long as the Corps has a use for me, I'll consider my options," the general responded.

"I was going to see a friend of mine in Pensacola about the time you would be getting settled. Would you like to have Andy stay with you while I'm away?" Chris said lying through his teeth.

"I'll talk it over with Edith since I don't know what she plans to do and we don't want to ignore Andy. The first two weeks in a new house are always hectic," the general replied.

Chris realized if Andy wasn't with him, Julia might decide to fly directly to Paris. On the other hand, if she came to Virginia despite that, it would be a big risk. Andy was aware Julia planned to visit them and he would certainly tell his grandmother.

He decided the best course of action would be to tell the Iverson's the truth, as long as they didn't tell Julia's parents. If she didn't want her aunt and uncle to know, then he would suggest she fly home without visiting him. Was it worth it to be deceptive on the one hand and disappoint Julia on the other? Chris felt, in the end, there would never be a romantic relationship between the two of them so he decided to nip it in the bud.

The next day Chris called Julia. He suspected she knew Edith was coming to Quantico in a few days to help her husband get settled. He told her of his quandary, actually her quandary. He said he wouldn't lie about her visit and he planned to tell her aunt and uncle about it. If she really cared about him, she'd tell them the truth. However, he knew she wouldn't take the chance of upsetting her parents, especially her stepfather who wasn't too fond of Americans. She was very unhappy with her choices. She couldn't be sure Edith would keep the secret from her mother.

He could tell she was crying when she admitted it would be best for her to go home without stopping in Virginia. That was what Chris thought would be the end of it.

Julian called back that evening.

"Chris, my aunt invited me to come to Virginia for a few days to see Andy and you before I go home. Isn't that great news?" She exclaimed.

Chris was certain that Edith was definitely playing matchmaker with the expressed purpose making sure Chris and Julia would have more time together alone. Chris winced at the thought of giving Julia false hope because between her family and his career, they had too many obstacles to overcome.

"Does that mean your parents will find out you are seeing me?" He asked.

"I've never mentioned you to them and my aunt promised not to say anything as well," Julia said.

Chris decided not to yield to temptation, even if presented with it. Julia obviously wanted to spend time with her American family and he was only on the periphery of it.

"I'm sure everyone will be happy to see you, Julia," Chris commented.

"Does that include you as well, Chris?"

"Yes, of course it does, Julia."

Chris was relieved when the conversation ended.

The following day he received a call that his orders were waiting for him at the school headquarters building. Chris was surprised and disappointed when he read his orders. They weren't his Hawaii orders but rather TDY orders to Marine Air Station Beaufort, in Beaufort, South Carolina. The purpose was to take a flight physical and re-qualify in the F-4 to have his flight pay reinstated. After a year out of the cockpit he had to recertify especially since he was injured on his last mission. The TDY was for seven days.

Chris wondered if the general had anything to do with it to keep him from an unnecessary entanglement with his niece. A good thought if he did arrange it. Chris had to report in two days, just one day before Julia arrived. Edith and the general would take care of Andy for a week at which time he hoped Julia would have returned to France.

Andy was excited to stay with grandma for a week. They had a very close bond.

When Chris visited the general in his new quarters at Quantico, he was surprised that Chris had to go TDY for a week. Edith hoped Julia would still be there by the time Chris returned.

"It seems as though fate is keeping me from seeing Julia again. She is really a very nice and is quite fond of Andy," Chris said to Edith.

"Chris, dear, you know we both love you very much. Somehow, you've had a significant impact on Julia. I don't know what you two spoke about the past eight months, but she is infatuated with you, I really can't explain it. She's always asking me questions about you, some of which I couldn't answer," Edith replied.

Chris was taken aback. Nothing in their numerous conversations on the phone revealed her feelings towards him or vice versa. What did Edith mean when she said Julia was infatuated?

"Edith, I can assure you neither of us ever expressed our feelings about each other. I like her very much but I am also realistic. My life wouldn't be compatible with her goals and lifestyle. I think she once told me her stepfather didn't like Americans. Am I missing something?" He asked.

"Perhaps, Chris, she never told you how she felt about you. As you know her mother and I both married American military officers. Unfortunately, her father died. I know both her mother and stepfather wouldn't approve of Julia following in our footsteps. I've communicated with my sister about my assessment of you, and what Julia has told me about her feelings for you. You have a special place in our hearts as the husband of my late daughter and the father of my grandson. Julia's mother understands how we feel about you. If Julia wasn't on a path to earning her degree in Art History and following her dream to work at the Louvre or another art museum, perhaps her mother would be pleased," Edith admitted.

Chris listened intently and agreed with Edith that he could derail

Julia's dreams if he pursued her. However, he didn't respond to what she said.

"I'm quite grateful you are taking care of Andy at a time when you are trying to get settled in your new home," Chris said, changing the subject.

"Chris, I'll always be there for Andy whenever I'm needed. He's all I have of Camille."

Chris noted a tear in her eyes. He hugged her and thanked her. He said good bye to Andy who was helping his grandfather unpack some boxes.

I'll see you in a week, Chris. You should stay with us until you leave for Hawaii. We have plenty of room," the general said.

"Thank you general. I've already checked out of my apartment. Is it okay if I leave some of my stuff here until I get my orders?" Chris asked.

"Yes, of course, use the second bedroom down the hall. Edith will get it set up before you return.

Chris was on the road to Beaufort by noon. He looked forward to flying again.

The drive to Beaufort was uneventful. Chris checked into the BOQ and slept until his alarm went off. He reported to the squadron headquarters and was told to take his flight physical and return as soon as possible.

The exam went well though the physician was focused on the scars on Chris's back. He took X-rays to check on whether there was any shrapnel still embedded, fortunately it was clear.

Chris was surprised when the physician escorted him to the psychiatrist's office for an additional fitness exam. The first dozen questions appeared routine and then the psychiatrist focused on Chris's emotional fitness with questions about his first wife's death, his divorce and coping as a single parent.

He was angered by those questions. He told him he was finished with the interview and stood to leave. He turned back and suggested the psychiatrist read his service record.

Chris spent the following six days boring holes in the sky and making dry bombing runs simulating close air support. There weren't enough funds to provide for live bombs. So much for peace time military life.

He took his time on the drive back to Quantico. He wanted to see his son but wasn't in a hurry to see Julia though he had growing feelings for her. He arrived early Monday morning just in time to greet the general on his way out the door. Andy brushed past his grandfather to jump into Chris's waiting arms.

The general greeted him warmly and reminded Chris, he wanted him to meet with his task group to obtain his input before he left.

"By the way, Chris, beware of the young woman in love. You don't want to make the French side of the family upset with Edith and me," he said with a chortle.

Andy accompanied Chris to his bedroom. While Chris undressed for a much- needed shower, Edith called out for Andy to come down for breakfast. After his shower, Chris crawled into bed and fell asleep.

Three hours later, Edith knocked on his door and woke Chris up.

"I'm going out and taking Andy with me. Please get up and spend some time with our house guest. She really came here to see you," Edith said with a broad smile.

Chris reluctantly got out of bed and quickly dressed. On his way to the kitchen to grab something to eat, Julia called out to him.

"Hey stranger, I'm in the living room. Do you want me to make something for you to eat?" She asked.

Chris turned, retraced his steps and greeted Julia with a kiss on each cheek. He told her not to bother, he just wanted some juice. He returned to the living room to find Julia seated on the floor looking at photo albums. She beckoned him to sit beside her while she pointed out the photos of her parents, Camille and her in France when they were teenagers.

Chris made some remarks and then pushed the albums aside.

"Let's talk about us. You can't leave tomorrow until we talk about our feelings,"

She looked down without saying a word

"Okay, Julia, I'll speak first. I've spent the past eight months suppressing my feelings for you. I know that sounds strange but I must tell you why. Before we met, I knew very little about you. All I knew was you were an art history student on an exchange program in San Diego. Then when we met, you told me you would graduate next year and try to get an internship at a major museum. My desire is not to disrupt your career by interfering in your goals," Chris said.

Chris watched as Julia slowly picked up her head and looked at Chris with tears in her eyes.

"Unlike you, Chris, I spent the past eight months falling in love with you."

He felt like shit.

"Yes, I want to get my university degree and become an art historian but I can always do that. I can't push aside the man I fell in love with. My step father wants me to marry a wealthy European man. But wealthy men want heirs and I can't have children."

Chris was stunned.

"I was raped by two North Africa immigrants when I was 15. I was badly beaten. I was in hospital for a week. About two weeks later I got very sick and ran a high temperature. Blood tests revealed I contracted a virulent venereal disease. The various anti-biotics used weren't effective. My stepfather only knew I was very sick but was never told about the attack. He was on a business trip at the time. After consultation with a medical expert, they decided to operate and examine one of my ovaries. They found it to be destroyed by the bacteria so they removed the second one as well. The chief surgeon told my mother it would be best to do a complete hysterectomy. My mother reluctantly agreed."

Julia sobbed uncontrollably so Chris pulled her to him and held her in his arms. He didn't have any words to comfort her. He held her head to his chest and kissed it. Julia raised her head and kissed him on the lips.

"Chris, I want you to make me feel like a woman, I need to know I can please you."

He knew what she wanted but he didn't want to make love to her under pressure.

"It's not the right time or the right place. Your aunt may walk in on us, he replied.

"My aunt will call me at four, we have two hours alone."

She kissed him again with an open mouth inviting their tongues to touch. He carried her to his room and locked the door. As he turned to face her, she was undressed and on the bed.

"I've never made love before so if I seem hesitant or don't do the right thing, please be patient with me," she cautioned.

Chris undressed and reassured her not to worry. He proceeded to stroke and kiss her breasts and then kissed her on her stomach. She moaned and moved her body towards his mouth. He continued the foreplay until she reached an orgasm. He was afraid to penetrate her not knowing if she would recoil because of the rape.

It was a wonderful experience for her. Julia's tragic attack was submerged in countless orgasmic spasms. She finally felt like a woman. After they made love, they took a shower together during which time they made love again. Their eyes locked on to each other during the entire time.

Chris had to resolve the issue he discussed before they made love. After they dressed, they returned to the living room.

"I didn't plan on making love to you. It was wonderful but it doesn't change what I said to you earlier. You have to make the decision to return home and finish your education. My feelings for you won't diminish if you return to school," he said.

She looked at him like no other woman ever did before.

"I know you love me and I love you. I owe my family a lot. If our love is true, it will be there a year from now. It hurts me to leave you, but it is best. You don't have to say anything, I know how you feel," Julia admitted.

The phone rang precisely at four. Julia answered and then hung up.

"That was aunt Edith. She'll be here in 15 minutes."

"I assume she knows what we were up to. Let her revel in her own thoughts and act as though we talked all afternoon. If Edith knows the truth, she'll tell your mother," Chris cautioned.

Julia said she'd tell her mother about him anyway but agreed not to confirm her aunt's suspicions.

During dinner, the general wanted Chris to speak with his group before he left for Hawaii. Edith kept looking at Julia and then to Chris to see if there were any telltale signs of what might have transpired while she was out.

"Are you all packed, Julia?" Edith asked.

"I just have a few things left."

The general said he would arrange for a staff car to take them to the airport. Julia asked Chris not to come with them because it would be very difficult for her to say goodbye. Edith shot a glance at Chris but he didn't protest. He knew it would be difficult for him as well.

That night, Julia left her room and crawled in beside Chris and went to sleep. She really loved him.

After everyone departed for the airport, Chris felt empty. Had he fallen in love with Julia? He wasn't certain but he knew he'd miss her a lot.

The next day, Chris accompanied the general to work to respond to questions regarding close air support during the Vietnam War.

Chris's comments were fairly positive of Marine pilots' actions but made one major point. Who would support the Marines on the ground in the next war if there were no airfields available to launch aircraft as there were in Vietnam? No one in the room had an answer. The general asked Chris whether he had a solution, knowing full well he did.

"Whether we support Marines in combat or during training exercises, every aircraft carrier must have 20 percent of its aircraft dedicated to close air support. Every Marine pilot should be carrier qualified," Chris answered.

One member of the group asked if that was feasible. Chris said yes but it would be up to the Navy. He wanted to continue giving his opinions but felt he should end it.

The following day, Chris received his assignment and travel orders to Hawaii. He departed from Dulles airport on July 29th, 1973.

16

HAWAII

Upon arrival at Camp Smith, Hawaii, Chris and Andy went directly to the military housing office where they were informed there was a two-bedroom, one bath house available but it was one of the older units. If they preferred, they could be put on a waiting list and live in temporary housing. Chris didn't want to move again so he chose the older house.

The house was adequate but needed renovation. The appliances seemed a bit newer. It was all that he could get as a junior officer. Once he was promoted, perhaps he'd rate better quarters.

Chris arranged for child care until school started. The primary school was near the housing area. Chris enrolled his son in second grade and met one of his teachers. The after-school program was very good but ended at 6 p.m. There was bus service to Chris's house but he didn't know if he'd be home on time. Perhaps he could arrange for a neighbor to watch him.

As soon as Chris received his mailing address, he phoned Edith and gave it to her to send to Julia. Edith promised to get Julia's address for him.

On August 1st, Chris reported for duty. He met his new boss, Lt. Col. Steve Davis, a Vietnam veteran who spent one tour at Da Nang airbase in 1970. They didn't know each other but had mutual friends. Davis told Chris he had one year left and hoped to command a squadron when he left.

Davis took Chris to meet his boss, Col. Bud Foster, who flew combat missions in Korea and Vietnam. Foster knew about Chris though they never met.

"Welcome aboard, Chris. We are very glad to have you. Your position hasn't been filled since March when many of our experience pilots were given their pink slips. I'm sure you'd rather be in a flying squadron than sitting behind a desk for a few years. You'll have the opportunity to fly a few hours about every six weeks," the colonel said.

"I'm glad to be here after sitting in classrooms for a year and I look forward to flying again, Chris replied.

"I'm familiar with your family situation and my wife assured me she will support you any way she can. Did you get military housing yet?" The colonel asked.

"Yes sir, one of the older units reserved for junior officers,"

"Since you will be promoted soon, I'll let the unit commander know to arrange for field grade housing. You might have to wait a while since there are so many senior officers assigned here."

"Thank you, sir."

"Steve will take you around to meet the folks who work for me and then he'll show you where you'll work, and of course what you will be working on," Foster said while shaking Chris's hand.

Steve and Chris made the rounds meeting about 12 junior officers and enlisted Marines. Over lunch, Steve explained Chris's responsibility. Basically, he would compile all the incoming data from squadrons assigned or deployed to the Pacific region and maintain the daily operational readiness status. Each Friday he would brief the general staff.

Steve's job was to take action on any negative information regarding Marine aviation readiness. Chris thought he morphed into a mundane numbers cruncher but he had to get his headquarters' ticket punched to move ahead.

Chris's windowless office was small, one desk, two chairs and a wall lined with file cabinets.

That afternoon, Chris and Andy discussed their first day's activities. During their conversation, Andy remarked that he missed Julia a lot, Chris did as well. He penned his first letter to Julia and included a note from Andy.

On the first Saturday in August, Col. Foster's wife, Alice paid Chris a visit. She was very pleased to meet both Chris and Andy. She said her husband had to do something to get them better quarters as soon as possible. Since Chris was a single parent, she said she'd let the other wives know when Chris needed help, especially if he had to travel or wasn't able to get home to greet his son. She warned him that everyone would probably try to match him up with a relative since he was single. She wasn't a nosey person, just curious, so Chris explained the two marriages and their untimely endings. She was very sympathetic. Alice told Chris not to hesitate to call her if he needed something.

Chris received his first letter from Julia a week later. She told Chris she never thought she could please a man after her assault or even achieve the excitement she had during their brief sexual experience. She felt better about herself and gained new confidence in her life. She professed her love for him and then wrote what she would be studying during the new semester.

He received two letters a week filled with the same level of intensity regarding her love for him. Chris tried to match her feelings but fell short, in his opinion.

At the end of September, Chris, went to Marine Corps Air Station, Kaneohe Bay on the north coast of Oahu. Since the drawdown of military forces, he was a welcome addition even though it was only for a day. Most of the pilots were young, only a few had combat experiences. Chris knew from his day job that many squadrons were in the same situation. Chris flew his assigned mission as the squadron commander's wingman. He was at home in time to pick up Andy from school.

Chris's job was interesting but not challenging. He was dismayed by the slow deterioration of the command's combat readiness due to budget cuts and the loss of experienced crew members and enlisted technicians.

Andy did well in school, he became one of his teacher's favorite students. Chris was informed, he was a real gentleman.

On November 1st, Chris was promoted to major. A week later, he and Andy moved into a bigger house with a third bedroom, a second bathroom and modern appliances. He lived on the same street as both Steve and Bud. It wasn't too soon after that Bud introduced Chris to his 20-year-old daughter who attended the University of Hawaii. Liz became Andy's favorite babysitter the first time out. She was attractive, friendly, but too young for Chris who still had strong feelings for Julia.

The general called Chris to congratulate him on his promotion. He said Edith and he would come to Hawaii on official business in January. In fact, his whole team was coming to interview Marines in Hawaii and Japan to complete the team's review of the Marine Corps role in the Vietnam War.

Edith spoke with Andy and then to Chris.

"How are things between you and Julia these days, Chris?" She asked.

"About the same though she doesn't write as often. Why did you ask?"

"I think you should know she is spending the holidays with one of her professors at his family home in the Alps. She told her mother she was going with a girlfriend but I question that," Edith continued.

"I assume he is much older than she is. Is he married?"

"He is a widower with two small children. Now do you see why I have concerns?"

"I see, well it seems to be something I can't control, Edith. I never thought things would work out between us in the long run. I'm not too upset, Andy and I are doing quite well," Chris replied.

After he hung up, he thought about what Edith said. It seemed like a perfectly good match for Julia. A man with the same career interests and a ready-made family. He wished he could find a woman with his same interests. The only potential candidates were the daughters of other military personnel in Hawaii but he didn't have time to meet them.

In early January, 1974, Chris led a flight of four aircraft on a routine training mission. He received information that a storm was fast approaching the northern coast of Oahu and they had to return to base. Just as they turned to head back, one of the aircraft encountered an unidentified problem. Chris ordered the other two aircraft to head back; he remained with the troubled aircraft. He gave the pilot instructions he should have learned in flight school about trouble shooting various problems.

The pilot seemed to panic and screamed he couldn't control his aircraft. Chris told him to settle down, he could make it back if he had enough fuel.

Suddenly the pilot blew the canopy and ejected leaving his weapons officer stranded. The aircraft was still at level flight at about 6,000 ft., only 50 miles south of Honolulu.

Chris told the weapons officer to punch out immediately, which he did. Chris alerted the tower at Hickam Air Base of what transpired giving the position of the pilot and his back-seater. He told them the aircraft was headed toward Honolulu with no one onboard. Chris knew immediately a major disaster was about to occur.

He maneuvered his aircraft under the pilotless F-4 to determine how to either turn the aircraft out to sea or get it to plunge into the sea on its present course. His weapons officer said it would have been great if they had ammo so they could shoot it down. Chris wanted to push the aircraft under its wing to change course. He moved under the right wing and positioned his canopy under it. He made a slow turn to the left forcing the aircraft to turn in that direction. They were about 20 miles from Honolulu. Chris didn't know his actions had been observed by a C-130 returning to Hickam. The pilot told the tower what he witnessed.

Chris continued his efforts to turn the aircraft out to sea and away from Honolulu. His weapons officer monitored their position since Chris was focused on maintaining contact with the F-4's wing above their canopy. Once they moved the aircraft about 180 degrees, Chris had to carefully slide out from under the aircraft. He dropped altitude enough to change his direction then turned to watch the F-4 safely plunge into the sea. The weapons officer hooted out loud and congratulated Chris.

After reporting he was low on fuel, Chris was told Kaneohe was closed due to weather conditions. He was cleared to land at Hickam to refuel and wait for the storm to pass. By the time Chris landed, the Hickam Air Base wing commander had been briefed and waited on the tarmac to speak to Chris.

It was difficult for Brig. Gen. Greeley to believe what he heard, however since there were eye witnesses, he realized what Chris had accomplished; he saved countless civilian lives.

Chris and the general had a brief planeside conversation. The wing operations officer took Chris's statement after he received a message that the downed pilot and his back-seater had been located and would be picked up as soon as possible. Neither Chris nor his weapons officer mentioned that the pilot ejected first and left his weapons officer to fend for himself. They agreed not to mention it back at Kaneohe unless asked directly. If reported and verified, the pilot could be grounded for his actions.

Two hours later, Chris flew back to Kaneohe. It was dark when he landed. The squadron commander waited in his staff car until the two crew members left their aircraft. He beckoned them to get in with him.

"I think we have a problem, Major Harrington. The media wants to know what happened this afternoon and we aren't prepared to discuss it with them yet. I want you to return to Camp Smith and contact Col. Foster as soon as possible. You will not speak to any reporters, is that understood?" He said raising his voice.

"Yes sir," Chris shot back.

He changed his clothes and drove back to Camp Smith. He went to Col. Foster's house to pick up his son. The colonel was home and asked Chris to stay for dinner.

"The Hickam wing commander contacted Brig. Gen. Kurtz about three hours ago to inform him of your actions today. He requested the both of us see him first thing in the morning," the colonel said.

Chris didn't know whether he was going to be grounded or worse based on what the Kaneohe squadron commander said to him or what the colonel said.

"I understand, sir. I did the right thing under the circumstances. I only had a few minutes to make my decision," Chris said with confidence.

The colonel smiled and clapped him on the back.

"You're a fucking hero son, but no one knows it yet. Now let's eat and not mention this until tomorrow."

The TV news accounts of the F-4 crash were fairly accurate but didn't report the names of anyone involved. The following morning, Chris and the colonel reported to Kurtz' office. Another colonel was present and was introduced as the MARFORCOMPAC public affairs director.

"Nice to finally meet you Major Harrington. You've had quite a career of significant achievements since you graduated flight training. Even as you are here sitting behind a desk, you managed to accomplish something that one might call impossible. I don't know what to make of you," the general said.

Col. Foster said he believed Chris was a gifted pilot with great decision-making skills. Chris remined silent.

"Major Harrington, I want you to spend some time with one of our public affairs officers to review what the Kaneohe Air Base commander recommends we tell the press. My boss wants to keep his command out of the picture, unfortunately you belong to him. He wants you to refrain from whatever attempts are made to drag you into it. He has directed the Kaneohe commander not to release you name. Is that clear, major?" The general directed.

"Yes, sir, I will remain invisible," Chris replied.

"For the record, major, your actions yesterday were extraordinary. My boss would prefer to extoll your heroism but we must wait until the accident board concludes its investigation. You will be interviewed here and not at Kaneohe for reasons I can't discuss with you," the general said.

Chris met with the public affairs officer. It was obvious from the media statement that Kaneohe had protected the pilot and falsely stated he had flown his aircraft away from a populated area before he ejected.

"With all due respect, colonel, this is a complete fabrication. It makes the pilot out to be a hero. Too many people know the truth including the Hickam Air Base wing commander," Chris said.

"The Marine Corps can't afford to look bad here, major. The brass knows the truth and has bought off on this statement. I'll let my boss know you have voiced your objection to this press release," the public affairs officer said as he rose to leave.

When Chris and Col. Foster returned to the office, Chris told him the press statement was total bullshit and could backfire on the Corps. He explained that too many people knew the truth.

"Just go with the flow, Chris. It's not in our lane," Foster said.

Chris clenched his jaw and refrained from responding.

"By the way, Chris, the post-Vietnam lessons-learned team will visit here next week to interview members of our staff. Your name is on the list. Are you familiar with the team?" Foster asked.

"Yes, sir. I met them briefly before I left Quantico."

"The team is led by Lt. Gen. Iverson. According to my boss, Iverson is a no nonsense general so be careful, Chris," Foster said.

It was obvious he didn't know Chris's relationship to the general. The only person who could spill the beans was Andy. If he did, everyone would probably treat Chris differently and cautiously.

Chris returned to his desk job. Though the F-4 incident was a topic of conversation, no one knew Chris was involved. At the end of the week, the general called to say he and Edith arrived and wanted to invite them to dinner.

Andy was so excited to see his grandparents, he kept telling Chris to hurry up. Chris changed and drove to the VIP quarters. The reunion was exciting. Edith had a few things for Andy. At dinner, Edith handed Chris a letter she received from Julia. He put it in his pocket. It was obvious it wasn't good news based on Edith's expression.

"I heard about that F-4 accident; thank God no one was injured. Did you know anyone involved, Chris?" the general asked.

"I don't think they released any names yet," Chris replied.

He told the truth and hoped the general would drop the subject.

Andy spent most of the weekend with Edith. The general prepped his team for their week-long interviews. On Monday, Chris was interviewed by the accident investigation team. He and his weapons officer were interviewed separately. They both gave the accurate version of the events that occurred. The investigators had previously reviewed the statements from the Hickam wing commander and the C-130 crew that echoed their testimony.

Edith was the luncheon guest at the officer's wives club. Chris realized by the end of the day, everyone would know about his relationship with the general. What grandmother wouldn't brag about her grandson and his father.

The general and his team flew to Japan to continue interviewing Marines who saw service in Vietnam. Edith remained in Hawaii and spent the week with Chris and Andy. When Andy went to bed, Edith wanted to know Chris's reaction to Julia's letter.

"I was a bit confused, Edith. She explained her decision to marry her professor but still professed her love for me. I'll miss her and I wish her well."

Edith said her sister was relieved Julia would remain in France. For the rest of the week, neither of them mentioned Julia.

Col. Foster invited Edith, Chris and Andy to his house for dinner. The general would arrive the following day, he and Edith were scheduled to return to Quantico the day after. It was quite obvious from the colonel's behavior toward Chris during the week he and everyone else knew his relationship to Gen. Iverson. People were cautious about what they said in front of Chris.

He didn't know whether other officers were resentful or envious. In either case, Chris earned everything he had, including his early promotion.

17

ALICIA

A week after the general and his team returned to Quantico, Chris had a surprising visitor. His head was down buried in his work when someone knocked on his door and asked to see him. Chris looked up at the sound of a female voice. A young Marine lieutenant approached his desk and asked if he was the Cisco Kid. Chris smiled and stared at her but didn't respond. He noted the name tag on her uniform and immediately understood her question. He asked her to have a seat, took out his brief case and rummaged through it. He pulled out a worn photo of a young Marine officer and his younger sister.

"If this is you, Alicia, then I am the Cisco Kid," Chris said.

The photo was of Javier Cruz on the day he was commissioned, and his 15-year-old sister. She smiled and nodded. Cruz was Chris's best friend and was his weapons officer in Vietnam when he shot down two MiG's.

"You certainly grew up since this was taken," he said.

Alicia blushed.

"I am so happy you found me. I lost track of Javi when I returned from Vietnam in 1972. How is he? Where is he?" Chris asked.

"He's an instructor at Pensacola. He wanted to apply for pilot training but he got his RIF notice. He is heartbroken because you were his role model and he wanted to become a pilot," she said.

"When does he get discharged?"

"His last day is March 1st."

Chris was very upset.

"Does he have any plans yet?"

"He's hoping something will change. He doesn't want to leave the Corps.

You must know how much he loves it," Alicia said.

"Are you based in Hawaii, Alicia?"

"I arrived three weeks ago. I'm on the second floor in the intelligence group."

"How did you know I was here?" Chris asked.

"I didn't, but I overheard your name mentioned so I looked you up in the headquarters' directory. I took me two days to get the courage to speak to you," she responded.

"Since Javi and I are like brothers, then as my sister, would you feel okay if I invited you to dinner this weekend?"

"I thought you were married, sir," Alicia said.

"I forgot, Javi never knew about my divorce. I'm unattached but I have a seven-year-old son living with me. Besides, as my sister, married or not, you can accept my invitation to dinner. But if you want to think about it, I'll understand," Chris explained.

"Thank you, sir. I want to tell my brother I found you and of course get his approval. We, Cubans are old fashioned," she said looking down.

"Old fashioned is good. My son can serve as your chaperon," Chris said with a laugh.

She said she had to get back to work. Chris stood to shake her hand. When she left, he couldn't get over how beautiful she was. He resolved to contact the general to ask him for a favor. He was the only one who could help Javi.

Chris couldn't get Alicia off his mind. He knew he had to play it slow and with discretion. People in a close-knit organization notice everything and love to gossip.

Later in the afternoon, Chris called the general at home. Edith answered to tell him how much she enjoyed his hospitality and spending time with Andy. The general was surprised to hear from him. Before Chris had a chance to explain his call, the general mentioned he learned of Chris's role in the F-4 incident the previous month. He was upset the brass in Hawaii covered their asses at Chris's expense. He assured him that he'd make sure the Marine Commandant knew the truth. Chris thanked the general and then asked for a favor.

"Sir, my weapons officer in Vietnam who helped me get two of my kills, wants to become a pilot and has submitted his request. Unfortunately, no action has been taken because he received his RIF notice. Is there anything you can do to help him?"

"You know the head of Marine Aviation is a friend and a neighbor, but we've agreed to stay out of each other's business. I'll speak with him but I'll tell him the request is coming from you. You probably have more influence in this matter than I do. Have you mentioned this to Brigadier General Kurtz, after all you work for him?" The general asked.

"It's complicated, sir. Captain Cruz has a younger sister who was just assigned to Camp Smith. I'd rather not involve her," Chris said.

"I see. I hope she's an officer, you know the rules about fraternization," the general said with a laugh.

"We met once to talk about her brother," Chris responded.

"I'll see what I can do. Give me his name and where he is stationed."

Chris gave the information to the general and told him Javi had less than a month on active duty.

A few days later, Chris received a surprise call from Javi.

"Cisco, this is Poncho, I'm happy to have found you. I spoke to Alicia yesterday and she told me she located you. I'm sorry about your divorce. I thought Katie was a keeper," Javi said.

"I'm so glad you called. Alicia told me about the bad news. What will you do?"

"It came at a bad time. I got married last year and my wife is pregnant. There aren't a lot of civilian jobs for weapons officers," Javi lamented.

"Where did you meet your wife.? Chris asked.

"She's a friend of the family. You know Cubans like to play matchmaker, so I finally succumbed. Alicia joined the Corps to escape the pressure. My father wants her to marry a rich Cuban boy. She is very strong willed and refused to play the game.

"I must say she turned out to be a beautiful young woman. I think she'll survive, after all she made it this far," Chris said.

"She asked me a lot of questions about you. Be careful, my brother, if she sets her sights on you, you will be in trouble."

"I think my experiences with women, especially wives, has made me gun shy no matter how tempting a woman can be. I don't need any complications in my life, I have to focus on my son," Chris said.

They talked for a while longer. Chris never mentioned he was trying to help him. Javi asked Chris to watch over his sister.

The following week, Brig. Gen. Kurtz asked to see Chris. He told him the Air Force Pacific Forces commander spoke to the MARCOMPACFOR commander about Chris's heroic action. He wanted to make sure Chris was recognized despite what the official Marine Corps press release stated. He offered to endorse whatever the Marines awarded Chris.

Chris expressed his gratitude. The general said Chris's requirement to fly minimum hours every six weeks to maintain his flight status currency and pay had been waived. He said no one could question his abilities as a pilot even after nearly two years away from an operational assignment.

Chris was disappointed. He'd have to wait nearly two years to fly again.

A week after he spoke with Iverson, Javi called Chris with some good news. His RIF notice was delayed pending his approval for pilot training.

"I don't believe in coincidences, Cisco, did you have anything to do with this?"

"I don't have that much clout, Javi. However, it doesn't hurt to have friends who do. I just need to caution you about how things work. You aren't guaranteed anything unless you finish near the top of your class. Play by the rules and keep your eyes on the prize," Chris warned.

Chris was surprised Alicia hadn't contacted him since he was certain Javi told her the good news. Perhaps she thought Chris's two marriages and a son were too much for her. He understood.

When Alicia finally called him, it was a conversation he didn't expect. She told Chris she was TDY to Japan for a week during which time she had a very emotional experience.

Her boss, Lt. Col. Sykes, requested she accompany him on the trip, something she didn't expect since she was new to the group. Her immediate supervisor, Maj. Jennings was scheduled to go but Sykes cancelled his trip. Alicia felt very uneasy about going since she'd been told the colonel had a bad reputation. Chris listened intently without interruption.

Alicia said on the third night, the colonel had too much to drink and made some offensive comments to her. On the fourth night, he attempted to touch her but she rebuffed him. On the last night he pounded on her hotel door. She didn't open it but he forced his way in breaking the security chain. He grabbed her and attempted to kiss her. She punched him in the eye and nose. He cursed at her and said her career in the Marines was over and left.

Chris wanted to know what had happened since she returned. She said she told Maj. Jennings about it. He too knew about Sykes' problems with alcohol and women. He told her he was probably too drunk to remember what he did.

"That's all he said to you?" Chris asked.

"He said to keep quiet about it since no one would believe her," she replied.

Chris was very angry but didn't tell her he was going to do something about it. He asked if she was doing okay with the situation. She said no, it wasn't right but she couldn't do anything about it.

He asked if she spoke with her brother.

"Yes, and he told me the good news. Thank you if you had anything to do with it."

"Did you mentioned what happened in Japan?"

"Of course, I did. He was very angry and told me to tell you."

"I'm glad you did. Have you considered my dinner invitation? I won't be upset if you say no, I don't even know whether you are engaged or have a boyfriend, on the other hand, let's wait until things settle down."

"I'm not engaged and I don't have anyone in my life. I just want to be successful in my job."

He told her he understood and she should call him anytime she needed someone to talk to.

Chris made an appointment to speak with Col. Foster. When he learned it was for a personal matter, the colonel told him to come to his quarters around 6 p.m.

That night, over drinks, Chris explained his relationship with his former weapons officer and his sister who was assigned to the intelligence division. He also mentioned that her brother asked him to watch over her.

Chris asked the colonel if he knew anything about Sykes.

"I suppose your question has something to do with Lt. Cruz."

Chris told him the story of Sykes' behavior while in Japan.

"Sykes is an alcoholic and a cheater, and my wife says he abuses his wife. So, I'm not surprised to hear what happened in Japan," Foster replied.

"May I ask why he is still in the Corps?"

"The truth is the Corps is led by combat tested men, some of whom have done the same things. I know that's a lousy answer, but that's all I can say," the colonel replied.

"What do you know about his boss? Is he aware of Sykes' reputation?

"His boss is a friend of mine. You must have met him in Vietnam. He was a wing commander at Da Nang."

"I remember a Colonel Sunderland. He was injured when he ejected from his aircraft," Chris said.

"That's him. His injury took him out of the cockpit. He still walks with a limp. He was reassigned to Intelligence to give him a shot at a promotion to flag rank. He is one of us and was highly decorated during the Korean War."

"Do you think he knows about Sykes?" Chris asked.

"Hard to tell. He just got here three months ago. Sunderland is a religious man and doesn't drink, so I don't think he'd tolerate it if he knew."

"What should I do, colonel? Should I speak with Sunderland or take Sykes' head on?" Chris asked.

"I can't tell you what to do. You do what your mind tells you to do. I know your career is safe so long as you keep your head. My only suggestion is not to see Sunderland. Let me speak with him first. I want to make sure he knows about Sykes' past behavior. I'll get back to you in a few days," Foster said with a wink.

Three days later, Col. Sunderland met with Chris and Foster.

"Thank you, Chris for bringing this matter to our attention. I heard allegations that Sykes has a drinking problem but no disciplinary action has been brought against him. You were in my wing at Da Nang for a brief period of time. You know my reputation as a no-nonsense commander. I plan on taking the first steps to remove Sykes from the Corps either through early retirement or by disciplinary action. He is sticking around to see if he gets promoted. I'll make certain that doesn't happen," Sunderland said.

"I think Colonel Foster explained why I came to him. I don't think attempted rape should be tolerated especially since the victim is a Marine lieutenant assigned to his group. The rest of the allegations would be enough to kick out an enlisted man but yet Sykes is still here."

"The Corps has to change now that more women are enlisting and more female officers are coming onboard as well. I can assure you I will collect all the negative information that has been recorded on Sykes' behavior. I have a meeting tomorrow with the headquarters unit commander, who has the legal authority to take whatever action is required, and I'll speak with the shore patrol's garrison commander, NCIS and JAG. I suspect any information on Sykes has been buried," Sunderland explained.

"Thank you, sir. Not many senior officers would take point on this matter," Chris replied.

"Not too many pilots would have taken the risks you have taken. I was just like you in Korea as a young lieutenant," Sunderland remarked.

When Foster and Chris went back to their office, Foster said he had confidence that Sykes' days would be numbered.

A few days later, Chris called Alicia to find out how she was getting along. She seemed to be in a good mood. She said Sykes hadn't spoken to her since they returned. She thought he didn't remember what he did since he was so drunk. Chris said that drunk or not, his behavior was dead wrong.

"Have you heard from Javi recently?" Chris inquired.

"I speak to him twice a week. He is still waiting for news about his application. He is quite nervous about it," she said.

"I'll call him this afternoon to keep his spirits up," Chris said.

"What has he told you about me?" She asked.

"Nothing much except you are stubborn, a fighter, defied your parents by not getting married and when you want something you go out and get it. Is that about, right?"

"That's Javi. He makes me sound like a monster. Did he have anything nice to say about me?"

"That's between us brothers."

"Well, for the record, I am very nice to some people. I'd like to cook a Cuban meal for you and your son this weekend. Am I still invited?" She asked.

"Do you have a car?"

"Not yet. You'll have to take me to a super market so I can buy the ingredients. How about picking me up in front of my quarters at noon on Saturday?"

"No problem, Alicia. I'll see you Saturday."

Chris was surprised by Alicia's change in behavior. Perhaps Javi convinced her he was someone she should get to know better. It was nice to have a good character reference. Chris knew she needed her big brother but he was in Florida. He would fill that role for the time being.

On Friday, someone from NCIS called to make an appointment to speak to him. Col. Sunderland must have stirred up some shit. Chris held him off until he had a chance to speak with Alicia.

Saturday, Chris and Andy met Alicia at her quarters. Andy asked her a lot of questions which she politely answered. They drove to a large shopping center to buy what Alicia needed to make dinner. Since Alicia hadn't been to Honolulu yet, Chris drove to Waikiki and took the highway toward Diamondhead.

They returned to Chris's house around three in the afternoon. Before Alicia headed for the kitchen, he took her aside and asked if she was contacted by NCIS.

"They called yesterday and asked to see me but they didn't tell me why.

I meet them on Monday. I think it might have something to do with my security clearance," she replied.

"I have to tell you that Sykes is being investigated for a lot of bad behavior, among which is what he tried to do to you."

Before Chris could finish his explanation, she showed her temper.

"What did you do, sir? I can't put my career in jeopardy. What if he finds out I mentioned his behavior to you?"

She was visibly upset. Chris tried to comfort her. He touched her for the first time and held her hand.

"He brought this on himself. You aren't the only one who will testify about him. Hopefully you'll be the last one. He can't hurt you; I'll be there for you as will other decent Marines. Tell NCIS exactly what happened as best as you remember."

"I won't forget and I'll tell them how I defended myself," she added.

Alicia calmed down when she realized this was her only way to fight back and get even.

She was a wonderful cook. Andy had two helpings. Alicia was pleased her meal was so well received. Chris thought she fit right in though he hadn't contemplated Alicia being more than a friend. He still had feelings for Julia but they were rapidly fading into the nether region.

"Please don't take this the wrong way, Alicia, if you ever want to get away from the BOQ, we have a third bedroom. You are always welcome. It's not much but it's quiet and you can do what you want. You can take my car and go to the beach or to the shopping center," Chris offered.

"I told my brother you were so nice to me and I felt safe with you. Men are usually very aggressive, pushy and obnoxious around me. I seem to attract the wrong type, even back in Miami. Cuban boys think they are Latin lovers, it made me sick. My parents were always introducing me to the sons of rich Cubans. That's one reason I joined the Marines. Unfortunately, I haven't avoided the men that are so aggressive in their behavior towards me. So, thank you for your kind offer to escape the reality of my life," she said.

"You can trust Andy, he won't come on to you," Chris said with a chuckle.

"What about you, Chris?"

"My life is dedicated to my son and the Corps. I've been hurt by loving someone whom I trusted, not once, but twice. I'm sure Javi told you about my first marriage. Before I came here, I developed a special relationship with my first wife's cousin. She went home to France and surprisingly got engaged to one of her professors. You'll forgive me if I don't want to get hurt again," Chris responded.

Alicia looked at Chris with compassion. He didn't want to make her feel sorry for him, but he did.

"I'm so sorry, Chris. You sought love and happiness and got hurt and I resist seeking the same. We are so opposite. As long as we can be friends, I'll be satisfied. But if anything changes, one way or the other, let's be open about it."

Chris knew she wanted to keep that door open. If she found someone to love, she wanted to be able to tell him without rupturing their friendship.

"Of course, we should be open and honest about everything," he said.

Chris drove her back to the BOQ after dark. They had to be discreet until the investigation was over.

Alicia didn't speak with him on Monday though he expected her to tell him about the interview. The investigator probably warned her not to discuss anything with anyone.

On Tuesday, Chris met with NCIS in his office. Since the investigator was in civilian clothes, people in the group became curious. The Sykes investigation was not well known around the command. However, rumors and gossip were plentiful in the military world.

Chris was asked a lot of questions about Alicia. He made it clear how he came to know her, what he knew about her first hand and from her brother. He iterated there was no involvement with her, she was a friend and the sister of his best friend. He had to explain why he went to Col. Foster about the incident which eventually went to Col. Sunderland. Chris was candid and told the investigator he would rather have visited Sykes and dealt with him in a direct way, but Foster advised him to stay away from him. Chris ended by saying he's never laid eyes on Sykes and was hopeful the Marines would seek justice.

The interview lasted 20 minutes after which time he was told not to discuss it with anyone. Chris didn't know if NCIS knew about his relationship with General Iverson, if they did, they might feel the investigation could attract high level interest.

Chris didn't contact Alicia because he wanted to maintain his distance until the investigation was over. He also didn't ask questions about the status of the case.

Foster met with Chris and informed him that Lt. Col. Davis decided to retire because his wife's health wasn't good. Steve and Chris worked closely together but he never discussed his personal life so Chris was surprised to learn of his retirement.

"Chris there isn't a replacement in the pipeline anytime soon. I'd like you to assume Steve's responsibilities," Foster said.

"I'm grateful you have confidence in me, sir, but I am too junior to do the things Steve did," Chris replied.

"Are you concerned that when you visit our squadrons to review them and to discuss problems you find with senior officers that your rank isn't sufficient enough to earn their respect?" Foster asked.

"Something like that, sir,"

"I thought you were displeased on how our squadrons performed during inspections, but then on the other hand, you rarely did anything by the book. It doesn't matter, no one will question the highest decorated Marine fighter pilot during the Vietnam War and a Navy top gun; a number one top gun," Foster said like a proud father.

"There is another issue that is of a personal nature. I shouldn't bring it up but...."

Foster cut him off.

"Don't worry about Andy when you go TDY, Liz and my wife will take care of him," Foster said.

Chris smiled with relief. He wanted to see how post-war fighter pilots performed rather than read all those boring reports and statistics.

"I will do what is needed to be done, sir. Thank you for considering my personal situation," Chris said.

"Steve will be with us for 60 days and will take you on his last inspection in a few weeks. Until then, it's business as usual."

Chris called Javi to find out if he had any word on his application. He was very happy to hear from Chris. He told him he had been accepted for pilot training but didn't get a start date yet. He was so grateful for whatever Chris did to make his dream come true.

"You deserve this opportunity, Javi, you earned it. I hope we get to fly together again, Chris said.

"Thank you, brother. I spoke to Alicia a few days ago. She told me about how you've treated her. She has a tough time with men because she is so beautiful; she is turned off by their comments and other behavior. She said you are so different. I think she likes you very much but she fears you have built a protective wall around you. She asked me for advice. I told her not to let you get away," Javi said.

"I don't know what to say, Javi. I like her very much but what kind of life would we have if we are in two different sides of the world? I promise I won't hurt her by pushing her away. However, my career might take me places she can't go and I have a son who needs me. It's so complicated and I think she knows it," Chris replied.

"Remember I told you once, if Alicia wants something, she'll find a way to get it," Javi said.

"Yes, I remember. Please call me when you get your class date."

Chris sat back in his chair, took a deep breath and exhaled to calm down. He had so much on his mind. Alicia crossed his mind often. He liked her a lot; he could probably fall in love with her but would either of them benefit from such a relationship?

The following week, Chris was told to report to Brig. Gen. Kurtz' office. When he arrived, he was meet by Maj. Gen. Cassidy, the MARFORPAC deputy chief of staff for aviation, Col. Foster, and Gen. Curtis Taggert, MARFORPAC commander-in-chief.

There were a few other senior officers present that Chris never met. He was told to stand between Cassidy and Taggert. Chris didn't know what was going on. Taggert addressed the small group.

"When we recognize our Marines for extraordinary achievement, we usually call the media to publicize the event. Unfortunately, today we are not going to publicize something that should be told to every person residing in Honolulu. I'm sure Major Harrington understands the reasons as most of you do,"

The general's aide read the citation of Chris's heroic effort to save lives by diverting a pilotless F-4 from crashing into a populated area. Taggert stepped in front of Chris and pinned the Distinguished Flying Cross on his jacket pocket. Everyone applauded as Chris saluted him.

"Thank you for this honor, sir. It was a well-kept secret. I was told a few weeks ago not to discuss that day and to become more or less invisible. Therefore, I'm not here this morning, no one has seen me and I've kept my word," Chris said to laughter and applause.

Taggert asked Chris to accompany him to his office. Once inside the spacious office, the general asked Chris to sit down.

"I've known General Iverson for more than 20 years. We served together in Korea and Vietnam. He is one of the finest infantry officers I've ever served with. He is so damn proud of you, major. He told me you're like a son to him. Since his daughter died, you have been even more significant to him."

"I assume he's told you I lost my father when I was seven. He was shot down in Korea. I've come to realize he's filled that void though I didn't meet the general until I was 16," Chris said.

"You've honored your father and the general by your achievements."

"Thank you, sir, for sharing. The general doesn't say a lot to me about things like that. We mostly talk about his grandson."

"In a few minutes, Rear Admiral Ben Weiss will visit us. He is the deputy JAG for Naval Forces, Pacific. He has reviewed the NCIS investigation and we've made a decision that you might not like. Sykes should have been dealt with several years ago. Almost everything he has done wrong was because of his drinking problem. That's no excuse for his behavior, but there is a mitigating factor. Sykes was estranged from his son when he went to Vietnam in 1969. When his son turned 18, he joined the Marines. He, too was sent to Vietnam while his father was still there. To make a long story short, he managed to meet up with his father. It was a very emotional reunion. Three weeks later his son was killed."

Chris listened intently but kept quiet.

"Sykes returned from Vietnam and was assigned here. He drank heavily and blamed his wife for allowing his son to enlist, Of course, his wife didn't know about his enlistment until he came home from boot camp."

There was a knock on the door. Ben Weiss was introduced to Chris. Taggert said the admiral wanted to inform Chris of the decision as a courtesy to him since he started the initial inquiry.

"After reviewing the testimony from 30 witnesses, 28 of which were negative, we concluded there was enough factual evidence to bring charges against Lieutenant Colonel Sykes. The most compelling testimony was from his wife, also a victim of physical abuse. In hindsight, people covered for Sykes which was the worst thing they could have done. He needed help," the admiral said.

"My decision is based on our failure to deal honestly with Sykes. I've decided, and Ben agrees, that Sykes will be sent to an alcohol treatment facility in San Diego for 90 days. At the end of that time, he will retire from the Corps," Taggert said.

"Does he know about your decision, sir?" Chris asked.

"He knows he was being investigated but doesn't know the outcome yet. We will advise him he has two choices; retire or face several criminal charges," the general said.

"JAG was informed that Mrs. Sykes left for the mainland the day after she gave her deposition. She was afraid of her husband's reaction when he learned of the command's decision," the admiral said.

"Chris, you can't discuss our conversation with anyone in my command. As far as Lieutenant Cruz is concerned, she will find out in due time. I understand she is a fine officer and I hope she hasn't lost faith in the Corps," the general said.

Chris left with mixed emotions. Sykes should go to prison but he had problems that were ignored for at least three years.

18

NOT A GOOD DAY

Alicia called and said she had her toothbrush, could she crash with him this weekend?

Of course, he said yes. He promised they'd go out to dinner though he loved her cooking.

When she arrived, he noticed she brought a small bag probably with extra clothes.

"I've always wanted to go parasailing, what about you?" She asked.

"I did it in San Diego, I think Andy would love it," Chris responded.

They had a great time together. They found a place to parasail. Andy couldn't go alone so he was tethered to Chris. The next day they decided to go to Sunday brunch at the officers' club. Alicia was very good with Andy and very respectful to Chris. Neither Alicia nor Chris made any flirtatious remarks, in fact they were like sister and brother which suited Chris.

During brunch, people Chris knew came by to say hello to him and to Andy. Chris introduced Alicia by her first name. Not too many officers or their wives knew Alicia or that she was a Marine officer.

After brunch, Chris opened the driver side of his car to let Andy in the back and then walked around to let Alicia in. Someone in the parking yelled at Alicia.

"You bitch, you whore, it's all your fault, my life is ruined because of you."

Alicia turned to see Sykes approaching. Chris told her to get into the car and lock the door. Sykes stopped about 15 feet from the car and pulled out a hand gun. Chris shouted for Alicia to get down and for Andy to lay down on the floor. Chris turned to face Sykes as he fired a shot at the car hitting the right fender.

Chris charged Sykes as two other men raced to grab Sykes from behind but not before he fired another round that hit Chris. He stopped and fell to his knees. He felt a sharp pain in his right side. He fell forward and struck his head on the asphalt above his left eye. He remained conscious but had trouble breathing. Someone gently turned Chris on his back. Blood seeped from his chest. Another person yelled for an ambulance. Alicia raced over to him screaming his name. Chris told her to take Andy home. Col. Foster arrived and pulled her away.

"I'll have my wife take them home. I'm going with you to the emergency room," Foster said as he grabbed Chris's hand.

The ambulance arrived, an EMT put an oxygen mask on Chris's face and a pressure bandage on his chest. They place him on a gurney and then into the ambulance. The last thing Chris remembered was looking at a very concerned Foster.

Fortunately, the doctors in the emergency room at Tripler Army Hospital saw a lot of chest wounds in Vietnam and knew exactly what to do. They X-rayed Chris's chest to locate the bullet. Apparently, it grazed a rib and ricocheted into his lung. Chris was taken to surgery to remove the bullet during which time his lung collapsed. The surgeon noticed Chris's left eye was swollen shut. There was a large hematoma above the brow. When Chris left the operating room, he had a tube in his chest, a swollen eye, a broken rib, an IV for pain medication; all a result of protecting Alicia and telling the truth about Sykes' behavior. Chris spent two days in ICU during which time he had one visitor allowed; his mother, Bonnie.

She flew to Hawaii as soon as she was contacted by the Marines. Alicia picked her up at the airport and took her to Chris's house. Alicia stayed there to take care of Andy. Bonnie and Alicia got along quite well. Col. Foster stopped by to see if they needed anything.

"I'm so glad you were able to come so soon, Mrs. Harrington. General Iverson called to inform me that Edith was in France visiting her family. He will probably want to speak with you tonight for an update on Chris's condition," Foster said.

Foster took Alicia aside and told her to stay with Mrs. Harrington. He said Sunderland gave her 10 days leave for personal business. She smiled and thanked him.

On the third day after the incident, Chris was moved to a hospital room where he could see his visitors. Bonnie brought Andy who was very upset by what happened on Sunday. He couldn't understand why someone would shoot his father. Chris made up a story about a bad man who wanted to hurt people and he was in the way.

Several officers visited him, one of whom was Taggert's chief of staff. He informed Chris that Sykes' deal was off the table and he would be charged with attempted murder. He also said Taggert had been on the phone with Gen. Iverson several times a day. Taggert had to explain everything to him and how Chris was involved. Chris had never mentioned anything to Iverson about Alicia or Sykes.

Alicia visited Chris for the first time. She was visibly upset and said it was all her fault. He told her not to blame herself, she was a victim as was he. He took her hand, the second time he ever touched her.

"I will recover, Alicia, and Sykes will go to prison. He did it to himself."

She nodded.

"How is my mother doing?" He asked.

"She's worried, of course. She's thrilled to be with Andy for a few days. We are getting along though she doesn't quite understand my relationship with you. I just said we were friends. She's leaving tomorrow."

"I want you to stay at the house until I get back. We can talk about what to do after that," Chris said.

The following morning Chris's mom and Mrs. Foster paid a visit. Bonnie was sad to leave but she had to get back home. She said Alicia was wonderful and thinks she has strong feelings for him. Mrs. Foster agreed based on knowing Alicia for a few months. Bonnie cautioned Chris to be careful and not hurt her.

On the fourth day, the surgeon told Chris he could go home in a few hours. He gave him a list of things to do and not to do for two weeks, sex being one of latter. Chris underwent a thorough physical exam. He was told what to expect and what not to expect, and to call if the latter occurred.

19

CONFESSIONS

Alicia arrived at noon to take Chris home. She brought a change of clothes and seemed embarrassed when she pulled out a pair of his underwear.

Chris didn't talk much on the way home. He had a lot of decisions to make and wanted them to be perfect. Alicia spoke very highly about Andy. She felt they were bonding and was concerned for him when she had to leave Hawaii.

That bit of information helped Chris with what he would say at home later.

Alicia urged Chris to go to bed. He decided to sit in the living and talk with Alicia about the things he thought about while hospitalized. She sat on an ottoman directly in front of him since turning to either side was painful for him.

"Alicia, I want to thank you for all you have done for me and Andy. I am grateful your boss gave you time off to be here full time. I wanted to take Sykes down. I had to get him to do something that didn't earn me a Court Martial. I guess it worked. I want you to consider moving in with us, unless you would feel uncomfortable."

"Are you afraid my reputation would be ruined?" She asked with a smile.

"I don't know how to answer you. Do you think our neighbors would think less of you?

"I suppose things are different nowadays, but we are Marines and we live under scrutiny in government housing."

"I want to say something that may make your decision a little easier. When I first met you, I considered you as Javi's baby sister. I told Javi I would look out for you and be your big brother."

Chris knew at once she didn't like what he said.

"It sounds lame as I hear myself saying it to you. After your incident in Japan, I knew I was wrong. You are a Marine officer that can take care of herself. I developed a great deal of respect for you and I began to see you in a different light. The bottom line is, I fell in love with you but was afraid to say anything to you. My previous relationships didn't end well and I'm not certain I want to put Andy through another disappointment."

Chris stared at her feet while confessing his love. When he looked up, Alicia had covered her face with her hands and was crying.

"I'm sorry I upset you. I should have kept my mouth shut," he whispered.

Chris handed her a few tissues. When he did, she grabbed his hand and pulled it to her lips.

"Chris, I've been in love with you for three years," she confessed.

"But we've only met a few months ago."

"Javi wrote to me about your relationship during the war. He said he considered you his brother. When he came home, all he spoke about was you. He hoped we could meet someday. He didn't know you married again. He showed me many photos of you. I thought you were so…."

She couldn't find the words.

"I hope I didn't disappoint you, Alicia. What you've witnessed the last three months isn't the real me. If you move in with us, you'll probably get a different impression. Now that I know how you feel about me, I'll have to be on my best behavior. By the way, since I had little knowledge of you or any expectations, all I can say is you overwhelmed me in so many ways."

"Don't you want to kiss the woman you love?" She said in a shy way.

"Of course, I do, many times before today, but I couldn't do it without some idea of how you felt about me."

Alicia stood up to face Chris. Their lips met. They embraced as they explored each other's mouth for the first time. Though Chris still had considerable pain, he had a strong desire to make love to her. Alicia noticed Chris was sweating and asked if he was in pain. He said he wanted to lie down.

"Are you trying to get me into your bed, Chris?"

"At the moment, anything like that wouldn't be good for either of us. Where did you put my pain pills?" He asked.

"I'll bring them to you, just go lie down. Andy should be home from school soon. He will be thrilled to see you."

"I can't wait to see him. Has he talked about what happened last Sunday?"

"Yes, several times. I tried to tell him not to worry, your father will be home soon. It would be better to hear it from you," she said.

The bedroom door was open. Chris saw something that warmed his heart. When Andy came flying through the front door, he ran to Alicia, jumped into her arms and kissed her. Apparently, she won him over as well. He asked if his daddy was home. She said he was resting in bed.

Andy came to the bedroom door quietly.

"Daddy are you sleeping?"

Chris opened his eyes and held out his hand. Andy approached the bed and grabbed his father's hand. Chris pulled his son toward him and told him to lay down with him. Andy kissed his father and snuggled beside him. Alicia saw everything from the door.

"Is there room for one more?" She asked.

"Lay down on daddy's other side," Andy said.

Chris waved to her. She was thrilled to join them.

Alicia put her head on Chris's chest and positioned her body as close to him as possible.

"Your son is responsible for this. You didn't have the courage to invite me," she whispered and laughed.

"You have an open invitation so you can accept whenever you want to. Are you okay with that, my love?" He replied.

"Only if you are a hundred percent," she said laughing.

Alicia asked Andy if he's ready for his snack. He said he didn't want to leave his daddy. She insisted by telling him his daddy needed to sleep.

Five minutes after they left the room, Chris was out cold. He didn't wake up until it was dark. Alicia asked if he was hungry. She said Andy was ready for bed and she left something for Chris to eat.

Chris got out of bed. He was unsteady on his feet. Alicia grabbed his arm and they went to Andy's room. After she kissed him good night, Andy asked his daddy to stay with him.

"What's up, my big boy?

"Can Alicia stay with us all the time?"

"I asked her today and I think she wants to stay with us."

"Can she be my mommy; I love her very much."

Chris was caught off guard but realized he and his son had the same desire.

"Let me work on it for a few weeks. I can't promise you anything right now but I want what you want. Get some sleep, sweet dreams."

20

THE FIRST NIGHT

When Chris returned to the bedroom, he heard Alicia singing in his shower. A really shy young women probably wouldn't do that unless she was deeply in love with someone. He decided not to join her but to wait until she was finished.

Chris tapped on the door and asked who was using all his hot water.

"There's plenty left. Come in, Chris," she said sweetly.

Chris opened the door a crack to see if she was covered or not. She was, so he walked in and saw a vision wrapped in a fluffy white towel.

Chris hesitated before he started to undress. He wasn't embarrassed but he didn't want to shock Alicia by revealing his shrapnel-scarred back and legs.

"Oh my God. You never told me about this. Does it hurt?" She asked.

Alicia reached out and gently touched his back. Her caress stimulated him.

"You have such a gentle touch. It's something to look forward to," he quipped."

He turned on the water, dropped his underwear and stepped into the shower. She told him they'll have to coordinate bathroom time better. He said he was sorry he was 20 minutes too late. They both laughed.

By the time Chris opened the bathroom door, Alicia was asleep in bed. Chris smiled and told himself he was the luckiest man in the world. He quietly slipped in beside her and stared at her beauty. Though his brain knew what his little friend wanted to do, his heart said to let Alicia rest until another day.

On Saturday, Chris and Alicia had to get up early to prepare Andy for his outing with the Fosters. Liz Foster's high school boyfriend was arriving on an aircraft carrier from the South China Sea. He joined the Navy after college and became a helicopter pilot. Liz hadn't seen him in over a year. The Fosters invited Andy to join them to see the ship. Chris believed Bud wanted to give them some private time.

All three of them were invited to a BBQ at the Foster's home later that afternoon. As soon as they deposited Andy at the Foster's, Chris and Alicia retuned to bed. Chris didn't know if he should pursue his basic desire immediately or wait until Alicia said or did something to suggest he take the first step.

It was quite obvious to Chris what Alicia wanted as she slipped out of her clothes and climbed under the covers 'au natural'. She pressed her body against his and pulled his face to hers. They kissed, and with no conversation their love making swept them up. They went from deep animated and satisfying sex to shorts naps and another sexual encounter that definitely eliminated any uncertainty that might have lingered earlier in the day.

They showered and got dressed for the BBQ across the street. The Fosters returned from Pearl Harbor before Chris and Alicia walked across the street. Mrs. Foster answered the door and looked at the couple, from one to the other.

"I know what you two have been up to," she said with a smile and a wink.

Alicia blushed; Chris looked over Mrs. Foster's shoulder to search for Andy. Most of the guests were either neighbors or colleagues the colonel knew at work. He greeted Chris and Alicia and introduced them to everyone. A few asked Chris how his recovery was going.

It was a fun night. Alicia chatted with the wives, though she was one of the men, Marine-wise. After the BBQ, Chris noted Alicia was having some discomfort. He took her aside and asked her how she felt. She said she had terrible cramps which she attributed to the onset of her period. Chris decided to take her home claiming it was past Andy's bedtime.

After putting Andy to bed, Chris found Alicia in the bathroom bent over in pain.

"I don't think it's my period. The pain is on my right side."

Chris thought it could be appendicitis though he didn't mention it to her. Alicia spent a restless night as the pain grew worse. At five in the morning, Chris called Tripler Army Hospital's emergency room to find out who was on duty. He knew most of the physicians there. Dr. Roy Fisher spoke with Chris who told him what was going on with Alicia and what he suspected.

"Bring her in right away, Chris, I'll be happy to examine her," he said.

Chris woke Alicia who was in considerable pain and told her they were going to the emergency room. He got Andy ready for the short trip to the hospital.

Alicia had trouble walking. Once they arrived at the hospital he asked if someone could find a wheel chair. Dr. Fisher took Alicia to an examining room. Chris and Andy waited outside for what seemed several hours.

"You were right, Chris, we have to operate soon or risk the chance of a burst appendix. Dr. Grossman is the surgeon on call. He should be here in a few minutes," Fisher said.

Dr. Grossman arrived, went to the operating room while the staff prepared for Alicia. She was mildly sedated but managed to hold Chris's hand as they took her gurney to the operating room. Chris kissed her as did Andy. They were shown to a nearby waiting room.

Andy was very concerned about Alicia. Chris explained what was taking place but before he finished, Andy fell asleep.

An hour and twenty minutes later, a nurse told Chris the operation was successful. Alicia was moved to the recovery room. The nurse showed Chris where Alicia would be taken after she woke up.

Since they had to wait at least another hour, Chris decided to take Andy to the cafeteria for breakfast.

They returned to Alicia's room and arrived 10 minutes before she was wheeled in on a gurney. She was awake but groggy. She smiled when she saw Chris and Andy.

"That was one hell of a period, sweetheart," Chris whispered in her ear. She smiled and touched his face. Dr. Grossman took Chris aside and told him he couldn't have waited a moment longer since the appendix was inflamed and could have ruptured. Chris thanked him and asked how long she'd be hospitalized.

"If there are no complications, perhaps Wednesday morning."

Chris was relieved. He went to the nurse's station and called Col. Foster to tell him what happened to Alicia. He asked the colonel to let Col. Sunderland know that Alicia had surgery and would be out about two weeks.

"Of course, Chris. If he's shorthanded, I'll tell him he can have you as a temporary replacement," he said laughing.

By the time Chris returned to Alicia's room she was asleep so he decided to take Andy home and get some sleep as well.

Three days after her operation, Chris brought Alicia home. She looked good but felt weak and tired. Chris made her comfortable and let her sleep the rest of the day.

The next day, Foster called to say Sunderland wanted him to give the morning intelligence briefing. Alicia's boss, Maj. Jennings, was on leave and there was no one else Sunderland trusted to brief the general staff. Chris had to report at seven in the morning.

When Alicia woke up, Chris explained what he had to do in the morning. She said she was well enough to get Andy ready for school.

Chris was handed his notes 15 minutes before the briefing. He knew most of the senior staff so he wasn't nervous. Sunderland introduced him and made some comment about the unavailability of his briefers so he had to steal someone who could walk and chew gum.

The summary of events in Asia was rather boring. Only the activity in South Vietnam drew any interest. Intelligence analysts believed the South Vietnamese could delay a North Vietnamese victory for at least 18 months. Most of the folks in the room were quite skeptical at the projection.

After the briefing, Chris called Alicia to find out how she felt and how the morning went. She was upbeat and even cooked something to eat. He missed her very much.

Chris went to his office for the first time since he was shot. Foster told him to move into the deputy's office and review the six personnel folders on the desk.

"I've been given permission to bring two pilots on the team to support you. Unfortunately, we didn't get any top guns. These six officers are all on the early out list. We can save the two best ones; it's up to you."

Chris read through the six files to look for the positive contents. He ranked the six and then read the files again to search for any negative comments. Three of the four captains had combat experience. The two lieutenants had less than three years' service.

There weren't any red flags, nothing negative in their job performances. Chris concluded the six were placed on the RIF list because of force reductions.

He returned the folders to his boss in rank order. The colonel quickly looked them over, nodded his head and asked Chris to contact them about coming to Hawaii if they wanted to remain on active duty.

Chris had to contact the first three on the list because the second one said he had accepted a job with an airline. The other two gladly accepted the offer. Chris told them their PCS orders would be available in a week.

Foster gave Chris more responsibility over the next several weeks. He hinted that some changes were about to occur and not be surprised how it would impact him.

The two newly assigned officers reported to the colonel's office on the same day. After he explained how they were selected, and by whom, he introduced them to Chris.

"They are all yours, Chris," he said.

Both thanked Chris for selecting them from the RIF list.

"This job is not a substitute for an operational billet but it gives you some breathing room for a few years. If you demonstrate my faith in you, I'm sure your fitness reports will keep you on active duty," Chris said.

Chris described their duties in detail and then gave them some of the reports he generated over the past several months.

In his new role, Chris would have to go on every operational readiness inspection to Marine aviation facilities throughout the Pacific.

21

CHANGE HAS TWO ROADS

Whenever he thought about Alicia, which was all the time, he convinced himself it was never too soon to ask her to marry him. He went to a recommended jeweler in Honolulu to buy an engagement ring. He spent a lot of money, but she was worth it.

The next task was to find an appropriate place and time to ask her the big question. He not only wanted it to be totally unexpected, but he'd ask her in Spanish. He never told Alicia he was fluent.

On an especially wonderful cool evening, he invited Alicia and Andy to take a walk where they could view the lights of Pearl Harbor. As an added surprise, Chris taught Andy to say he wanted Alicia to be his mother, in Spanish.

Chris's heart was pumping so hard he thought she could hear it. He wasn't nervous, just excited. They found a bench where all three sat to enjoy the view. Chris got down on one knee and asked Alicia, in Spanish, to be his wife. She put her hands over her face and cried.

She replied in Spanish that she would. She embraced and kissed him while Andy tugged at her to get her attention. Alicia knelt down to face Andy who looked at his father for encouragement. In perfect Spanish, Andy asked Alicia to be his mother. She broke down and cried again.

"I want to be your mother more than anything else", she said in English.

That wasn't so bad, Chris thought. He tried to compare it to his first two marriage proposals but he had no clear memory of them. Now the newly engaged couple had to pick their wedding date. More importantly, they had to decide whether to marry in Hawaii or in Miami. Alicia had a big family to placate which made the decision a lot harder.

Alicia called her parents to tell them the good news. Her mother was thrilled as was her father. They even began planning the wedding over the phone.

Alicia's father preferred to speak Spanish so Chris surprised him with a 15-minute-long conversation with a belated request for permission to marry his daughter. Chris continued in Spanish when he spoke to Alicia's mother.

Chris tried to contact Javi but he wasn't available. He'd learn about it from his parents.

Since Chris knew there were lots of changes were in the near future, he suggested they get married around Thanksgiving.

It didn't take long for word to get out at Camp Smith that the beautiful Cuban lieutenant was betrothed to Chris. There were lots of smiles among his friends, filled with envy Chris surmised.

In early May, the changes were announced to everyone's shock. The Marine Corps chain of command was about to churn in a big way. The current Marine Corps commandant was selected to become the head of the Joint Chiefs of Staff. The deputy commandant retired leaving the two top Marine leadership positions open. The current MARFORCOMPAC commander, General Taggert was selected to become the new Marine Corps commandant. The rumor was that Chris' former father-in-law would get his fourth star and become the deputy commandant. There must have been an interesting backstory to this move because the deputy commandant wasn't announced until a week later.

When the new MARFORPACOM was announced, Chris was ecstatic. When he told Andy, that grandpa was coming to Hawaii to stay for a long time, he was so excited. The general called the following day to tell Chris he was given two choices. He turned down the deputy commandant job since he'd never be considered for the top job in the future because of his age. He said Edith was ecstatic to be with them for at least the last year of Chris' tour of duty.

Other news involved Alicia's boss, Col. Sunderland was selected for his first star and promoted to the MARFORPACOM staff as the deputy chief of staff for Intelligence. The best news was about Col. Foster, Chris's boss, also selected for his first star and assigned to the MARFORPACOM staff as the deputy chief of staff for Aviation. He replaced. Maj. Gen. Cassidy who was selected for his third star and assigned to the Marine Corps commandant's staff as deputy chief for Aviation.

All of these announcements had little impact on 90 percent of the men and women in the Marine Corps. But to Chris, all of his friends were suddenly in the right places.

Chris feared Alicia would be assigned to work directly for Sunderland and therefore would never have any time as his wife or Andy's mother.

From June through August, there were lots of social events that celebrated all the senior officer changes. Chris and Alicia were invited to every event.

The phone calls between Alicia and Miami became more frequent and intense as the wedding date neared. Alicia was a bit stressed because she was so far away; she was a hands-on person.

In late September, Chris, Foster and numerous other staff officers and NCOs departed for Japan to conduct a no-notice operational readiness inspection.

It was the first time Chris and Alicia were apart, except for their respective brief hospital stays. On day three of his TDY, Chris received a message that Lt. Col. Dan Ryan called his office in Hawaii on an urgent matter. Chris expected the worst news from his former brother-in-law, it was as he expected.

"Chris, you have to go to Reno as soon as possible. We have a major problem here and you are part of the solution," were the first words spoken by Ryan.

Over the next 30 minutes, Chris learned that Katie, his second wife, had a devastating psychological meltdown and was in a psychiatric ward at a county hospital. Her daughter, Annie, who regarded Chris as her father, was with her grandmother. Unfortunately, the grandmother had stage four pancreatic cancer and could no longer care for Annie.

Chris was surprised to learn that Dan separated from his wife after she gave birth to their third daughter. The separation was a matter of convenience rather than a permanent breakup. Dan's wife, Shelly, wanted him to retire at 20 years. Unfortunately for their marriage, Dan was selected to command an F-111 squadron in Idaho with a chance for promotion to colonel if he didn't retire. That move was the last straw for Shelly who told her husband when he hung up his wings, she'd welcome him back home.

Dan told Chris with his huge new responsibility, he couldn't take his niece and become a single father. In addition, Shelly couldn't take her since she had a newborn and two other children. Chris wasn't happy at all. He thought the Ryan's were selfish.

Chris began to feel like the go-to guy, but he wasn't legally or biologically related to Annie, though he loved her dearly. Chris expressed his reservations about being forced into something he believed would impact his relationship with Alicia. Dan said the only other choice was to place Annie in the foster care system. That choice made Chris's stomach churn; it was a terrible option.

Chris informed his boss about the conversation immediately since he had to get permission to go to Reno in a few days to help resolve the situation before it became be too late to save Annie.

Foster was very empathetic to Chris's untenable situation.

"Chris, you have to do what's best for Annie, your concerns about Alicia's reaction, if adverse, can be sorted out later," Foster advised.

The following day, Chris boarded a C-141 bound for Hawaii. Chris hadn't yet spoken with Alicia. He was uncertain as to how to handle her anticipated objections.

Alicia wasn't expecting Chris for another two days. Though she was thrilled to see him, when he told her what happened and where he was going later that evening, she was very upset, but she remained silent until she heard the whole story.

"Chris, I had a difficult time accepting a ready-made family when we first met. I love Andy very much, but I am only 23 years old now you want to saddle me with two school-age children. We hardly know one another; it's been less than a year. When will we have time for each other?" She said.

Chris knew she was right but Annie's future was at stake.

"I am going to Reno to see what I can do. I will only agree to take Annie as a last resort. My feelings for you will never change, we will have time for each other. Edith will be a great help to us," Chris said knowing Alicia was no longer listening.

After Chris showered and changed his clothes, he found Alicia on the phone speaking with Edith. He didn't know whether she would provide any solace to Alicia.

Chris hugged Alicia and told her not to worry, their relationship would not change because of another child to love. He apparently didn't convince her.

Chris arrived at Travis Air Force Base in northern California. He rented a car and headed for Reno where he met Dan for breakfast. Apparently, Dan didn't tell Chris the whole story which he didn't appreciate.

"Last year, when Katie began to have a few psychotic episodes, she became very concerned about Annie. She visited a lawyer to make arrangements for Annie if anything happened to her. She was well aware that our mother had terminal cancer so she made you Annie's guardian if something happened. In addition, she expressly stated in her legal document that if she died or became severely incapacitated, she wanted you to adopt Annie," Dan said.

"She did all that without contacting me?" Chris blurted out.

"I'm afraid she lied when she told the judge she informed you of her decision," Dan continued.

Chris was extremely upset because to get out of this predicament, he'd have to show cause why he wouldn't be a fit father.

"We have an appointment with the family court tomorrow morning. I am so sorry this happened so fast. I know you have big heart. Annie will be better off with you," Dan added.

"You know, Dan, unlike you I am a real single father. I have a fiancée that is not happy about this and I don't blame her," Chris shot back.

"One other thing, Chris. The hospital psychiatrist would like to transfer Katie to a private facility where she would get better care. I can't pay for it alone," Dan said reluctantly.

Chris, who always had success at the gambling tables in Las Vegas, asked how much Dan needed.

"You expect me to hand you twenty-five thousand dollars and also give up the woman I love because you are a lousy uncle?"

Dan looked down at the breakfast table in silence.

"I don't have that much money laying around these days," Chris lied.

He explained to Dan he'd have to win that much over the next 24 hours and if he couldn't do it, Dan would have to make up the difference. Chris wasn't about to use his gambling largesse safely tucked away in his Las Vegas bank account.

Chris went to his room to get some sleep before taking on the house odds on the eve of becoming a father again. Before he did anything else, he had to call Edith to explain everything to her. He knew she had spoken to Alicia so he needed to tell her what was going on from his perspective.

Edith listened intently without interrupting. After he presented his side of the situation, she told him Alicia had come to her seeking her advice.

"Chris, she loves you so much, but she is scared. She may be a hard-nosed Marine officer, but she is still a young woman who is just beginning to find her way. She told me she was thinking of resigning her commission next year to become a full-time wife and mother. But you threw her a curve ball she wasn't prepared for. Can you understand that, Chris?"

"Of course, I do, Edith. Unfortunately, I am backed into a corner. I can't let a beautiful, vulnerable seven-year-old girl fall victim to a cruel foster care system. Believe it or not, I am the only father she knows. I can't abandon her."

"You are a wonderful human being, Chris. I have a little secret to tell you. The general loves you like a son and so do I, God bless you."

Chris was certain she was crying because she hung up abruptly without saying goodbye. The phone rang just as he was about to fall asleep. It was Edith.

"I'm sorry to bother you Chris, but Alicia just called to let me know her father had a heart attack. She is flying to Miami this evening. She will drop Andy off and I'll drive her to the airport."

"Does she know anything about his condition?" Chris asked.

"Maybe she'll get an update before she leaves. Poor girl, I promise not to discuss your situation with her. She is probably stressed out to say the least. Call me tomorrow if you can. I might have more news for you, goodbye, Chris."

Chris's problem just paled before the one facing Alicia and her family. He decided to speak with Javi as soon as he returned to Hawaii. In the meantime, he decided to start his day at the blackjack table.

Six hours later, Chris had won a paltry seven hundred dollars. He wanted to be three thousand ahead before heading to the craps table; it was his normal *modus operandi*. He reached his goal just after midnight. Dan bumped into him at the late-night buffet. Chris was on empty for more than 12 hours.

"How are you doing?" Dan asked.

"I'm ahead and about to wander over to the craps table. What time is our appointment in court?" he asked.

"We have to be there at 9:30 in the morning. It shouldn't take too long. I have all the paperwork including my mom's prognosis, Katie's diagnosis, and Katie's declaration giving full custody to you," Dan replied.

"I feel as though I just fell through a trap door. What will the judge rule, do you know?"

"I spoke to Katie's attorney two days ago. The judge will rule on custody, but she will probably discuss adoption so you'd think twice about changing your mind. The lawyer agrees that foster care isn't the right choice."

"If I win enough money before we head to court, I won't hand it over to you. It's not that I don't trust you, but I want to be part of the choice of facility for Katie. I want to know the annual costs, and I want to be billed directly for my share. How much are you investing, Dan?" Chris asked.

"I can only afford eight thousand the first year. If I get promoted, I'll bump it up to ten. It seems unfair, I know that. I wish I could do more but I am supporting a wife and three children," he responded.

"If and when I ever marry, I will demand a fifty-fifty split of the costs. I think that's the fair thing to do. Just for the record, that's my bottom line. Do you have any information on Katie's chances of returning to a reasonable state of normalcy?" Chris asked

"Her psychiatrist told me she may never return and will likely need to be institutionalized for the rest of her life."

"I understand. I hope when you retire you find a good paying job because I can't foot the bill for years. I suppose you inquired about VA financial assistance or other government assistance programs," Chris asked.

"Not yet. It's on my to-do list for when I return to Idaho."

Chris was not a happy camper. He knew he'd have to gather the information about government financial resources. He had to get the burden off his shoulders and onto Dan's.

Around four in the morning, Chris's winnings reached twenty thousand dollars. He decided to quit and wire the money to his Las Vegas account after his court date. Chris fell asleep as soon as his head hit the pillow.

Dan knocked on his door at 8:30 a.m., in time for a cup of coffee and a quick shower before their court appointment.

The judge wasn't happy that Annie's family couldn't do what Chris had decided to do. The judge inquired into Chris's military service as well as his role as a single father for several years. She made sure to put her comments into the record. Before she made her ruling, she told Chris she had given her decision a lot of thought. She held up a file that contained adoption papers.

"I recommend you sign these today and walk out of my courtroom as Annie's legal father and not just her court appointed guardian."

"I'm happy to become Annie's legal father, after all, I'm the only father she's ever known."

After signing more than a dozen documents, Chris became Annie's father. A few spectators in the court applauded which surprised the judge.

"Today you saved this young girl, your daughter, from an uncertain future. Now, Chris Harrington, you do right by her," the judge said.

She came around the bench to shake Chris's hand while ignoring Dan. She told him to file the paperwork with the family court in Honolulu.

The only thought that ran through Chris's mind was did he trade a fiancée for a daughter? Dan thanked Chris for stepping up where he failed to accept his legal responsibility.

"Dan, all you need to do from now on is to make sure Katie is in good hands. Don't ignore her like you would have done with Annie", Chris said with an attitude.

Dan was about to say something but Chris cut him off.

"I lost the woman I was about to marry. This was a painful choice for me, not a convenient one like you made. You separated from your wife for a fucking shot at a promotion? What's that worth, another few thousand a year?"

Chris took Annie's hand and walked out of the court room.

"Why are you so angry with Uncle Dan?" She asked.

"I'm sorry it looked that way, Annie, we are still friends."

After Chris wired his winnings to his Las Vegas bank, he drove to San Francisco to fly home. Annie was quiet. Chris felt so bad for her. Now he had two sweet children whose lives were anything but normal. They both needed a mother more than anything else.

Annie slept most of the way on the plane. When she got up to have something to eat, she asked a lot of questions about Hawaii. She spent all of her life in Nevada and never saw the ocean or ever walked on a beach. She was excited to see Andy again.

Chris grabbed a taxi and went directly to his house. He wanted to spend some time alone with Annie and to get her settled in her room. He called Edith to tell her he was back and also to find out the latest about Alicia.

"She was quite distraught. Her father's heart attack together with your situation, has really impacted her. I asked her if she was coming back and she shrugged her shoulders. I told her I understood why she had to go but I beseeched her not to abandon you and the children."

"Perhaps when her father recovers, she'll change her mind," Chris said.

"Unfortunately, Chris, I think she made up her mind before she learned about her father."

Edith invited Chris to the house. Before he left, Chris called his boss to let him know he was home. He explained what had occurred since he left Okinawa. The general said he did the right thing but he wasn't happy about Alicia though he thought she probably wouldn't leave him.

By the time Chris arrived at Gen. Iverson's house, Edith had a phone conversation with Alicia.

"She's in Miami at her father's side. He is in ICU but will recover. She gave me her home phone number so I could call her later. She is with her brother and mother. I didn't say anything about Annie. She didn't ask about you, I'm sorry," Edith said.

Chris felt like someone punched him the stomach. He looked at Annie knowing he didn't have a choice. Andy heard his father's voice and ran to greet him. When he saw Annie, he gave her a big hug and asked if she could stay with them.

"Andy, Annie is your sister now and will always be with you. You are her big brother so you have to take care of her," Chris said with a smile.

He looked at Edith who seemed very happy and greeted Annie with a hug and kiss.

"Annie, this is your new grandma, Edith," Chris said.

"Grandma, I'm hungry," she said.

Edith laughed and hugged Annie. She took both children to the kitchen. She looked over her shoulder and suggested he call Alicia. While dialing her home in Miami, Chris hoped Javi would answer the phone. Instead, it was Rafael, Alicia's older brother. Chris introduced himself and asked about his father. He also inquired about his mother and Alicia. Chris didn't think Rafael knew about his engagement to Alicia but he did say the family had mentioned him.

"Did Javi get time off to come to Miami," Chris asked.

"Yes, he did. He's in the shower now," he replied.

Chris gave him Edith's number and asked Javi to call as soon as possible.

Javi called ten minutes later.

"Ola Cisco, where are you?"

"I'm in General Iverson's house with my children. I'm sure you are aware of my latest addition," Chris inquired.

"Oh yes I am. Alicia called me twice before our father had a heart attack. She was very unhappy and angry at the same time. She understands what transpired but she thinks it is very unfair to her at this time in her life. I just listened to her without comment. Hey, brother, you have a lot of repair work ahead of you. I can only tell you not to give up, she loves you very much. Right now, she is focused on our father so if you speak to her, focus on him," Javi advised.

"Thank you, Poncho. I'll wait until there's good news about your father before I talk with her. I'll be home in about an hour if you want to chat again."

Chris went to the kitchen to see his kids. Edith asked if he spoke with Alicia.

"I spoke to her older brother and then to Javi. He said I have a lot of work to do. Unfortunately, I can't change what happened. If she can't accept both of these wonderful children, I'll just remain a single father. I know it will be a hardship on all of us, but I am responsible for them. I think Alicia's biggest concern is that we won't have time for each other. To inherit two school-age children at 23 years old, is a lot to ask. I really can't blame her. However, if she became pregnant in a year or so, having a new born would certainly take up more of her time."

"You make a lot of sense from your perspective. She said the same things about not having time with you. I told her I'd always be around to help out. I really didn't know if she was listening." Edith replied.

At that moment Chris was resigned to never seeing Alicia again. Falling in love with someone you really didn't know obscured the reality of what was occurring around you. Alicia might have thought Andy was nothing more than an appendage with respect to Chris. He was always present but never got in the way, but two children were too much. This was what Chris believed and he didn't have a clue how to change the reality of two children ever present in their lives.

"Perhaps I should have said something sooner, Chris," Edith said.

"About what, Edith?"

"When I learned about you and Alicia, I didn't want to say anything that might interfere in your budding relationship. I think now is the time to tell you about Julia," she continued.

"She was a wonderful young woman but we lived in two different worlds," Chris said.

"Please hear me out. As you know, Julia married her art professor, an older man with two children. Since she couldn't have children, it was a perfect situation for her personally and professionally. About a year ago, her mother confided that Julia was unhappy. Apparently, her husband was really looking for a live-in nanny and not a wife. He treated her like a servant. He came home late or went on trips allegedly related to his work. Julie called me in May to tell me she was divorcing her husband. She provided all the details of their sham marriage."

"I'm really sorry for her. She must have been devastated," Chris added.

"After she ended her tragic story, she asked about you. I didn't know what to tell her. I thought you were engaged to Alicia so I told her you and Andy were doing great in Hawaii. Then she asked if you could ever forgive her."

"Forgive her for what? We both knew we would never be in the same place at the same time. Besides she was under a lot of pressure from her parents to marry a wealthy European man," Chris replied.

"Yes, I knew what she would face from her father, especially if she married you. I spoke to her mother last month. She told me Julia was very depressed. Though she obtained her art degree she wasn't motivated to look for a position with a museum. She asked about you. I didn't know what to tell her so I avoided going into details. What do want me to do, Chris?"

"I don't know if I could go through another serious relationship and lose the woman I love. This situation with Alicia has broken my spirit. I feel so bad for Andy. He barely knew his mother but he got attached to Katie, Julia and now Alicia. What do you think, Edith?"

"Perhaps I should speak with Julia to determine how serious she is about you and what she'd have to give up, or at least postpone her previous career goals. I won't tell her you are free from any entanglements; in fact,

I won't discuss your situation at all. Can I tell her about Annie?" Edith asked.

"Julia would probably love the idea of two children, it may even encourage her to pursue me," Chris said with a smile.

"Just be prepared to have two women or no women in your life. Either way you won't be happy, Chris. If you open up pandora's box with Julia, you better be certain because you haven't heard the final word from Alicia."

Chris understood he had to make a choice. Whether Julia was interested or not, he had to know if Alicia would marry him. Both women were young, beautiful and loved Andy.

Chris took his children home. Seeing the two of them getting along so well, he was such a proud father. Whether he was a candidate for father of the year or not, they still needed a mother. He desperately wanted a wife to share his children and his life. For the rest of the day and night he thought of both women. He was lucky to have a choice, but in reality, the choice wasn't his to make.

The following afternoon, Javi called to update him on his father's condition.

"The doctor told us this morning that dad needs a triple by-pass. He is scheduled for surgery the day after tomorrow. Mom can't take care of him by herself because I have to return to Pensacola and Rafael has business in Argentina. Alicia is going to ask for a 30-day emergency leave."

"How is she? Did you tell her we spoke?" Chris asked.

"I did and she said she'll speak with you soon. She asked me if it would be possible for her to get a compassionate discharge since she already served three years. I suggested she should ask her commander."

"I assume if she can get one, she won't return to Hawaii," Chris replied.

"Alicia is the closest to our parents being the only girl and the youngest child. She won't leave until dad recovers and is back to normal, and that could take months," Javi said.

"I suppose the marriage is off the table. Your father's situation only compounded a relationship that took a recent nose-dive."

Chris explained the adoption and Alicia's reaction to it.

"She hasn't discussed it with me, Chris. I am surprised by her reaction because she's always been a very giving person and loves children."

"When you complete pilot training, what's next for you?" Chris asked.

"I graduate before Thanksgiving. I understand most of the class is going to F-4 training though there are rumors it has a short life in the Corps. I'm sure you know about that," Javi said.

"I heard we were supposed to get the F-14, but that plan has been scrapped in favor of the Harrier. My guess is the Marine Corps realized it won't always have land-based support aircraft in close proximity to our troops like in Vietnam. The thinking is to employ small carriers with rotary aircraft and VTOL aircraft like the Harrier. These smaller carriers can project Marine combat aircraft to support the land battle at a safe distance," Chris added.

"Well, whatever happens in the near future, I hope to serve with you again as your wingman. As far as Alicia is concerned, I'll encourage her to speak with you as soon as my father's surgery is over," Javi said.

Chris returned to his normal routine getting the kids off to school and going to work. In late October, he received an unexpected TDY assignment to join a carrier group operating in the Philippine Sea. Apparently, a dozen Marine pilots had completed carrier training and Chris was selected to command the group during operational training during naval exercises. Why they selected Chris and not a Navy commander was a question Chris felt was a Marine Corps decision.

Edith took charge of the children. Chris left on November 10th, 1974. He still hadn't heard from Alicia. Javi's last conversation was good news about his father. The surgery was successful and he was going home.

Chris flew to Subic Bay and took a COD to the carrier. The twelve Marine pilots joined the carrier when it was in Yokosuka, Japan. He didn't know any of the pilots but they heard of him.

The 10-day exercise began two days later. His squadron participated in simulated ground support on a few outlying Philippine Islands. Chris joined them for the first three days to see how they performed. The forecast for bad weather interrupted the exercise, at least for air operations. The weather improved enough to continue the air activity for the last two days of the exercise.

The day before Thanksgiving, the carrier air wing commander wanted to test the Marine pilots in a less favorable flying environment. With a Typhoon looming south of the Philippines, the commander selected a small window of opportunity when there would be some considerable chop before the storm to test the pilots' ability to handle a rolling deck.

Since the exercise was over, Chris wanted to know why the commander decided to endanger the pilots for no apparent reason. He was told since his Navy pilots have faced rough seas; the Marines should prove their ability to handle it.

The typhoon picked up speed and whether the commander knew that or not, Chris's squadron took off and flew a prescribed track that would bring them back within an hour. The seas were more than a chop by the time the aircraft returned. The carrier was about 70 miles off the nearest Philippine islands.

It began to rain hard; visibility was poor. The first six aircraft made it down before the skies darkened. The carrier deployed its landing lights. The next five aircraft managed to land without incident. The twelfth aircraft was missing or not acquired on radar. Chris thought the pilot was just ahead of him but couldn't locate him. He circled back to where he last saw him and caught a glimpse of the aircraft. Chris approached it and made sure he followed him back to the carrier. By the time they reached the pitching carrier, it looked impossible to make a safe landing. Chris flew with the aircraft and talked him down to a rather ugly landing; nonetheless a safe one.

By the time Chris overflew the carrier he didn't have enough time to get back to the carrier and land safely, and he didn't want to eject in a turbulent sea. Rather than risk anyone's life on the carrier's deck, he decided to fly west as far as he could hoping to close the distance between the carrier and the nearest island.

Chris was aided by a strong tailwind. He figured he traveled about 50 miles closer to shore. Unfortunately, Chris had to punch out of his aircraft because he ran out of fuel. The typhoon's outer winds whipped Chris as his chute deployed. He came down almost horizontal rather than vertical. When he hit the water, his parachute was picked up by the strong winds and dragged Chris through the violent sea for a few minutes. Chris finally settled on the fast-moving water. Fortunately, the current was hurling him toward the Philippines.

He was fearful of hypothermia so he kept awake as long as possible. Chris's eyes were swollen shut from the sea water. He drifted about 10 hours until he suddenly crashed into rocks, slammed his head and ribs and became unconscious.

Chris eventually washed up on a beach. He woke up for a moment. He could feel the sand beneath him. He couldn't open his eyes but he could feel the sun on his back. He passed out again.

He heard voices, children's voices. He felt hands and feet prodding him to see if he were alive. Then he heard loud adult voices and the children stopped touching him. There was a lot of commotion. People were shouting and giving orders to people. He felt a dozen hands on his limbs lifting his body above the sand. He passed out from the pain.

He felt a light touch on his face, a woman's touch. Someone put a cup to his lips. He knew his soaked clothes were being removed. He shivered constantly. Someone wrapped him in a blanket. Whoever was with him looked at his bleeding head wound and tried to wash it. The greatest pain was from his ribs, but he couldn't tell them anything.

Chris fell asleep. He was warm but in a great deal of pain. He didn't know how long it was since they found him. Chris had no recollection of what happened. In fact, he didn't know who he was. Apparently, the villagers' called a local doctor who placed warm wet rags on his eyes to wash the salt out. Chris didn't know if he would live or die, he felt an emptiness like being lost in space.

The Navy couldn't begin search operations for six hours. At dawn, the carrier launched search planes. They were aloft for four hours and found no traces of the F-4. The air wing commander realized he fucked up by putting the squadron in harm's way. He delayed reporting the missing aircraft for 12 hours. When he finally did, he didn't release the pilot's name.

Thirty-six hours later, Chris was taken aboard a small boat for a two-hour ride to a medical facility. There was only one doctor at the facility. He focused on Chris's head wound which was still bleeding. When Chris was undressed, the doctor saw the black and blue marks on his right side. His examination was quite thorough. Chris had two broken ribs. A nurse wrapped his ribs to prevent further internal damage. The doctor also treated his eyes with a solution that enabled Chris to see images though very opaque images.

As he became more clear-headed, Chris realized he had no frame of reference with respect to time, location or even to who he was. He saw people dressed in white shirts looking at him, making gestures and talking to each other. He couldn't understand their language.

The doctor conferred with the local police chief regarding the disposition of the patient. The facility could no longer accommodate the patient's injuries. The police chief contacted the local military commander for guidance. He suspected Chris was an American sailor who went overboard during the recent storm.

The doctor continued to attend to Chris's head wound which was quite significant. He checked his body for other bruises or possible broken bones. The staff cleaned Chris from head to toe and then put fresh hospital clothes on him. They brought him to a room, placed him in a bed, and started an IV to hydrate him. Later that day they offered him warm soup, his first nourishment since he left the carrier.

Chris fell asleep until he was awakened by the sound of a helicopter outside the medical facility. Two men that looked like Chris, came to his bedside. They asked him questions in English. Though he understood them, he couldn't answer. His memory was completely void of any information except for his comments regarding pain from his injuries.

The medical staff placed Chris on a stretcher and carried him to the helicopter. Two hours later, Chris arrived at another hospital. He was surrounded by men and women who looked like him. They rushed him inside and placed him on an examining table. He understood everything they asked about his condition. After they x-rayed his head and ribs, he was taken to a room with other patients. He asked one of the patients where he was. He told him he was in the hospital at Clark Air Force Base.

The emergency room physician said he had a significant head trauma. There was fluid on his brain that was putting pressure on the inside of his skull. He told Chris not to worry, they had someone on staff who knew how to deal with traumatic head wounds.

Later in the day, another doctor sat by his bedside. He introduced himself as a psychiatrist. He spoke to Chris in a calm, low voice. He asked him a series of questions that he couldn't answer. He didn't even know his age.

Chris was left alone for a while. A nurse offered him something sweet to drink. She fed him a few pieces of fruit and a cookie. Chris tried to sit up but the nurse restrained him. When she realized he had to use the bathroom, she helped him to his feet. He leaned heavily on her at first until he got his balance. It was the first time he stood up since he walked to his aircraft, but he had no recollection of it.

The next morning Chris was taken to surgery. The head trauma specialist decided to put a shunt into the lower back part of Chris's cranium to drain fluid to ease the pressure.

The hospital commander put out a query to the Navy as to whether they lost anyone at sea east of the Philippine Islands. Luckily whomever received the message knew about the missing F-4 that crashed a week earlier. The Navy requested a description of the patient which it passed on to the Marine Corps.

A few hours later, the reply from the Marine Corps asked for a description of the patient's back and front right rib cage. On the tenth day after Chris was presumed dead, General Iverson received a call from the hospital commander describing the scars on Chris's back and bullet scar on his lower right rib cage. The general was at home standing next to his wife. Edith saw something she never saw before. Her hard-nosed 34-year Marine husband started to cry.

"Edith, they found him, Chris is alive."

He hung up the phone and grabbed his wife, another surprise for her.

"He's safe in the air force hospital in the Philippines but has been seriously injured. He has severe head trauma, two broken ribs and has amnesia," the general said.

"Thank God," she muttered through tears of joy.

"I am sending Bud Foster to the hospital to see him. Perhaps Chris will remember him.

While all this was going on, Javi heard rumors that Chris had been lost at sea. He was hesitant to tell Alicia because of the confidential news she told him the previous week. Alicia was pregnant, two months pregnant; it was Chris's child. Even after she told Javi, she didn't commit to returning to Hawaii to marry Chris. She was conflicted, more so than before. She didn't tell her mother about the pregnancy yet because she knew she would force her to go back to Chris.

Javi called Chris's office to find out the latest on Chris. Foster told him that there was nothing new to report. An hour later, Iverson called Foster and told him to pack his bags. He decided not to call Javi until he made a positive identification.

Foster flew to Clark Air Force Base on a C-5 aircraft which was the first available direct flight. Eighteen hours after he received the call from Iverson, Foster stood at Chris's bedside.

"Hello, Chris, I am very happy to see you. Do you remember me?" Foster asked.

Chris stared at the general, there was no sign of recognition on his face.

"I'm sorry, sir, I don't know you."

"You work for me in Hawaii. I'm also your neighbor and friend. My daughter sometimes took care of your son, Andy. Do you remember Andy?"

"Yes, Andy is my son. How is he?" Chris said.

The staff psychologist was surprised to hear that. He urged the general to continue mentioning people in Chris's life.

"I spoke to Javi Cruz the other day. He doesn't know you are alive. He is your best friend."

"Poncho?"

"Who is Poncho?" the psychiatrist asked.

"Poncho is Javi's callsign," Foster replied.

"General Iverson and Edith are very worried about you. Do you remember them, Chris?"

"Yes, they are Camille's parents," Chris replied.

"Who is Camille?" Foster asked.

"She's my wife," Chris replied.

"Who are you?" The psychiatrist asked.

Chris looked at them both as if he were searching for the answer.

"I don't remember. Am I the person you call Chris?" he asked.

"You are Major Chris Harrington, a Marine pilot," Foster said.

"I think we should talk, general." The psychiatrist said.

As they left the room, Chris asked about Camille. They both turned around in surprise. Foster whispered to the psychiatrist that Camille his first wife, died in 1968.

"She's okay, Chris," the psychiatrist replied.

"Apparently Chris recalls some things from his past like his son's name, Javi's callsign and his wife, Camille. Both from six to eight years ago. Nothing from before or after. That's quite unusual," the psychiatrist remarked.

"He also doesn't know who he is, even though he can recall people from his past. How do you proceed from here?" Foster asked.

"I'm not certain, general. I will continue testing name association. I'll need the names of people in his life after his wife died until the present."

"I'll try to help, but I think General Iverson's wife knows more about Chris than his mother does. I'll call her later. I'll be in the VIP quarters making a few calls about the incident at sea," Foster said.

One of the general's calls was to Iverson and his wife. He confirmed the patient was Chris and he had some recall of Camille, Andy and Javi Cruz. Edith gave him several names including his second wife, Katie, her daughter, Annie, Julia and Alicia.

"There doesn't seem to be any men in his life other than general officers," Foster quipped.

"We are praying for his recovery and his memory," Edith said.

"Bud, I've heard some scuttlebutt that the carrier's air boss ordered Chris's squadron to practice severe weather landings for no reason other than to see if they were as good as navy pilots. I want you to look into that for me. I have the name of the carrier's commanding officer. He should be in Subic Bay. I want a full report but don't let him know what I told you. They may try obfuscate the truth," Iverson said.

Foster decided to give Javi a courtesy call with news about Chris. He realized that Javi would tell his sister. Foster didn't want to interfere into Chris's personal life, but Alicia was a terrific young woman and the two of them were right for each other.

Javi was relieved Chris was alive but dismayed by his condition. He kept the information to himself for a few days until he saw his sister. He never told her Chris was missing because of her condition. Perhaps he shouldn't tell her anything. If she doesn't return to Chris, she'll never know of his ordeal. He decided not to tell her unless she wanted to go back to him.

After Alicia's emergency leave was up, she requested an extension. She was turned down but told she could be attached to the south Florida Marine recruiting district on temporary duty to make public appearances to help recruit women and Cubans. She was a perfect role model for both demographics.

By mid-December, Alicia began to show. She didn't know how much longer she could hide her pregnancy from her mother. She decided to tell her at the family's Christmas dinner. She was prepared for a barrage of questions except for the important one. Though pregnant with Chris's child, the thought of taking care of three children overwhelmed her. She knew in her heart she loved him and that she was being terribly unfair to him. She needed someone's counsel so she decided to call Edith.

When Alicia called to discuss her dilemma, Edith wasn't aware Alicia was never told about Chris. She assumed she didn't know anything because she didn't ask about him. Edith was faced with a difficult chore. Her heart told her Alicia should return and marry Chris. Her mind told her Chris needed her and his unborn child in his life, regardless of his condition. But what about Alicia? Was she strong enough to care for three children and a man who lost his memory?

Edith believed if she told Alicia about Chris's condition, it would convince her to remain in Miami. Love may be very powerful, but there is a limit to its power. Since Edith didn't know Alicia as well as Chris knew her, she couldn't determine Alicia's commitment to him. One thing was certain, if Alicia returned, she'd have to resign her commission to become a fulltime mother and wife.

Edith wanted to ask Alicia a very important question. How committed was she to Chris, despite the fact she would have three children? Edith thought it wasn't the right question at the time.

"You are carrying Chris's child. Chris has two children, one of them is my grandson, who you love very much. If you can walk away from them because you don't think you can cope with all that responsibility, then why did you join the Corps?" Edith said

Alicia began to cry.

"You are a strong woman who was trained to be a leader. There are three people, soon to be four, that love you. You can't give them up because it's too difficult to contemplate the impact on your life. If you choose to become a single parent, you will be alone and that, my dear Alicia, is a lot of responsibility." Edith remarked.

"I understand, but I still have to deal with my parents because I haven't told them about my pregnancy yet. I'll call you after Christmas," Alicia said.

Edith thought she might have been too hard on her. On the other hand, being a hard-nosed Marine's wife, she believed Alicia needed a swift kick in the ass.

Since Chris had made some progress in recognizing names from a three-year window in his life, the psychiatrist sent for a hypno-therapist. It took four days for the Navy to approve the cost of bringing in a well-known professional from California. If Chris had been anyone else's former son-in-law, the request wouldn't have been approved.

A week before Christmas, the new doctor explained to Chris what he did and how he did it. Chris was anxious for it to work so he could get on with his life.

Once under hypnosis, Chris was asked to talk about the earliest thing he could remember. After several minutes, Chris spoke about working in the vineyards with his Mexican friends. He mentioned they taught him Spanish. Chris smiled when he spoke of the fun times he had with them.

The doctor recorded the session so when Chris woke up, he could listen to his own voice talking about his past.

Chris moved forward in time to when he was in high school at which time, he worked at the winery packing bottles in boxes. He also spoke about playing baseball and basketball in high school and having a lot of girlfriends.

"What do you remember about the two hours under hypnosis?" the doctor asked.

"Two hours? It seemed like a few minutes. I think I talked about working in the vineyards and learning to speak Spanish. My mother got me a job packing wine bottles when I was in grade school," he said.

"What is your mother's name."

"Bonnie."

"What is her last name?"

"I don't remember," he replied.

"What is your name?"

"Everyone calls me Chris, but I don't remember."

When Chris returned to his room, the doctor recorded his observations. He thought it unusual that Chris recalled events in his life but had no recollection of himself.

The doctor continued the session the following day. He had Chris remember what he did in college, playing sports, meeting Camille and having a son. Once he got to Andy's birth, he shut down. When the doctor asked who married Camille and who was Andy's father, Chris said he was. But when asked his name it was evident Chris couldn't associate the person, Chris, with himself as discussed under hypnosis.

When the doctor brought Chris back, he asked if he remembered Camille and Andy.

"Yes, I do," he replied.

"Are you Camille's husband and Andy's father?"

"Yes."

"What is your name?" The doctor asked.

"I don't remember."

Whether Chris was under hypnosis or not, he remembered two people and his relationship to them, but not his name.

The doctor was frustrated. He contacted a few colleagues to get their input. It wasn't unusual for someone to disassociate himself from the past or present while remembering events and people. The question was why?

The day before Christmas, Alicia told her mother she was pregnant. Her mother was calm and direct.

"You are a grown woman who made a decision that will be with you the rest of your life. If Chris is the father, please God he is, you should be with him. I think you aren't telling me the whole story, Alicia," her mother replied.

Alicia told her mother the truth about her misgivings regarding, Annie's adoption. She said before that happened, she thought about resigning her commission and becoming a full-time mother and wife. She said she was confused and scared.

"So, you'd rather be a single mother rather than marry the father of your child who you love very much?"

"I don't know, I have to be sure I will be happy raising someone else's children. I don't want to let Chris or his children down if I can't do it," she said.

She wrapped her arms around her mother and cried.

"You know what your father would tell you?"

Alicia knew what he'd tell her; the same thing Edith told her.

"Let's not tell your father until you are ready to go back to Chris," her mother whispered.

Chris's recovery was problematic though he remembered people in his life, he didn't associate himself with them. The hypno-therapist decided to force the issue by making Chris say who he was, his relationship to the people he recognized and what happened to him.

During two hours under hypnosis, Chris repeated everything the doctor told him about himself from his childhood to the present. How much of the information Chris could remember and how much he would accept as reality, had to be determined over the following few days.

When Chris was brought back to consciousness, the doctor asked only one question.

"What is your name?"

"Chris Harrington," he replied.

The doctor smiled.

Over the following two days, Chris related everything he knew about himself including the last time he flew his F-4. At that point, Chris could no longer remember the four weeks between that night and the present. The doctor was enormously pleased and accepted the fact the four missing weeks was normal during an event punctuated by severe head trauma.

On December 27th, Chris spoke to General Iverson and Edith. He also had a few minutes with Andy and Annie. The general mentioned he ordered an investigation into the events leading up to his accident. He said Foster was his point man to get the facts.

"Bud will return to the hospital when he completes his interviews with the Navy. He will accompany you back to Hawaii on a C-9 Nightingale within a day or so. You will spend New Year's Eve with your family," the general reported.

When Chris spoke with Edith, he asked about Alicia.

"I'm sorry to say we haven't heard anything from her or Javi."

The following day, Foster returned to Clark Air Force Base. He informed Chris of his findings which he expected would result in the carrier's air boss being reprimanded, or perhaps worse.

Since Chris was still a patient enroute to Hawaii for continuing medical care, he had to fly as litter patient. On December 30th, they went to the Pearl Harbor medical facility. After reviewing his records, the doctor on duty released Chris so he could spend the holiday with his family.

Bud had a staff car waiting at the hospital to take them to Iverson's house for a wonderful family reunion.

22

NEW WIFE, NEW LIFE

When Alicia told her brother, she was returning to Hawaii on January 1st, he was forced to tell her about Chris's situation. Alicia was stunned and became distraught.

"Is he dead, please don't tell me he is dead?" She pleaded.

"He is in a military hospital in the Philippines but he has amnesia," he replied.

"I have to call Edith right away," she yelled.

"Don't do that, Alicia. Let me call to find out the latest news. I still think you should return to Hawaii as planned. The children need you and you need them," Javi said.

"Okay, I'll go there even if I don't hear from you. I have to report for duty right after the new year."

Javi's phone call came the day after Chris returned. Edith answered the phone but instead of speaking with Javi, she told him to call Chris's house.

The two best friends spoke for nearly an hour before Javi remembered to tell Chris that Alicia would return to Hawaii the following day. Chris said he wanted to surprise her so he shouldn't say anything to Alicia before she left.

Chris decided to leave his children with Edith so he and Alicia could have some time alone. When he approached the gate, he was very nervous. Javi had told him what she went through with respect to her concerns about being a mother of two children so early in their marriage. Javi also told Chris that Alicia was pregnant but he should be surprised when she told him.

Chris was still unsteady on his feet and suffered occasional headaches. He was on heavy duty pain medication. When he first spotted Alicia, his heart jumped into his throat. Since she wasn't expecting him, she practically walked past him.

When Chris stepped in front of her she shouted in excitement. She threw her arms around his neck and embraced him.

"I've been such a fool for not returning sooner. I love you so much. I want to get married as soon as possible," she said through tears.

"I'm sorry young lady, but I don't remember you," Chris said laughing. She pulled back and looked into his eyes.

"How could you forget your Cuban fiancé?"

She continued in Spanish with litany of reasons why he should never forget her. She told him she was the mother of his three children.

"It's coming back to me now. I think I remember having two children, is the third one with you?" He laughed.

They kissed and embraced each other for several minutes. He led her to his car. Once inside, she said they'd have to get a bigger one. He looked at her, patted her belly and leaned over and kissed it.

They sat in silence for a moment starring at each other.

"I never thought I'd see you again. Even when I regained my memory, I believed you weren't coming back. When you left, we were three; now we are five," he laughed.

"I'm anxious to see Andy and Annie. I truly missed him and I hope to get to know and love her," she said crying.

"Before we go home, I think we should talk. I don't know if I'll ever be cleared to fly again. If I can't, I will resign my commission. I have some ideas about the future that we can discuss later. If you decide to stay in the Corps, that's okay with me, or if you want to get out, I'm good with that," Chris said.

"Let's see how things work out with our two children and if everything is as usual, I want to wait until the new one arrives. Is that a sufficient answer, sir?" She said with a smile.

"When do you want to get married?" He asked.

"As soon as possible," She replied.

"It's still early, let's go to City Hall and apply for our license before we go home," Chris said.

They embraced and kissed.

"We do need a bigger car, I'm not as agile as before," she said laughing.

They were fortunate in their timing because there was a short line at the licensing office. They received the schedule for civil weddings. If they waited an hour or so, they could get married. They looked into each other's eyes, both teared up.

"Let's do it," she said.

The newlyweds drove home knowing they did the right thing at the right time. The families on both sides would probably feel cheated, but the little one in the oven couldn't wait for a formal church wedding.

Chris decided not to mention what they did until all the hoopla settled down. The focus had to be on Andy and Annie who finally had a mother and father.

The Iverson's' affection for Chris and Alicia was if they were their own children. Perhaps Alicia filled the void of losing a daughter. Chris was certainly the son the general never had.

Andy jumped into Alicia's arms while Annie stood aside, perhaps she was shy. Alicia knelt down and put her arms out. Annie slowly walked toward her and embraced Alicia.

"She is so beautiful," Alicia exclaimed as tears rolled down her cheeks.

"I promised to call Javi as soon as I arrived," Alicia said.

"He's probably worried since it's been nearly four hours since you landed," Chris added.

As she walked toward the telephone, she grabbed Chris and whispered she would tell Javi what they did. Chris gave her the thumbs up.

During dinner, Chris stood to propose a toast.

"I want to propose a toast to the woman in my life, whom I deeply love, who is now with child and as of late this morning, is my wife," Chris said raising his glass.

The Iverson's didn't react at first because the double-barreled news flash was unexpected. Edith ran over to put her arms around Alicia. The general congratulated Chris and then went over to Alicia.

"I never kissed a Marine officer, of either sex, so this will be my first time. I want to welcome all of you to our family. Edith and I could never be happier," the general said.

Alicia had a long day. Chris could see the fatigue on her face so he suggested they go home. The little VW bug held the family of four for the first time. It was obvious, they had to have a new car.

"I'll put the kids to bed, my love. Why don't you take a shower and get some sleep? You can kiss your children goodnight later," Chris said.

"I need a hot shower and a soft pillow. Being pregnant sucks. I feel as if I'm toting a 60 pound back pack wearing lead boots," Alicia quipped.

Andy was so happy Alicia was home. Annie said she thought her new mommy was very pretty. Chris told them both they were going to have a new brother or sister soon. So far, so good. Chris was pleased with his growing family. The Corps was no longer his primary consideration. Even if he could return to the cockpit, he was too junior to command a squadron, and frankly, training was boring.

Alicia was fast asleep. Chris took a shower and crawled alongside her. When he put his arm around her waist, he realized there was a new life with them as well.

They decided to skip the Sunday brunch at the club. Chris cooked pancakes and bacon. Alicia wasn't hungry which was something she got used to. She had morning sickness for about a week. Chris told her to stay in bed. They made their belated phone calls to advise their parents they were married. The Cruz' already heard the news from Javi. Chris's mother was elated and very happy with the new grandchild on the way.

Chris and Alicia returned to work for the first time in several weeks. Nothing changed much except for a few new enlisted folks. The news from Vietnam was bleak. Alicia was brought up to speed on all the intelligence reports that pointed to a complete NVA victory within a few months. Anyone who served in southeast Asia was dismayed that so many Americans lost their lives for nothing.

Chris's world was equally bleak. There was a significant loss of Marine aviation personnel. Several operational readiness indicators demonstrated a lack of leadership and training. Chris sensed a malaise within the aviation forces. The Navy was transitioning to the new F-14 Tomcat, the Marines were left with the older F-4's.

There was nothing to look forward to within the Corps, except budget cuts, low recruiting numbers, unfavorable media especially when Saigon fell to the NVA on April 30th, 1975. Ten years of young men and women fighting for a cause that no one could define, neither in the beginning, nor at the end.

All the military services had the same problems. Senior officers and non-commissioned officers retired as soon as they could. Junior enlisted and officers on their first tour of duty left as soon as they could. All of this weighed heavily on Chris as he considered leaving the Corps. He could make more money at the craps table in one night than the amount he was paid every month.

Alicia decided to make an appointment with a civilian gynecologist and deliver her baby in a local hospital. Chris drove to her appointment the last week in January. The new doctor ordered a sonogram because Alicia seemed quite big for a little over three months.

"Do you see what I see?" the doctor asked them.

"Look where I am pointing. There are two fetuses there. You are having twins. I can't tell the sex of one because it is hidden by the other one. But the one in front is definitely a girl," the doctor said

"I was worried I couldn't be an adequate mom for two kids and now there will be four of us," she exclaimed.

Chris was silent.

The doctor left the room while the nurse cleaned up Alicia's belly.

"We've outgrown our home, our car and soon we'll have to decide on our careers." Chris replied.

"I met you a year ago when you were a single father and now there are six of us. Can you love us all without any hesitation?" She asked laughing.

"Of course, I can. By the way, I thought we took precautions so we could wait a few years before having children. I guess we got carried away."

"I'm cutting you off until Andy and Annie are in college," Alicia quipped.

"I suppose I deserve it," Chris replied.

When Edith heard the news, she exclaimed she didn't know if she could babysit four children at one time.

"Don't worry Edith, as soon as I give birth, I am resigning my commission. I can't be a part time mom, it's not fair to them," Alicia said.

Chris was surprised at her comment.

"I don't want to put my babies in childcare. They need their mother more than the Marines need me," Alicia responded.

"The older kids won't be much trouble," Chris said.

The next several months were mundane and boring after Saigon fell to the communists. The Marines who served in southeast Asia were angry at the way Congress pulled the funding for the war. Though defeat was inevitable after the United States pulled their military forces, no one expected the war to end so quickly.

Between the news from Vietnam to the reduced defense budget, morale was quite low. This wasn't only confined to the Marine Corps, the other services felt it as well. Public opinion of the military was at a low, lower than during the war years. Since Hawaii was the home to several military headquarters and bases, the people in Hawaii still maintained a healthy respect for the military.

Chris celebrated his 30th birthday in March, Annie turned eight in April, and Andy turned nine in May. The twins were born in late June; two healthy identical girls, both looked like their mother.

Chris and Alicia struggled to find names that pleased them both. Finally, they decided on Rose Marie and Lily Ann. Alicia picked the first name and Chris the second. They laughed when they realized they had two flower girls.

The two girls became the center of attention in the family. Edith spent as much time helping Alicia as she could. Chris's mom visited in August. Alicia's father wasn't well enough to travel, but her mother visited in August. She finally met Chris, Andy, Annie, and of course the twins.

Chris and Alicia hired a full-time nanny to take care of the twins when

Alicia returned to work. She was very apprehensive at first, not unlike any mother that had to place their newborn in the care of someone else. It worked out well. The nanny was the wife of a Marine corporal based at Camp Smith.

Alicia was determined to get her weight down so she ran two miles every morning at six. Chris couldn't accompany her because there were four children to look after. In addition, Alicia joined a competitive women's soccer team that played on the weekend. Chris tried to take all four children to watch their mother, but it was difficult to do. Again, Chris and Alicia were apart for a few hours on the weekend.

As Chris began his third year in Hawaii, he was torn between staying in the Corps, or resigning his commission. Since he wasn't in an operational billet, he didn't have to schedule his fitness exam. He reported to the hospital once a month to have his head x-rayed. The concussion was gone and the membrane around his brain returned to normal. He still had no memory of the events that led to his being hospitalized in the Philippines.

Before Chris pressured Alicia into making a decision about staying or leaving the Corps, Chris called his detailer to get some early thinking about his next assignment. The feedback he received was to the point and unrefutably accurate.

"Considering you have four children, Chris, your wife is still serving with you, your father-in-law is the Commander, you aren't eligible for promotion yet, and Hawaii is a great duty assignment, why the hell do you want to leave? Extend for a fourth year, enjoy your life and keep the family together," he offered.

Chris had no response other than to say thank you. He realized that his situation was really a great one, probably one that most Marines would kill to get. Truthfully, he couldn't financially afford to leave the Corps until he had another opportunity.

As the twins became more active, Chris noticed Alicia spent less time with them, from the time she came home from work, until she put them to bed. He didn't think it was normal for a new mom, but on the other hand she hardly interacted with the older children, except during dinner. Chris helped with homework and was the parent they came to with a problem or a question. He thought he was making a big deal of it, but he began to realize there were two families living under the same roof. Added to that evolving situation, he and Alicia were not having sexual relations, not once since she gave birth. He didn't know if it was a physical problem or an emotional one. He never pushed it with her because she was always so tired, and frankly they never had time.

Chris thought he could talk things over with Alicia, but there was never a good time. They were rarely alone, whether it was at night, or the weekend, she was always busy with soccer or other things. He had to do something or the marriage would dissolve due to lack of effort.

One day on the drive to the house after work, he took the bull by the horns and let his frustration out.

"Are you aware of what I've just brought up?" He asked.

"I'm not sure what you are talking about. The kids are fine, I'm busy and you're busy. Isn't that enough?"

"What about us? What about Andy and Annie? We aren't in your life. You have the twins, your job, and your sports. When was the last time you even hugged Andy and Annie?"

"I have enough to do with the twins. Besides, Andy and Annie have you, they're your kids anyway," she said as a matter of fact.

Chris pulled off to the side of the road and stopped the car.

"What did you just say? My kids? Aren't they yours as well? Aren't the twins mine as well?" He shouted.

Alicia looked surprised at what she heard. She hesitated to process what Chris said.

"Is that how you see it? You expect me to be a mother to four children."

Chris couldn't believe what came out of her mouth.

"You better believe it, and I expect you to be my wife as well in name and in fact and all that goes with it!" He yelled.

"Take me home now. I can't handle this. You are being unfair. I never wanted to have four children at my age. I can't do what you expect of me."

Chris knew he didn't imagine what he had observed for several months. Alicia was no longer the wonderful woman he fell in love with. Perhaps the only remedy would be for her to resign her commission and become a full-time mother. On reflection, however, that wouldn't solve the problem as he saw it.

"Okay, I'm going home, but I want you to consider what I said and especially what you said. If your world doesn't include Andy, Annie and me, then perhaps we don't belong together," he said in a calm voice.

From that moment, until she went to sleep, Alicia didn't say a word to Chris. Over the next two weeks, nothing changed in their relationship. They only spoke to each other when necessary.

A week before Thanksgiving, Alicia's boss called him unexpectedly.

"Chris, did you know Alicia submitted her resignation a few days ago. When I spoke with her about it, she said it was a personal decision. When I asked what you thought about it, she said it wasn't up to you. I thought that was a strange response," Sunderland reported.

"Well sir, I didn't know about it nor did she discuss it with me. However, it wasn't unexpected.

"That's not all, Chris. When I asked if she was doing it because of family responsibilities she said yes, my family in Florida needs me. I was surprised and dismayed, but I didn't pursue it," he continued.

"Now that's unexpected. I suppose I'm the last to know. Thank you for the heads up, sir," Chris said with a lump in his throat.

That evening, Chris asked Alicia the burning question.

"When are you leaving me?"

"As soon as my paperwork is signed off," she responded curtly.

"What about us and the twins?" Chris asked.

"Over a year ago I told you I didn't think I could be the mother of children that weren't mine, especially school-age children. Nevertheless, I decided to give it a try, even after I knew I was pregnant. It's not working out for me and I don't see anything changing the way things are."

"I suppose you don't care about you and me or the fact that the twins are my children as well. Are you committed to destroying a family that loves you just because you can't cope? Why haven't you discussed your feelings with me? Are you no longer in love with me?" Chris asked.

"It's not about you, it's about me and what I want in life. I need to be me, a woman who wants her own identity. My mother has agreed to take care of the twins while I get my graduate degree. I want to go home to my family. I don't want to be a Marine or a Marine's wife any longer."

"Well, you certainly blindsided and hurt me very much. You are taking my daughters from me, from our lives, you are very heartless, Alicia. Something has gone terribly wrong and if I'm to blame, I'm sorry. If you are doing this because of Andy and Annie, I will never forgive you. I love Lily and Rose, but you are the most cold-blooded person I've ever met," Chris said raising his voice.

From that day, until Alicia left for Florida, the two of them barely spoke to each other. Chris had a difficult time explaining to Andy and Annie why Alicia and the twins left. Edith helped Chris with an explanation that seemed plausible. The general and Edith were heartbroken. Chris told them the entire story. Of course, Edith knew how Alicia felt a year earlier but thought she had a change of heart.

The general was concerned Chris would resign his commission. There was nothing he could offer him to remain in the Corps. Chris considered his options but didn't want to change anything yet to further disrupt Andy and Annie's lives.

23

NEW LIFE, NO WIFE

Chris called Javi after Alicia left for Florida and gave him the details of the final days of their disintegrated marriage

"I don't know where she's getting those ideas. After all, she had every opportunity to become a leader in the Corps. No one held her back." Poncho said.

"I think that's the reason she wasn't too keen on having two children in her life so soon. She probably felt a potential loss of freedom. I wish she would have told me before we took the relationship as far as we did," Cisco replied.

"I agree, and the twins were the last straw, God Bless them," Poncho said.

"What do you think she'll do after she gets her degree? Will she let your mother become their *de facto* parent?

"My mom couldn't handle it. My father still isn't 100 percent," Poncho responded.

"Every time I check my mail, I expect to see divorce papers. Why do you suppose she stays married to me?" Cisco asked.

"I have no idea. I don't think she's doing it for any unsavory reason like if you pranged another aircraft and didn't survive. You know, insurance and benefits."

"She has a plan, I'm sure."

Chris could never be angry with his 'brother', Javi. After speaking with him, it was quite clear; Alicia wanted her independence, to find her own way without the responsibility of being a wife or a mother.

Andy and Annie seemed to adjust to having one parent again, but if it wasn't for Edith's help, Chris would probably have failed as a father. Both kids were very active in sports and other activities. His weekends were spent driving to, waiting for, and driving from sports venues as well as various school activities.

Chris's interaction with his former father-in-law was waning for very good reasons. The general had his hands full keeping his forces at peak levels, in a peacetime environment, and with a reduced budget. Though Marine aviation didn't shrink that much, it didn't follow the Navy's transition to the more modern F-14 Tomcat.

Chris thought Congress believed the world's toughest warriors could be cocked, aimed and fired at a moment's notice. The Pols didn't understand the need for training, readiness operations, modernization of weapons, and the stress of constant sacrifice on families of a deployed Marine.

The media was no friend of the military either. Their constant badgering about the loss of Vietnam to the communists as a military defeat. The two American presidents after the war, Tweddle Dee and Tweddle Dumb, both of whom were formal Naval officers, were clueless and spineless, in Chris's opinion.

Whenever Chris looked into the eyes of a Marine rifleman who served in Vietnam, he wanted to hug him because of all the great things Marines stood for, their fidelity to the Corps and what they sacrificed for God, country and family. Americans must never forget; Marines are human beings with the same emotions as everyone else. They aren't automatons that operate on batteries. If they were, God forbid, the government wouldn't fund replacement batteries.

Chris was angry for both personal and professional reasons. He loved the Corps to death. Every day and night he anguished about his future without the Corps, though he'd always be a Marine, his concern was being financially successful so he could provide a stable future for his children. How could he accomplish both?

If he remained on active duty for the foreseeable future, he had to find someone to complete his family. Though still married to Alicia, she wasn't the person to fill that role. Whenever he opened up to Edith, which was often, her niece's name was ever present in the conversation. Chris had to admit it, Julia was the only woman he knew who could love his kids, be a great mother and wife; the one person he felt most comfortable with unless she too had changed since he last saw her.

In May, 1977, Javi called to let Chris know that Alicia earned her MBA with honors. Though she majored in finance she focused on the hospitality industry. A major resort chain in Miami hired her as an assistant CFO. Javi reported she spent less and less time with the twins as she worked toward her new career.

"What's your mother's reaction? How long can she take care of the girls?" He asked.

"Fortunately, my father is a little better and has more interaction with the girls. I suspect they'll keep them until they are ready for school. What are you thinking?" Javi asked.

"Unfortunately, I am in no position to take the girls. I couldn't contemplate taking care of four children without a wife. I am still married to your sister, so I don't date anyone. Besides, my tour of duty is over in the fall and I don't have a clue where I'm headed. What about you?"

"You mean take the twins?"

"Yes, what's so bad?"

"My mom discussed that with me but we can't afford it," Javi said

"It's so damn tempting to resign my commission, but I love the Corps," Chris said changing the subject.

"Good luck, my brother," Javi said

After he hung up, Chris considered where he could go as a single father and a Marine, so he could remain with his children. He knew his former father-in-law would send him wherever he wanted to go. It seemed as though Miramar, MCAS near San Diego, was the closest. It would put him back in the cockpit, but he would be faced with deployments. He was lucky to have choices, but were they good for a single father?

Chris was getting antsy about not hearing from anyone regarding his next assignment. What he didn't know was his father-in-law's post-Vietnam assessment of the Marines' role in the war was being integrated into an advanced degree program at the Naval Post Graduate School in Monterey, California, for select Naval and Marine officers, other United States military officers, senior Defense Department civilians as well as foreign military officers. The school offered numerous think-tank type post-graduate degrees related to national security and other defense issues.

In late July, when the general asked Chris to come to his office to discuss his next assignment, Chris was taken aback. If the general had any news, he could have discussed it with him at home.

The general was very happy to see Chris again. They hadn't seen each other in about a month. There were two other men in the office.

Chris was introduced to Navy Capt. Jess Phillips, the Naval Post Graduate School's commander and Dr. Howard Bloom, the chief academic officer.

The two men discussed the new post-Vietnam war courses that were going to be added to several degree programs. They came to Hawaii to advise the general as to what portions of his assessment were being used.

Chris jumped to the conclusion he was being recruited as a student, but he already earned a graduate degree from George Washington University. He didn't think he had the smarts or time for a PhD.

"General Iverson has recommended that you, Major Harrington, should be appointed the lead subject matter expert for the courses regarding Marine Aviation close combat support tactics in Vietnam. We've reviewed your academic qualifications and your extraordinary military record. Frankly, there is no one else we would consider, so please don't turn us down," Phillips said.

Chris looked to the general and told him he was proud of the work he and his team accomplished which was to be discussed in an academic environment and outside the purview of politicians.

"In case you gentlemen are wondering why a major is telling a general that he is proud of him, perhaps needs an explanation. Chris is the father of my grandson and he has been like a son to me. If you hadn't come up with his selection, I would have, because he is the best damn pilot in the Corps and knows the good, bad and ugly of the air support efforts in the war."

Everyone looked at Chris in anticipation of his response.

"Just where is the school and how long is the assignment?" He queried.

They all laughed considering those questions were not at all expected, at least not at first.

"The school is in Monterey, California, just south of San Francisco, and the assignment is for three years unless you want to remain another year," Dr. Bloom replied.

Chris smiled. It was a perfect place for a single father and it wasn't too far from San Diego. He looked at the general who gave him a 'thumbs-up'.

"I think you should know I am very opinionated about the war, not from a political perspective, although that as well, but I am disappointed, and frankly disgusted that the greatest military force in the world couldn't defeat the NVA? Gentlemen, we weren't defeated on the battlefield but rather in Washington DC," Chris said hoping not to be rejected.

"Do you know why, major?" Dr. Bloom asked.

"Yes, two reasons. We are a democracy run by politicians who didn't want to win at all costs, and we had leaders with no balls!"

Everyone was silent or perhaps stunned.

"If you could be more tactful in the future, I think your classes would be quite fascinating, and perhaps a great inspiration for our students," Dr. Bloom replied.

He reached over to shake Chris's hand and said welcome aboard.

The general walked them to his outer office. Chris heard the general tell them that people will be knocking down doors to hear his son-in-law speak.

When the general returned to the office, he patted Chris on the back.

"Did we solve your single father issue? I think you should resolve yourself to the fact that you'll never fly again as a Marine pilot, but you will come home every day to be a father who sees his children grow up," the general said.

"Thank you, sir, I am very pleased and I won't disappoint you. When do I have to leave?"

"In about three weeks. I know it will be tough on Edith and me, but we will retire in San Diego which isn't too far from you. Dr. Bloom left the course outlines for the three courses you will teach. I want to give you the Marine aviation section of the official post-Vietnam assessment regarding its role during the war. I also included the interview notes but redacted the names of those interviewed. You can fashion your own lectures from these documents," the general said.

Chris walked out of the building with a big smile. Someone up there had been good to him.

He broke the news to Andy and Annie about moving to California. Annie said she wanted to go to Disneyland; Chris made the right decision.

24

NEW LIFE, SOME STRIFE

The Monterey Peninsula and Carmel Valley are two of the most beautiful places to visit in California. In addition to being a favorite tourist destination, the area was the home to very rich and famous people, as well as having several world-class golf courses.

Chris decided he didn't want to wait for a three-bedroom house to become available in one of the military housing areas. He decided to invest in a home where real estate values continued to increase.

Dr. Bloom introduced Chris to other faculty members, most of whom were civilian PhD's. The few military faculty members were senior military officers with post-graduate degrees.

"Dr. Bloom, when I was a student at the staff college in Quantico, I earned my master's degree at the same time. It was difficult because I had to complete it in one year. Since I have at least three years here, is there a possibility of earning a PhD while a member of the faculty?" Chris asked.

"I anticipated your question. It would be difficult, but you could do it. I assume you have an idea for a thesis, in fact, it's probably already in your head," Bloom replied.

"I have some thoughts about it. I'll wait until I have more experience as an instructor since my courses will be the basis of my thesis," Chris replied.

"Please call me Howard, I'm not very formal with my faculty. I will give you a list of the required courses that should take about two years to complete. The other courses we offer cover areas of national security and military strategy. When you are ready, you can select the 12 elective courses that support your degree and supplement your thesis. The course work is quite difficult and will take up most of your free time," Howard said.

The following week, Chris met with a realtor in Carmel. She was very well dressed, attractive and quite professional.

"I should have introduced myself earlier; I'm Libby Scott. I have been here about 12 years and I know this market quite well. This is a good time to invest because the economy is not doing well and people are selling their homes at affordable prices. They are the second homes for most of the sellers who live in Los Angeles and the Bay area. The vast majority of military personnel from the installations in the area rent or live in military housing. Since you will be here for at least three years, you are doing the right thing."

"I hope you can find something near good schools and close enough to my work," Chris said.

"Please tell me how many children you have and their ages. Will your wife be working?" She asked.

"My wife and I are separated. She lives in Miami with our twin daughters. I suppose you want to know how much I could afford," Chris replied.

"I guess I wasn't too subtle. We can look on this side of the peninsula where the homes are older and less expensive. Your commute would be shorter. On the other side, we could check out Carmel and Carmel Valley, but the prices are quite high and the commute would be longer."

"I never owned a home before so I don't know what I could get for my budget which is about two to two-fifty."

"I think we should look on this side. I will start with Pacific Grove which features great older homes and beautiful views of the bay. The schools are quite good anywhere around here," she added.

"I don't have the time to get involved in a fixer-upper, it has to be move-in ready."

Libby drove Chris around Pacific Grove and presented about five houses for his consideration. The following day they went from Monterey to Seaside near Fort Ord, a sprawling army training base.

Chris wasn't overwhelmed by what he saw. Though he was never a home-owner, he knew what he wanted; it had to feel comfortable. He went to the school's housing office to see if any students or faculty had houses for sale. He found two in his price range, both near the school. He called both sellers and visited each one on the weekend. He took his children to get their opinions.

Both houses interested Chris who polled his kids for their opinion. The house they selected met all of Chris's requisites. It was high above Monterey Bay overlooking both sides of it. The elementary school was less than mile away. Since it was listed with a realtor, he had to call Libby.

Chris faced the same problem he had before; who would take care of his kids until he got home? He had to find a sitter who could meet their school bus and make them a snack. Again, he returned to the family assistance office to find a sitter. He preferred an older person or a college student. The clerk gave him a short list of available sitters. He preferred to hire a military family member.

He returned to his hotel and called the names on the list. The ones that answered either had another position or didn't want to work five days a week. Since the sellers had small children, he called to ask if they knew anyone. They provided two names of high school students who lived nearby.

Chris interviewed both girls in-person. Both were high school juniors and daughters of military officers assigned to the area. Only one of them wanted an everyday job, the other one said she was involved in after-school activities. With one candidate available, he made his choice. Selena Vargas was the daughter of the staff adjutant at the Defense Language School, located at the Presidio of Monterey.

When she accepted Chris's offer, he told her he wanted to meet her parents. Selena thought the request was a bit unusual but she gave Chris her father's office number.

The sellers accepted Chris's offer and agreed to vacate the premises within two weeks. The meeting with Selena's parents was for lunch at the Presidio's officer's club. Major Juan Vargas and his wife, Victoria greeted Chris at their table.

"This is the first time we've met someone that hired our daughter to take care of their children," Victoria said.

"I think it proper because of my unusual circumstances. I am a faculty member at the Naval Post Graduate School. I want you to know I am a single father, but I have a wife in Miami who is pursuing a career that is not compatible with my current assignment. I want to make sure the both of you can trust me. My children are 11 and 10 and are quite capable of taking care of themselves. However, I would feel better if I knew someone was at my house when they came home from school," Chris explained.

"We appreciate the fact you want us to feel comfortable with your situation. Since we'll practically be neighbors, we expect to get to know you better," Juan said.

After lunch, Juan invited Chris to visit the language school when he had the time. Chris reciprocated but said he was new to the post-graduate school and didn't know much about it yet. Chris left with an invitation to dinner the following week.

Chris was involved in several faculty meetings, including how to approach a diverse class of military officers, both foreign and domestic, as well as civilian defense employees. Other techniques besides lectures were to get the students involved to have them contribute to the discussion, and everyone was entitled to an opinion. Chris was told even if he was the expert on his subject matter, other folks may have knowledge beyond his and he should respect it.

Other faculty members discussed their past experiences at the school. One thing Chris learned was the students were very smart and knowledgeable based on experience in the field and at higher levels.

Chris spent most of the first week before class began preparing his lectures and showing the kids around the Monterey area. He registered them in school and had dinner at the Vargas' house. Selena spent time with Andy and Annie while Juan and Chris talked about their experiences in Vietnam.

Dr. Bloom handed Chris his class roster an hour before class began. There were several last-minute changes due to military commitments.

There were 18 students in the class, 16 were U.S. military, one Canadian officer, and one civilian that worked for the Secretary of the Navy.

Most of the degrees offered were in science and engineering. Chris taught in the School of International Graduate Studies, for the Department of National Security Affairs. The courses covered current and emerging national security issues.

Chris's area of expertise was southeast Asia with a focus on lessons learned and how to strengthen bi-lateral relationships with allies in the region. Though the Vietnam War was over, the communist government posed a growing national security threat to southeast Asia.

During the first few weeks, Chris stuck to his syllabus omitting his personal opinions even when asked by students. He also avoided debating a student even when it was obvious he had to. Apparently, he lost the fire in his belly as the memory of the war faded.

Chris spoke with Alicia's mother each week to check on the twins. Mrs. Cruz seemed unhappy that Alicia spent less time with them. She disclosed that Alicia was being considered for an executive position at a resort property in Spain and probably wouldn't take the girls. She suggested that Chris file for full custody if that happened.

He never contemplated being a single father of four, especially with his demanding schedule. Chris also called Edith once a week so Andy could speak with her. Edith was excited to tell Chris the general would retire on December 1st, and they would be home in San Diego the following day. Chris relayed his conversation with Mrs. Cruz about the fate of the twins.

"I know it is a tough decision for you, Chris. However, I would file for custody and a divorce, if I were you. Your marriage is obviously over," she said.

"I don't know Alicia any longer. I suppose that's the best thing to do and get on with my life."

Edith admitted she was quite sure Julia would make a wonderful wife and mother to his children. She disclosed that she has been speaking with Julia about visiting them in San Diego for Christmas.

"Did you tell her about my situation? Does she know about the twins?" He asked.

"Yes of course, she wanted to know everything. Let me be clear on one point. If you still love Alicia, don't encourage Julia. She may never come back into your life if that happens," Edith warned.

Edith said she would visit Chris before Christmas.

Chris was a very determined person and never wavered in the face of a dire situation. This time he couldn't pull the trigger. He was still in love with the old Alicia. He didn't particularly like the new Alicia and hoped she'd have a change of mind, especially about her daughters. Though Mrs. Cruz said Alicia didn't spend much time with the twins and was entertaining an offer to work in Spain, without the twins, Chris still had hope for reconciliation. He needed to speak to someone other than Edith because she was biased.

Chris called his mother. He brought her up to date on everything. Her response was a shock.

"Chris, if you gain custody of the twins, I'll come live with you and take care of the children," she said.

Chris didn't contemplate an offer like that. She went on to say she would retire in a few months and could live with him until he found someone, but didn't mention Julia.

"I don't know what to say, mom. I have the room for everyone but are you up to it?" He asked.

"Andy and Annie will be easy to take care of. The twins will be a handful but what other choice do you have? Don't forget, I'm the grandmother to all of them," she added.

The green light just flashed; the game was on. He'd file for divorce first to see if Alicia puts up a fight. If he succeeded, he'd file for custody of the twins once his mother moved in with him.

Dr. Bloom recommended a top-notch divorce lawyer in Carmel who had several famous clients. Even though Bloom said he'd be expensive, Chris made an appointment.

Sidney Sachs was an affable person with a big smile and a sense of humor. The first thing he told Chris was that he was expensive. After Chris said he knew that, he explained his situation, Sidney suggested to save money, he should ask for custody and a divorce at the same time.

"One court fight, one lawyer, one fee is my recommendation. Your wife deserted you and by her past and current actions she's an unfit mother," Sidney said.

"What if she fights for the children but agrees to a divorce?" Chris asked.

"She'll lose on both counts; you can take that to the bank. Will her mother support your actions?"

"She is in my corner, especially if Alicia takes the job in Spain," he replied.

"Let's hope she does, but we have to file before she leaves the country or this will be a very expensive case," Sidney said.

Chris filled out several documents including the names of people that would be deposed like Edith, and Mrs. Cruz. Chris didn't include Javi but would speak with him if he needed his testimony. Chris gave Sidney a $10,000 check with the admonition that he wasn't a wealthy man. Sidney smiled and said he knew what he was paid as a Marine officer.

A week before Edith's visit, Chris called Mrs. Cruz to check on the twins and to get the latest news about Alicia.

"My daughter is leaving for Spain at the end of January and she's leaving the twins with me. I want you to file for custody," she begged.

"I will, but I have to know if you would support me in court," Chris said.

"The family will support you, Chris. My daughter is not a fit mother and I pray for my grandchildren," she added.

Chris called Sidney to advise him of the conversation with his mother-in-law. He was elated by the news and said he'd already filed the case in Miami and was awaiting a court date for the initial hearing.

"Will I have to be there for that?" Chris asked.

"No, but you will have to be present at the divorce and custody hearings. Unfortunately, those matters are handled by two separate courts. I'll try to schedule the cases for the same week due to your circumstances," Sidney added.

Edith's visit went very well. She felt very sorry for the torment Chris was undergoing. She said the general was having a hard time being retired after 37 years on active duty. She was happy to be home for good.

"I sort of put Julia's visit off until your legal problems were solved. I hope you don't mind," she said.

"It's for the best. I haven't seen or heard from Julia in nearly five years. We both married since then and divorced so who knows how we'll get on," Chris replied.

Three weeks later, Sidney called with information on the two cases.

"We are scheduled for court appearances on March 10th and 13th. I've spoken to Alicia's lawyer. He said she won't contest the divorce but hasn't decided on the twins."

"If she leaves them with her mother, who can't take care of them any longer, how could Alicia keep custody?" Chris asked.

"She could offer to give you temporary custody until she returns from Spain," Sidney replied.

"No way, Sidney, full permanent custody, that's my demand."

"I knew you'd say that. We will go for 100 percent custody. There might be a little problem with your status as a single father of four," Sidney continued.

"My mother is moving in with me to share the raising of my children," Chris replied.

"Well, that should do it. By the way, don't rush into another marriage, you have bad luck it seems," Sidney said laughing.

"Three strikes but I'm not out. At least I have four people who still love me."

Chris was allowed to take a week off and flew to Miami. The first hearing was held the afternoon he arrived. It was a quick divorce with no contest and no settlement. The following day he visited Mrs. Cruz and the twins. He hadn't seen them in 18 months. They were identical and beautiful. How could Alicia leave them?

Sidney and Chris spent the next day going over all the documents to be presented in the custody case. Sidney spoke to Alicia's lawyer about full, permanent custody. The lawyer said Alicia still wanted visitation rights with proper notice; they agreed. Sidney said his mother's affidavit stating she moved in with him was a crucial part of the hearing.

The following afternoon, Chris and Sidney returned to Monterey with the twins. Chris's mom fell in love with the girls the moment she saw them. Andy and Annie were also very happy to see their sisters. Chris looked upon the scene with tears in his eyes. He marveled at how much the twins looked like Alicia, though he lamented his children still didn't have a mother they could bond with.

25

A SINGLE FATHER OF FOUR

Chris realized he couldn't have survived one week without his mother living with him. She had a magic touch with the twins who thought she was the same person as grandma Cruz.

Together they celebrated Andy's 12th birthday, Annie's 11th and the twins' third. Chris's first year teaching at the Naval Postgraduate School ended without any major problems. Chris kept his personal opinions to himself and kept to the lecture notes. His students were respectful though most outranked him. His student evaluations were excellent.

Edith visited about once every six weeks. In July, the general and Edith spent a weekend in Carmel. It was the first time the general had an opportunity to see Chris and his children in a year. The general was scheduled to play in a pro-am golf tournament to help raise funds for the USO.

The general mentioned that Chris's good friend, Javi, was promoted to major. He also mentioned Chris was on the promotion list for lieutenant colonel. The general advised Chris if he ever expected another promotion, he'd have to go back to operations. Since the general was retired, he could no longer help Chris's career though he might be able to help find a good spot for him after the school assignment ended.

Chris's life got complicated when Grace Abbott called to invite him to Las Vegas for a weekend. She wanted to interest him in working with her when he left the Marine Corps. Grace mentioned she wanted a good right-hand person since she was getting on in years and needed fresh eyes and ears.

He accepted the invitation as it was very important in his decision-making process about either retiring from active duty, or accepting Grace's offer.

Chris's weekend with Grace opened his eyes to what he could have if he left active duty. She said her husband had left numerous securities and bonds that he purchased 20 years earlier. They were worth over $10 million. She bought a lot of property based on what she knew about the future growth in Las Vegas. Grace didn't exactly pressure Chris to take her offer, but he felt she truly wanted him to have a more prosperous life as a civilian. It was a choice that would mean leaving active duty sooner than he planned to though he wanted to remain on active duty until he was no longer promotable. The general specifically told him to return to operations or he would no longer be promotable, so his choices narrowed.

Mrs. Cruz called to check on the twins. She said Alicia had sent birthday gifts for them and she needed his address to forward them. Other than the gifts, Mrs. Cruz had no other contact with her daughter.

Chris called Javi to congratulate him on his promotion. Javi was deploying to Japan soon, something that made Chris jealous. Javi said he spoke to his sister once since she left for Spain.

"She said she loves her job and was upset that you went through with the custody law suit. She only expected you to file for the divorce," Javi relayed.

"If she loves her new life as a career woman with nothing holding her back, why would she care about the twins?" Chris asked.

"She said she still loves you," Javi said.

"I don't believe it, Javi. Before you know it, she will marry again to some European businessman and live the life she planned for herself."

"If I know my sister, she will get tired of the life she's leading. She has to have some feelings for her daughters. Would you ever take her back, Chris?"

"I have too much on my plate to think about that. I am contemplating leaving active duty and joining the reserves. I am being offered a great business opportunity in Las Vegas by a long-time friend. I need to think about a stable future for my children," Chris said.

"I'll touch base with you when I return in three months," Javi said.

In July, Dan Ryan made his annual call to update Chris on Katie's condition. He also asked for Chris's contribution to maintain Katie in a private facility'

"Are you still on active duty, Dan?" Chris asked.

"I got out six months ago when I failed to get promoted. I fly for an airline on the west coast. It's not as exciting as flying at tree-top level in an F-111," he said.

"Is your sister making any progress?"

"There's a problem. She's catatonic and doesn't acknowledge anyone around her. They can't treat her. I was advised to move her to a state hospital since they couldn't do anything for her. They said I should save my money."

"That's your decision, Dan. You have to realize she will physically deteriorate in a state hospital. The money isn't that important to me, but I think she should stay where she is." Chris advised.

With the possibility that Edith would play matchmaker and invite Julia to San Diego for Christmas, Chris felt he had to have a long-overdue talk with Andy. He was his only child who didn't know his mother.

On the weekend before school started, Chris and Andy drove along the Pacific Highway for several hours before heading back home. Andy was 12 and a half and turned out to be an outstanding young man. He was a straight A student and an excellent athlete.

When they stopped to eat lunch at a very picturesque location, Chris tried to find the right words to engage his son.

"Andy, you know I love you very much and I'd do anything for you. But I failed to do the most important thing and that was finding a wife who wanted to be your mother,"

Chris almost fell off the bench when his son replied.

"Why did Katie and Alicia not stay with you? Was it your fault or do you suck at picking out a wife?"

"Katie betrayed me with another man when I was in Vietnam. Alicia didn't want to be married with a family because she wanted her own life as an independent woman. When she had Rose and Lily, she tried to make it work. The rest of the story you know quite well," Chris explained.

"So why are we having this discussion now?" Andy asked.

"Before I answer your question, I need to know if you cared for anyone I met, or married, or someone else in our lives you met and liked."

"I didn't like Katie but I never said anything to Annie. I liked Alicia very much until she left us the first time. I never thought she'd return. But she left us again."

"Anyone else?" Chris asked.

"There was only one other, and now I understand why we are having this talk. I don't remember her very well but grandma Edith always mentions her name."

You are so smart, son. Cousin Julia is grandma Edith's niece and your mother's cousin. She lives in France and is an art expert that works for various museums and private collectors. About two years after you met her, she married an older man with two children. The marriage didn't work out so grandma Edith is trying to get us together. That's why I had to find out how you felt about having Julia in your life."

"Dad, do you really think two people who had failed marriages could make it work?" Andy asked.

Chris was surprised at his son's question because someone his age wouldn't normally ask it.

"I can't answer that, Andy, but I won't meet her again if you don't want her in your life." Chris replied.

"She'll always be in my life, dad, she's family," Andy wisely stated.

"You are absolutely right. I suppose you think I'm stupid."

"I think you are afraid to get involved with someone again and that's okay with me. I don't need a mother now that I have grandma Edith and grandma Bonnie."

Chris was so pleased by his son's maturity and his ability to express his feelings in a direct way.

"Everyone needs a mother to love no matter how old they are. Besides you, there is Annie and the twins. They need a mother too," Chris added.

"Do you want me to ask grandma Edith to invite Julia to San Diego so we can check her out?" Andy said laughing.

Again, Chris laughed so hard, he almost fell off the bench. He grabbed and hugged Andy and told him he was the most important and smartest person in his life.

Chris didn't encourage Andy to ask his grandmother because he knew he'd mentioned it the next time they spoke.

School began again for Chris, Andy and Annie. Grandma Bonnie was left with three-year old twin girls to contain all day. Chris continued to keep his opinions at a low ebb since he couldn't afford any negative feedback from military brass.

On November 1st, 1978, Chris was promoted. The faculty hosted a party at the officer's club which was a very nice gesture. That evening the general called to congratulate him. Edith said she put the idea out for Julia to visit over Christmas. Apparently, Andy delivered his message. Chris invited them to Monterey for Thanksgiving. Since the Harrington house was fully occupied, the general said he'd make reservations at the school's VIP quarters.

Chris didn't think a lot about Grace's offer since he might have to factor Julia into whatever he decided to do. He was uncertain how she would react to his continued career in the Corps since his assignments could result in separations.

Thanksgiving was a real treat at the Harrington house. Two grandmothers and four grandchildren, provided a lot of time for the general and Chris to talk. The general wanted him to remain an active-duty Marine for as long as possible. He suggested what assignment would be most helpful to his career. They both agreed that commanding a fighter squadron was the best choice.

In early December, Edith called to announce that Julia accepted her invitation for Christmas.

"I didn't tell her you'd be here Chris. You haven't seen each other in nearly six years. I want to surprise her rather than scare her off," she said.

"What does she know about my situation, you know my marriage, the twins and my divorce?"

"I told her a year ago that you married again but I never mentioned the twins, or Annie, or the divorce."

"I suppose if you mentioned I had four children; she would have turned down your offer. What does she do for a living?" Chris asked.

"She explained she was an art acquisition consultant. When a museum or an investor wants to purchase art, she researches it to authenticate the painting. She works with a team of art experts. She travels a lot in Europe."

"That sounds like a great career. Why in the world would she give it up for me?" Chris asked.

"First of all, she always asks about you even while she was still married. Second, she's not Alicia. She loves children though she can't have her own. I'd think she could find work in America, don't you?"

"What's you plan? How should I approach her? Six years is a long time. I don't know if the chemistry between us is still there," Chris replied.

"I think we should start from the beginning. You two don't have a long history so let's make this an introduction. I suggest you leave the twins with your mother otherwise Julia may freak out," Edith said laughing.

Chris was nervous because he really didn't know the 'adult' Julia. She might love children but not at this juncture in her life. At just 26 years old, she might cherish her current lifestyle and not want to settle down. Chris decided to be attentive to Julia but not appear to be desperate for a wife.

Two days before Christmas, Chris, Andy and Annie flew to San Diego. The general picked them up so he could speak with Chris beforehand. He dropped the children in front of the house to Edith's waiting open arms. Julia wasn't visible from the drive way.

Before Chris got out, the general told him to sit a while.

"I've never been involved in matters of the heart unless I was part of it. Julia is a lot like Camille, physically speaking. But Julia is very sensitive. She has been mentally scarred by her attack when she was 15. Her marriage to her teacher was a traumatic experience. Edith had to tell her you were coming and when she did, her face lit up for the first time. I could see the change in her immediately. Another disappointment would probably crush her spirit. If you decide Julia isn't the one, please don't give her any false hope. If she thinks she's the one, don't encourage her,"

Chris was surprised the general had any opinion on the matter. If he saw a tragedy in the making and was worried enough to warn Chris, the few days in San Diego could be tense.

"Edith told me to listen but not be aggressive unless there was a sense of certainty on both sides. I promise to be on my best behavior. Has she changed much, general?"

"You will be surprised, Chris. Six years is a long time. You've changed as well. I hope you both see the good in each other."

Edith walked out to the car and asked if there was a problem. The general said he was giving Chris a last-minute mission briefing. Edith told Chris to follow his instincts and his heart, and let the other stuff take care of itself.

"Andy recognized Julia right away. She was thrilled to meet Annie. The three of them are sitting on the bed in the guest room talking up a storm. She asked about you. I think she is very nervous. I will introduce you two as if you've never met before,' Edith said.

26

JULIA ENCORE

As Chris approached the house, he had butterflies in his stomach. Even if he felt the same way about her as he did six years ago, he was unsure of her feelings. Even if she shared his feelings, he didn't think she'd give up her lifestyle to become a mother of four and a Marine's wife.

"Look who's here, Julia. I hope you remember him but if not, this is Chris Harrington," Edith announced.

Chris reached out to shake her hand but instead she kissed him on the cheek. She blushed and stepped back.

"I'm Julia, the young woman from Paris who fell in love with you six years ago. I haven't forgotten you, Chris," she said.

The general handed Chris the car keys and told them to go somewhere and talk. Until they were in the car, Chris hadn't said a word to her. He didn't know what to say.

"You look so different, Julia. Six years ago, you had long hair and looked like every other California college student. Now you have a wonderful French cut that makes you look so sophisticated. Either way, you are still beautiful," Chris said.

He was grasping for the right words. He drove to the harbor and found a parking spot where they could talk without being disturbed.

"You haven't changed much, Chris. I know you went through lot and so have I. I'm sure Edith told you about my marriage and divorce. I'm so sorry I did that. I never thought we'd see each other again. I was lonely and needed someone in my life. I guess I picked the wrong person," she said with tears in her eyes.

Chris spent 15 minutes relating what happened to him from the time he met Alicia until he filed for divorce. Julia listened intently.

"I wouldn't have married her if I thought there was a chance for us. When you married, I decided to give up and find someone else. Though we never made any promises to each other about the future, I had hoped something would change," Chris said.

"You said Alicia was pregnant, where is the baby?" Julia asked.

Chris smiled.

"She had twin girls and I have full custody. They are home with my mother. She lives with me now because I couldn't care for four children on my own.

Julia smiled.

"They are identical, beautiful and are now three years old. They wear my mother out but she still loves them."

They stared at each other for a few seconds. Chris felt she wanted him to kiss her. He touched her hand and held it, then put it to his lips.

"If there is a way, we could be together, I'd do anything for you. I think for both our sakes; we shouldn't repeat what happened the last time we were together. I promised Edith I wouldn't hurt you and I don't want to be hurt again," he said.

"I loved you for six years but realized we could never be together, but now things have changed. I have to follow my heart. If you still love me, I want to be with you. If not, I'll understand and pray for you to change your mind," she said.

Chris took her in his arms and held her tightly. She was perspiring, trembling and crying. It was the moment of truth. He realized what he did in the next five minutes would impact their lives forever. He had to be sure. This wasn't just a decision for the two of them to make, there were four children to consider.

Chris held her in front of him and kissed her beautiful lips. He had to find the right words. What if Alicia came back? He didn't know a lot about Julia to tell the truth. Did that really matter? He didn't know the true Alicia but he married her anyway.

"Julia, tell me how this will work? Would you give up your career and live with me? Is this something you thought about in case we met again?"

"Edith planned everything. She said I should be absolutely sure about you or don't come for Christmas. So, I thought about it for two months. I took a chance because Edith didn't know how you felt about me. She is very nervous about your reaction as am I. Have you thought about us at all?" She asked.

"There were times during the last six years that you were on my mind a lot. I worried about you especially after you married. When I heard about how your husband treated you, I was really concerned. I must admit, before I married Alicia, I was still thinking about you. Though we only spent a few days with each other, I knew more about you than I did about Alicia. I made a lot of mistakes. I don't want to make another one. I know that sounds bad, you wouldn't be a mistake for me, but could it be a mistake for you?" Chris postured.

"I made mistakes as well. I didn't follow my heart with you, I married because I was lonely, I didn't keep in touch with you though Edith was a great surrogate. I think we've both learned from the past," she replied.

"Tomorrow, you and I will fly to Monterey to meet my mother and the twins. I want you to understand what awaits you. Andy and Annie are both able to fend for themselves but both need a mother's love. I've tried to be both and I hope I haven't failed them. Sorry I sound like your former husband; I didn't mean to. I want you for me, I need someone to love and someone to love me. My mother will always be around to help. We won't be overwhelmed by four children, in fact if you want to continue your career, I'd be fine with that," Chris added.

"I don't know what to say. I look forward to meeting your mother and the twins. I really appreciate your willingness to allow me to continue my career. However, I'd like to see Andy and Annie graduate high school before I do that. The next five or six years are the most important ones for teenagers, especially for Annie," she added.

"Are we moving too fast, Julia? After a six-year hiatus, did we just decide to become a couple?"

"I should hope we'd be more than just a couple, Chris. I'd understand if you didn't want to marry again though I wouldn't feel secure in our relationship," Julia lamented.

Chris held Julia close to him. He whispered that he loved her and he didn't want her to leave again. He found her lips and welcomed her response.

"Let's spend at least a few days together before we say anything to Edith. One of us may have second thoughts," Chris said.

"It won't be me. I won't make the same mistake twice," she said.

They returned to the house where Edith was anxiously waiting for some news. Chris smiled and said they were going to Monterey so Julia could meet his mother and the twins. Julia said they had a good talk but didn't make any decisions.

"I'm glad you aren't rushing it, Chris. There is so much to consider," Edith said.

They had dinner and a few drinks. Andy and Annie were anxious to open their presents. Edith insisted they wait until Christmas morning. Chris booked the flight to Monterey for the afternoon.

Since Edith didn't know how things would work out between Chris and Julia, she arranged to have them sleep in separate rooms. Around one in the morning, Julia slipped in beside Chris and fell asleep. He knew she was there but didn't do anything but hold her around the waist.

The flight to Monterey was quite empty since it was Christmas day. Bonnie and Julia got along from the first minute they met. The twins charged into the room to great Chris. He introduced them to Julia who had trouble telling them apart.

"They must look like their mother; they are very beautiful," Julia said.

"I can't imagine how a mother could abandon these beautiful girls," Bonnie said.

Lily took to Julia while Rose shied away. Chris explained that Lily was more assertive. He urged Rose to sit on Julia's lap. He assured her Julia was his friend and would like to get to know her. Rose approached Julia and stood in front of her.

"Are you going to stay with us?" Rose asked.

"Do you want me to stay here?" Julia asked.

"I want you to stay," shouted Lily.

Rose shook her head in affirmation.

"It seems as though Julia won them over," Bonnie said.

"Mom, Julia and I have been discussing our future together. I think we both wasted six years waiting for things to go our way. If she moves in with us, I want you to stay for as long as you want. I may receive another assignment next year and we'd probably have to move, but I want all of us to move as a family," Chris said.

"Don't you think I'd be in the way? Wouldn't you want your privacy?" Bonnie asked.

"My answer to both questions is no, unless you prefer to live in Napa by yourself," Chris said.

"I love my home in Napa and I have a lot of friends there but I'll decide what to do after Julia moves in with you. I know you love children, Julia, but two pre-teens and two toddlers are a handful," Bonnie said.

Julia helped Bonnie with the twins, she sang a French lullaby to put them to sleep. Bonnie whispered to Chris that his friend Javi called the previous day. While Bonnie and Julia discussed their knowledge of wines, Chris called Javi.

"I just wanted you to know that Alicia married a wealthy businessman's son. He owns a chain of hotels in several countries. She told me she did it even though she still loves you. I really don't understand her, Chris," Javi said.

"I think I do, Javi. I hope her new husband doesn't want children," Chris added.

They spoke a few minutes longer about their respective careers, until Julia walked in and put her arms around Chris. She kissed him on the cheek and whispered she was tired and was going to bed.

Chris and his mother stayed up to discuss her options. Bonnie wasn't sure if she wanted to remain after Julia moved in. She felt there would be too much confusion with the children. Julia would have to assume her rightful position as stepmother from day one. She didn't know how Andy and Annie would react. Chris explained that Andy met Julia six years ago when he was told they were second cousins. Chris didn't think Julia would have a problem since Andy never knew his mother and Annie really like Julia.

"What about Julia? Do you think she can handle the children? The twins are getting more difficult each day. They don't mind me as much as before and I'm fairly strict," Bonnie said.

"Any woman that becomes my wife will face the same challenges. Do you expect me to live alone the rest of my life?" He asked

Chris realized he wasn't being fair to his mother. Maybe she wanted to find someone to spend the rest of her life with.

"I will receive orders by the end of the school year. Regardless of what Julia decides, you are welcome to stay as long as you want. If you want to return to Napa when we leave here, that's okay with me," Chris said.

By the time Chris went to bed, Julia was asleep. It was probably better they didn't engage in anything to cloud their thinking. Sex can often lead to bad decisions.

Julia returned to France on January 2nd. She promised to get her affairs in order and return as soon as possible. They spoke every other day, neither wavering in their commitment to each other.

The last six months at the post graduate school was very enjoyable. Chris felt less restricted on speaking his mind about the Vietnam war. Most of his students agreed with his opinion as to how it was led, fought and concluded.

The general kept in contact with Chris since he was very interested in his next assignment. He reminded Chris to get promoted again he'd have to command a squadron first. He contacted some of his active-duty friends to let them know Chris was up for an operational command. Chris was going to have to compete with his peers who were a few years older and probably had more flight time than Chris over the last six years. The general never told Chris he was acting as his agent.

The assignment's office for determining where aviators like Chris would end up contacted him in April. Chris could opt to stay in Monterey for another year, if he was unhappy with what was in store for him.

In May, 1979, Chris was offered a squadron commander's position at El Toro Marine Corps Air Station, Santa Ana, CA. The two fighter squadrons still flew F-4 Phantoms but would transition to the F-18 Hornet by the end of Chris's tour. Chris was highly suspicious of who was behind this assignment since El Toro was conveniently located 80 miles north of San Diego.

Chris's assignment was conditional since he was not in an operational unit for more than seven years. He had to go TDY to Pensacola to requalify as an F-4 pilot and to undergo an extensive flight physical. The latter was required as a result of his accident at sea where he almost lost his life and suffered a memory loss.

Chris put his house on the market when he left for Florida. In June, his mother returned to Napa with the children and would bring them to San Diego in a few weeks. Julia planned to move in with Edith in August to wait for Chris and to help with the children.

The transition from the academic classroom to the operations briefing room seemed to be on track. Chris had no problems qualifying to fly again. He also had significant training on his new role as a squadron commander.

The physical exam was quite thorough; Chris was cleared to fly. However, the psychological exam focused on his loss of memory which blanked out a few days of his ordeal. The flight surgeon believed the short loss of memory wouldn't cause any problems five years after the fact, however, one psychiatrist felt it could be a factor during a time of stress.

Chris's medical records were forwarded to Marine Corps headquarters for further review. Fortunately, everyone that reviewed the records was a friend of the general or Chris. He was cleared for the assignment in less than a week.

The general arranged for Julia and Chris to spend a week in Cancun to get reacquainted. Neither left the hotel room for three days.

27

IN COMMAND

After returning from Mexico, Chris left his family in San Diego until he settled in at El Toro, MCAS. As squadron commander, he was provided on-base housing that fortunately had a four-bedroom unit available.

One of Chris's first operational tasks was to ensure all his pilots were carrier qualified. The other fighter squadron at El Toro also had the same task. Unbeknownst to Chris, his squadron and the other one, would soon deploy to the USS Coral Sea operating with the Pacific Fleet. It would be the first time since World War II that Marines would provide the total air support on a carrier deployed to the Pacific.

Not every Marine fighter pilot was carrier qualified as was quite evident during the Vietnam War. Ground support fighter squadrons were usually situated at bases in close proximity to the troops they supported. Truthfully, the need for Marine fighter pilots was so great during the war, often carrier qualification training was delayed until the pilots returned from Vietnam.

Chris often voiced his opinion that all Marine pilots should be carrier qualified as soon as possible. He knew he was the best person to lead his squadron considering his carrier operations' experiences during and after the Vietnam War.

Two weeks after Julia and the children moved to Santa Ana, Chris deployed with his squadron for carrier training. While Chris was away, his mother stayed with Julia to help get the children enrolled in school. Julia couldn't have done it alone.

After Chris returned from deployment, Julia noticed a change in Chris. He was very focused on his new responsibilities and not as much on his children or her. At first, she didn't let it bother her but when the older children noticed it, she decided to approach the subject.

At first, Chris thought she was upset because they weren't as sexually active as when they were in Mexico. Julia emphasized it wasn't about sex at all. He just wasn't very loving to anyone and wasn't part of their daily lives. Chris was taken aback because he didn't detect the change. He attributed his behavior to the fact he never had command responsibility before and was probably too focused on his squadron. He felt very vulnerable to whatever might go wrong even if one of his men had a car accident. Chris also ascribed his conduct to not having worked his way up the chain of command through the various operational roles before becoming a squadron commander.

He told Julia she was right and admitted it was his fault. Two days later he had lunch with the other squadron commander to discuss his problem. His fellow squadron commander was three years older, senior in grade, had been in operations for most of his career, and was a family man.

Lt. Col. Alan Winters wasn't intimidated by Chris's wartime record or his relationship to Gen. Iverson. He was quite blunt and told Chris he didn't really deserve to have his command over so many men who had more flying hours than he did, and who had spent many months on deployments while Chris had cushy desk jobs.

Chris knew he deserved the admonition. He soon realized Alan wasn't angry or jealous, he was just being honest. Chris led a soft life for nearly seven years. He was concerned if his men felt the way Alan did, they wouldn't respect him. Chris was always the one everyone looked up to during the war. He instinctively did the right thing and was a natural leader. Somehow, he lost it. Alan gave him some good advice about prioritizing his family and his squadron. Chris never had to do that before.

Chris sensed his squadron didn't have confidence in a young commander who had fewer flying hours than many of them. The scuttlebutt was that Chris was some general's son who was given the command through patronage. He tried to ignore what he sensed but the feeling persisted.

Two weeks later, the family drove to San Diego to visit the general and Edith. Chris decided he would seek further advice from the general about his two new worlds in which he couldn't afford to screw up either one. Chris suspected Julia would have a similar conversation with Edith.

The children loved to be at grandma's house as did Julia. However, Chris wasn't relaxed being away from his squadron. He worried that something would happen to someone and it would be his fault. The general straightened him out.

"I'm sorry I never schooled you on how you are feeling now. I never thought you needed it but I understand your career took a very unusual path. In war, a lot of one's success is instinctive, you react to a situation and do the right thing. Today you are a leader, a role model, a motivator and someone who works to earn respect every day. You aren't the father of your men, however on the other hand, you might have to kick an ass or two, like a father. Each one of your men knows who you are and unfortunately knows how you got where you are. You have to make them forget the latter. When you are with your squadron, whether you are flying, working, meeting or having fun, you are the boss, not a friend. Make them feel good about themselves, not feel good about you. I wasn't the best loved commanding officer, but I saved lives and earned respect," the general said.

"I'm concerned about including my family in my world. Being a military parent is different than being a nine-to-five parent. I am convinced being a Marine, a commander, a father and a husband, and keeping all the wheels on, might be difficult. We are a different breed of men. The Corps is bigger than life. You can talk to a hundred Marine families and they will say the Corps comes first," Chris said.

"What you are telling me is that something has to be second and it can't be the Corps. I heard that all my life from Marines all over the world and I heard it in this house. If you can't love your soon-to-be wife and your children more than anything else in the world, and not be able to love the Corps as much at the same time, then I would advise you to resign your commission," the general said.

Chris remained silent.

"At the end of the road, never look back and say you didn't do your best for everyone. Too many of us regret we put our families second. Let me tell you something, son, there is no second place. You love your men and you love your family and don't ever forget that," the general added.

The general excused himself when he lost his composure. Chris realized his personal and professional life would have to exist in the same orb on equal footing. Too many people depended on him for him to fail.

Chris took a walk around the house. He found the general sitting on the back porch alone with a drink in his hand.

"I'm beginning to think I failed you, son. Instead of helping you, I might have hurt you. I want you to benefit from my ability to look in the rearview mirror because there is no way to predict the future. Every career Marine, and especially every Marine who commanded men, faced your dilemma. Most of us failed at either being the commander we were trained to be, or being the parent or husband God meant us to be. I might have met one or two Marines in my life who did both equally well," the general said.

"General, I don't know what to say. Everything I heard from Alan and you these last few weeks has been a revelation. Where was I supposed to learn all this?"

"First of all, you can stop calling me general; call me dad, Harold, Harry or whatever. For the record, the Corps trains men to become leaders, they don't train men to be husbands or fathers. Maybe there is more emphasis on the latter in the other services. But like you said earlier, Marines are a different breed. We fight wars, we die or get wounded; we don't get medals for being a dad. You have an opportunity to show the rest of us what a real man is. As I mentioned earlier, if you can't make both worlds work, leave the Corps. Too many before you did the opposite and left their families, or their families left them," he said.

"I wish I had you in my life when my father died. I am so grateful I have you now. I will call you dad, but perhaps Harold would be more appropriate when we are in public," Chris said.

"I will always call you, son," he said with tears in his eyes.

Julia found her two Marines in a somber mood. She just left Edith after getting the advice she needed to survive as a Marine's wife. She asked Chris to go for a walk to discuss how to make everyone's life the best it could be.

After Chris told her everything he and the general talked about, he made one modification. Though he agreed everyone in his two worlds had to be considered equal, equality was only in the mind; the heart was saved for the children and Julia. As far as Chris was concerned, there were no other equals. He said he hoped she would agree with him because he wanted to get married as soon as possible.

"We need another vacation, Chris," she said as she touched him in all the right places.

28

KEEPING IT EQUAL

Chris was determined to dispel any notion he was selected for his current command based on anything other than his achievements during and after the war. He called the entire squadron together for a beer and pizza meeting in the squadron operations room.

"I haven't had a chance to meet you informally as a group yet, though I have met with you individually over the past four weeks. None of us have crossed paths in our careers, so all you know about me is what the rumor mill has to say. I realize some of you have questioned my assumption of command at this time in my career. We all know pilots who would be a better fit here based on their records. Sometimes the best pilot doesn't make the best commander. We've all flown with great pilots who we thought were better than our incumbent squadron commander. I'm sure you know that a group of senior Marine Aviation officers select squadron commanders, wing commanders and other senior leaders assigned to Marine Corps Aviation. Those of you who don't think I was selected through this process are dead wrong. If you do, shout it out," Chris encouraged.

After an awkward 30 seconds, two pilots raised their hands.

"I appreciate your honesty so let me address you two. I was promoted to major two years early based on my Vietnam service. Since then, I was promoted with my year group. When I was assigned to COMMARPAC headquarters in 1973, it was for two reasons. The first was to get headquarters staff officer experience which helps your career down the road, and the second was I had some health issues and the flight surgeons wanted me out of the cockpit for a while. When I completed my tour in Hawaii, I wasn't eligible to command a fighter squadron since I was too junior and, as you all know, there were lots of good pilots that deserved a shot. Does anyone have any questions so far? Chris asked.

"In 1976, I reached a decision point in my life where I decided to resign my commission. I didn't think my career was headed in the right direction. I had a tremendous business offer to get out and make a ton of money and by 1976, I had four children and no wife." Chris was interrupted by laughter.

"My first wife died leaving me with my son. My second wife was committed to a mental health facility and requested I take her daughter and adopt her. My third wife was a Marine officer who didn't want any children before she was 30. She gave birth to twin girls when she was 23. She decided to leave the Corps and me with our twins. So, I don't really think my situation calls for any laughter. In 1977, I wasn't considered for an operational unit because I made it known I was contemplating leaving the Corps. Any further comments or questions so far?" Chris asked.

Someone asked why he didn't leave the Corps in 1977.

"I've asked myself the same question a hundred times. The answer is simple; I love the Corps; I love to fly. Unfortunately, I had very few options left if I remained on active duty because of an aircraft accident that resulted in some short-term medical issues. Luckily, I was offered a faculty position at the Naval Post Graduate School so the school could leverage my Vietnam experiences and observations to discuss future conflicts. I also wanted to earn a PhD, but my family situation was too demanding.

When I accepted the assignment, I was still a single father of four. Now for any of you that believe that a retired Marine infantry general, who was my former father-in-law, had any influence on me being here, you have been misled. As much as we both love the Corps, he urged me to get out and become a full-time father."

Chris stopped and looked at every man in his squadron hoping someone would challenge him or his story.

"I assume the question to be answered is how did I get from almost getting out to commanding this squadron. But that question doesn't have to be answered unless you doubt my ability to command this squadron. I don't think I have to prove to anyone in this room that I can still fly the shit out of a fighter. If anyone wants to challenge me on that point, we can arrange it some time."

At that moment, someone in the back of the room spoke up.

"By the way, gentlemen, Lt. Col. Harrington is the first and only Navy Top Gun graduate in the Marines."

Chris saw it was Winters who stood up for him. He must have been there the whole time.

"So, what's left to be concerned about? Ah yes, my ability to lead this squadron. That's something that will become apparent over time so I hope you stick around to find out," Chris continued.

A few men stood and applauded Chris, some approached and shook his hand. Winters walked from the back of the room and stood beside Chris.

"I've never seen a commanding officer have to defend himself right after he assumed command. You don't really know this man and what he's done for his country, for the Corps and for his fellow pilots. You probably don't know he's the most decorated Marine Corps pilot in the Vietnam War and that he downed three MiG fighters. You don't know he flew MIGCAP for two carrier-based squadrons over North Vietnam and never lost a pilot. When I told my squadron the whole story, they demanded we swap commanders," Winters said.

Everyone laughed.

"Thanks Alan. You didn't have to do that but I appreciate it," Chris said.

"Hey, command is a lonely job. We've got to stick together, Chris."

They shook hands and went to the club for a beer with some of Chris's men.

Chris might have convinced everyone he wasn't someone's fair-haired boy but he still had to prove his ability to command a combat fighter squadron. There was so much goodwill beer and pizza could earn. Leadership was never something Chris had to study up on. He assumed the role whenever it was required. During the war he led a flight of three to four aircraft on bombing missions against enemy targets. Once he returned to base, he was just one of the guys. Now, he is the commander 24/7 as well as a father of four and a soon-to-be husband.

Julia and Chris hadn't discussed marriage much. He wanted to give her enough time to acclimate herself to the United States, to being a step mom to four children and to being a Marine's wife. Thankfully, Edith helped with the latter.

It took a while for Chris to balance his two worlds. As a result, he became more loving to Julia and the children. There were times when Chris realized the children were taking a toll on Julia. She never complained but he could tell. Chris made sure every minute of every day he didn't have to be at work, he'd spend at home. There was only one exception to his routine. Whenever the squadron had a reason to go to the officer's club for a birthday, or a child's birth, or some other important event, Chris made sure to be there. The subtle bonding of Chris and his men was paramount to his success as a leader.

The subject of marriage was rarely brought up in a direct fashion. They alluded to it once in a while but they never nailed it down. In October, Chris asked Julia to marry him. He tried to make it a romantic gesture, but he botched it. Thankfully it wasn't a surprise so she excused his mumbling.

"I was beginning to have my doubts, I thought I failed my audition," she said laughing.

Chris held her close to him. She began to cry.

"I know this is much more than you bargained for. I wouldn't blame you if you turned me down. I love you so much, I want you in my life forever. If you aren't sure, I'll understand," he said.

"You are such a fool, Chris. I've loved you from the first time we met. If I were able to have children, we'd have as many as we have now. I wasn't sure you wanted me as much. Of course, I'll marry you," she said.

They held their kiss longer than usual. Chris didn't want to let her go.

"I think we should let Edith and my mother plan the whole thing. I'm sure my mother will want to come to see our big family. Too bad you didn't meet her before the wedding," Julia said.

"What about your step father?" Chris asked.

"I don't know about him. You know how he feels about Americans," she added.

Before we tell Edith and Harold, we should pick a date, don't you think?"

"The children are off from school by December 15th. Let's do it a week before Christmas," she said.

"That sounds perfect. I'll have to check the squadron's training schedule for that time," Chris said.

If there were any doubts about their love for each other or their commitment to each other, they evaporated in the heat of passionate love-making the rest of the night.

There were several short TDY's to Yuma Air Station, Arizona to use the bombing ranges. The squadron operations officer posted the bombing range results which had improved since Chris took command.

In early December, Chris got a troublesome phone call from Javi. The good news was that Javi was going to Iwakuni Air Base in Japan to assume the operations officer job of a fighter squadron.

The bad news was about Alicia. As Javi described it, Alicia didn't want to get pregnant but her new husband and her father-in-law wanted an heir to the family fortune. About three months after she married, Alicia got pregnant. She decided to have an abortion without anyone in the family knowing about it. She traveled to a Paris clinic where she aborted her child, Unfortunately, she gave the clinic her real name, which was a big mistake. Someone tipped off a journalist who investigated the situation. Word got back to Alicia's family and all hell broke loose. Her husband beat her, threw her out of his house, and annulled their marriage. Her father-in-law disowned her from any family inheritance and blackballed her from the hospitality industry.

Chris actually felt sorry for her even after what she did to him.

"Where is she now, Javi? Is she okay?"

"I'm not sure. After she pulled herself together, she tried to get a position with a large hotel in France but she was turned down. She told me she was staying with a friend in Spain but was considering returning to Miami.," Javi relayed.

"What about your parents, do they know what happened?"

"I told my mother. She was very upset but insisted it was Alicia's fault for leaving you."

"I don't know if this is what she deserved for leaving me, rather it's for abandoning her children."

"So, how do you like being the boss? I would love to fly with you again, Cisco but I don't think I'll see you in Japan soon."

"You are right. I have my hands full here with the squadron and four children."

"How are my nieces," Javi asked.

"They are wonderful and growing up to be beautiful ladies like their mother."

"What happened to your French girl, have you seen her?"

"She is living with me. We are getting married in December. I am very happy; she is a wonderful stepmother. It's been difficult for her to become a Marine's wife and to take over a family of four children. She has been the best for all of us."

"If I hear from Alicia before I leave, or any time after, I won't mention your marriage. I don't know how she will react and I don't want any harm to come to you or your family. I don't know much about Alicia's mental state since she left you. If Julia wasn't in your life, would you take Alicia back? You don't have to answer that, amigo."

"No, it's a very fair question, Javi. I will always love Alicia but I could never trust her again."

"I love my sister but she is a different person now. I agree with you."

"Like you said, neither of us knows her. Would she want to be the mother to four children? I doubt that. She'll land on her feet somewhere. I do feel bad for her and I'll always love her," Chris replied.

When Chris hung up, he thought about Javi's question. It bothered him for a few days. What if Alicia showed up before he married Julia? What if she went to court to get her children back? He decided to call his lawyer, Sydney to ask the many questions that suddenly filled his mind.

Chris was hesitant to select a date to marry Julia. He wanted to speak with Sydney first. He left a few voice messages but Sydney didn't respond. Chris though he might have died.

A week later Sydney returned the call. Chris was relieved to know Sydney was still around. He posed the two questions about Alicia.

"It would be better if you married as soon as possible because as a single father, Alicia may have grounds to get her children back," Sydney replied.

"If I get married this month, before she files anything with the court, will I maintain custody?"

"It depends on the judge's assessment of your lifestyle. I don't mean you aren't a terrific father, but as a military pilot who leaves his family for weeks at a time, the judge may believe a full-time biological mother is better than a stepmother of four children."

"Are you suggesting that I should leave the Corps to make sure Alicia has no grounds to reclaim her children?" Chris asked with alarm.

"Don't make any decisions now, Chris, I'm just giving you the worst-case scenario. A court gave you permanent custody of your twin daughters. It is unlikely another judge would overturn that decision without ironclad evidence to the contrary."

"Okay, Sydney, I'll stay the course unless I hear from you again," Chris replied.

Chris was somewhat shaken after he hung up. Like Javi said, he didn't know Alicia's state of mind. Chris decided to fly to Las Vegas and get married the following weekend

Before he made any arrangements, he had to convince Julia to forego a family wedding. However, Edith and Julia's mother would put pressure on both of them to have a proper church wedding. Chris didn't want to tell Julia about Alicia because there was no evidence, she would return to Miami and go to court to get her children back. He had to make up a bullet proof story to persuade Julia to get married in Las Vegas and not tell anyone in the family. They could still have a big wedding later in San Diego.

29

THE OFFER

When Chris mentioned getting married in Las Vegas, instead of having a family wedding, he gave Julia a flimsy, but truthful excuse. He told her she needed to be legally married to insure she could remain in America, and so the government could provide her all benefits as the wife of a military officer, including death benefits. Until she became a legal military wife, she had to continuously reapply for a temporary ID to enter and leave the air station and to use various facilities there. All of it quite valid.

Julia agreed and thought perhaps a family wedding would be too difficult to arrange for her mother to come. She was still excited. The problem of dropping off the children, without telling the general and Edith the truth, was problematic.

Chris suggested to tell them they wanted to have a weekend alone. Julia backed him up. In fact, she called Edith to ask if she could take the kids for the weekend. She answered Edith's obvious question with Chris' answer. After they checked into their hotel room, Chris called Grace to tell her he was in Las Vegas to get married. He wanted her to meet Julia. Grace was anxious to meet the lady who captured his heart.

Grace met them in the hotel lobby and was quite taken with Julia. She thought any young woman who would become the mother of four children and adapt to being a Marine's wife must be one hell of a lady.

At lunch, Grace asked Julia if Chris ever discussed the offer she made, and continued to make Chris. He was embarrassed because he never mentioned it to Julia. She prodded Grace to tell her about the offer.

"Let's discuss this later," Chris urged.

"No, I want to hear about it now," Julia replied.

Grace began when she first met Chris at Nellis AFB. She had a sense that he would have a better life if he had another option.

"I am getting on in years, I am a widow and have no children. I wanted Chris to learn my business and possibly take over for me when I retire."

At that point Julia interrupted to ask what kind of business.

"I am in real estate and insurance, have been for nearly 50 years. I develop residential apartments, town homes and single-family homes. Business was slow the past few years during President Carter's term. I took advantage of buying buildings, houses and property on speculation. If the economy turns around when President Reagan is in office, I'll never be able to handle my business alone," she continued.

"Julia, I never told you about this because I wanted to retire before I started a new career. But now I realize my retirement check each month would be pocket change if I accepted Grace's offer," Chris added.

"Unfortunately, Chris would have to serve another five and a half years to retire and I don't know if I'll still be here then," Grace said.

Julia looked at Chris and decided to make her point.

"Chris, I know how much you love the Marine Corps. I know you aren't in it for the money. Please consider our future and your children's futures when you finally retire. Try to compare five more years as a Marine officer to five years with an established real estate organization."

"Julia, I've gone over the advantages of accepting my offer many times over the last few years. Things have changed now for Chris, he has you and four children to educate and support. Perhaps Andy or Annie, or both would also join him in the business," Grace offered.

"I've considered your offer, Grace, but until now, I couldn't do it as a single father. I will consider your offer and discuss it with Julia in more detail. If I decide to accept, what would the timing be for me to uproot my family and move here?"

"I think you'd need about a year to learn the business, and another year assuming the role of president, while I am still around to help you before I can retire. If anything happens to me before, or shortly after you join me, you would be on your own. So, I think you should move here within the next six months."

"That's a lot to consider and I will make a decision with Julia next month. But first, we have to get married today," Chris said.

"Don't worry about it, I will arrange everything, just give me your driver's license, Chris, and Julia I'll need your passport," Grace said.

When Grace left, Julia asked Chris why he never spoke about his opportunity.

"After Alicia left us, I was a single father again. I seriously considered resigning my commission to give my children some stability. I really considered Grace's generous life changing offer. Then you came back into my life again and I felt I could remain in the Corps until I retired after 20 years of service. Until now, I hadn't realized how obtuse I had been. Grace is worth millions and she wants me to share her business. But I can't make this decision for you, though I know the children would be better off. So please let me know what you think," Chris said.

"I love you and the children more than anything. However, if I said as long as we can be together it doesn't matter to me, I'd be foolish. I know how much you love the Corps, but one day you'll have to leave it. You'll never get an opportunity like this again. Besides, Las Vegas is close to my aunt and uncle, and to your mother. You could provide a great education for your children. You could buy your own airplane if you still want to fly. Think of all our possibilities," Julia remarked.

Chris smiled; he knew Julia was right. He also remembered what the general told him. If he couldn't keep his family and the Corps on an equal level at all times, he should leave the Corps. The general was thinking of his own career during which time the Corps always came first, even in peacetime.

Chis and Julia returned to their room to wait for Grace to call with the wedding arrangements. They continued their discussion about Grace's offer. They made a list of the pros and cons. In the end, there was only one con; Chris' love for the Corps. He finally came to the conclusion that in peacetime there was nothing for him to do except to train the men in his squadron. He knew there were many exceptional Marines that deserved the opportunity to command a squadron.

30

ONCE A MARINE, ALWAYS A MARINE

On a cloudy, windy day on June 1, 1981, Lt. Col. Christopher Harrington submitted his resignation. It was a tremendous emotional event for Chris, who loved the Corps almost more than anything. He discussed his decision with his former father-in-law and his wing commander. Both men supported his decision based on his situation which included having a family of six, potential future deployments and of course the opportunity presented to him by Grace Abbott. He also knew five additional years would not be worth the risk to himself and to his family.

Everyone said they were sorry to see him leave and wished him luck. It was when he drove by the flight line on his way to his house that he teared up.

Chris had to remain on active duty for another week so he could take part in the change of command ceremony. He called Grace to let her know his schedule. She told him she'd find a large enough rental for his family after which he could decide where to live and what to buy. The market was a buyer's market, she added.

Julia knew Chris was feeling sad but confident he was determined to make a new life for their family. She greeted him with a kiss and a hug. The twins were about to be dropped off from school. Andy and Annie would be home later. Chris had a week to pack up, make arrangements to move and collect his children's school records.

During the first few days in June, Chris never second guessed his decision. However, he got a lump in his throat every time an aircraft flew over his house. He'd probably feel the same or worse on his last day. Though the general said he wanted to attend the ceremony, Chris asked him not to. The general had been part of his life since he was 16, and was with him for his entire 15-year military career. He felt he might lose it when the general shook his hand after the retirement ceremony. The general understood.

The day before leaving, Grace called to give him the address of the rental house she found. She said if they really liked it, they could buy it. That was the last thing on Chris's mind.

The change of command ceremony was very crisp as Chris handed the squadron colors to the new squadron commander. After the ceremony, Chris was the only one besides the wing commander on the platform. An officer read a citation and then called on Lt. Col. Winters to pin on Chris's final award of his career. Nothing could top the Navy Cross he received years earlier, nevertheless he was pleased he was awarded the Legion of Merit.

The following day, the family flew to Las Vegas where Grace met them at the airport to take them to a hotel she owned. She rented a car for them so they could see the new house and check out the area. Only Annie and Andy had ever been to Las Vegas. Chris made a point to call Shelly Ryan, Dan's wife, to let her know they had moved to Las Vegas. He knew Andy and Annie would be happy to see the Ryan kids again.

Grace had one of her assistants take the family to 'Circus-Circus' while she stole Chris away for his first introduction into the business world. Grace was prepared to discuss her organization in great detail but she tried not to overwhelm him. She was very upbeat that her real estate investments would become a windfall once President Reagan got the economy going in the right direction. She also knew, from inside information, that several new hotels were planned to be built and she owned the properties that were being considered. Her condos and apartment buildings were only half-occupied, but once the new hotels were under construction, she would benefit from the construction workers and later, the new hotel and casino employees.

Chris asked a lot of questions about his role which would be the primary sales executive and chief negotiator. Grace would continue to make additional investments. She was confident they would make a great team. She said in a few months she would rename her business from Abbott Real Estate to Abbott-Harrington Investments and give him the title of president. Chris was surprised and very appreciative.

During the meeting, Chris saw a formation of aircraft headed for Nellis AFB, just north of Las Vegas. It caught his immediate attention at the same time Grace told him about becoming president of a multi-million-dollar organization. He turned back to Grace and muttered under his breath, in with the new, out with the old.

Grace's assistant returned to the office with the Harrington family in tow. Everyone was hungry so Chris excused himself and went to a buffet dinner at a nearby hotel. The twins were surprisingly well behaved considering they had a full day of activity. Julia was anxious to speak with Chris but the children dominated the dinner conversation. They finally made it back to the hotel in time to put the twins to bed. Andy and Annie watched TV for a few hours while Chris and Julia talked about his new opportunity.

Julia was so elated when she learned about the new organization name and Chris' new position.

"Did she discuss your salary or did you forget to ask"? Julia said.

"It never came up. It has to be more than I was being paid in the Corps. I was too distracted by the enormity of the opportunity that I didn't ask." Chris replied.

Since Grace never mentioned meeting with Chris the next day, he decided to drive the family to the new temporary house. Julia got Andy and Annie ready for bed while Chris took a shower to relax and contemplate what he heard earlier.

When Julia came to the bedroom, she told Chris she was very happy and loved their family. She said she was so proud of them when they went to 'Circus-Circus'. Grace's assistant said she couldn't get over how well-mannered they were.

"That's all your doing, Julia," Chris said.

"You were a father to them long before I became their mother. The credit is all yours, *mon Cheri*," Julia responded.

"Come over to my side of the bed. I want to tell you how much I love you and that I am very happy to have you in my life," Chris said.

"Why Mr. Harrington, are you trying to seduce a poor French girl?"

"No, a rich one," he laughed.

They made love for the first time since Chris became a civilian.

31

REFLECTIONS

For 15 years, the Marine Corps was Chris's whole world. Yes, there were people who entered his world, Camille, his first wife, Katie his second wife, Alicia his third wife and of course his brother Marine, Javi. He had three children of his own and adopted one from one of the wives who briefly shared his career and life.

He never thought of leaving the Corps until the one woman who came into his life and had the most profound impact on him that changed him as a man, a husband and a father. Julia gave up her country of birth and her career to become the mother to his four children. She willingly accepted her life as a Marine's wife, never complaining or making any demands. It was because of her love for him and for the sacrifices she made that Chris thought his family deserved something more than he could provide serving in the military.

Most men with his record of accomplishments would have remained on active duty until retirement. However, Chris recognized the negative impact his former father-in-law's military career had on his daughter, Camille. He believed the general realized Camille's problems that led to her suicide were partly his fault. Chris knew that joining the Marine Corps and serving in Vietnam was too much for Camille to bear. He never wanted that to happen to Julia or to his children.

As the general once told him, you can't put the Corps ahead of your family or vice versa; they must be equal and if not, you must give up the Corps.

On a night when Chris had trouble falling asleep, he held his sleeping wife in his arms listening to and feeling her breath on his neck. He felt he had to give her the freedom to follow her dream of being a museum curator. He had the financial ability to build a museum in Las Vegas for her to fill with the art of her choice.

Las Vegas was growing. There were several hundred thousand residents that lived normal lives outside the entertainment and gaming industries. They had families who deserved something cultural that many similar sized cities had. He decided to take his idea to Grace to let her chew on it for a while. Perhaps the city fathers would support it or even better, hotel owners would consider it a civic duty to provide some culture for their employees and perhaps donate to it.

Chris had a lot of ideas on how to share his largess with people that needed assistance to reach their goals, like Grace did for him. Chris finally went to sleep knowing he would be a force for good.

Several years later, the Regan Administration requested the military services to scour their records for significant combat engagements where heroic actions of sacrifice or extraordinary bravery were not verified because witnesses had died in the war.

The furor over Vietnam subsided enough to consider highlighting the sacrifices service members made during the war. Service members that received the second highest award bestowed upon them by their respective services were also to be considered for an upgrade to the Medal of Honor.

During the Vietnam War, the United States government awarded the Medal of Honor to 239 recipients, of which 150 were posthumously awarded. The Army had 155 recipients, the Marine Corps had 57 recipients, the Navy had 15 recipients and the Air Force had 12 recipients. Approximately 2,644,000 personnel served within the borders of South Vietnam from 1960 to March 28, 1973. There were countless acts of heroism that resulted in the ultimate sacrifice. As in most wars, some acts were forgotten or the recommendation for an award got lost in the bureaucracy.

The review of all the records of such acts, and the recollection of veterans that might have witnessed them based on units, locations and dates, was a lengthy task. In the end, only three men would be presented with the Medal of Honor.

In 1986, Chris received a letter from the Secretary of the Navy advising him he was being considered for the Medal of Honor for the heroic acts for which he had previously earned the Navy Cross. Chris called Gen. Iverson about the letter. The general explained what had transpired in the Pentagon over the past two years.

"I survived the war, general. I don't deserve anything more than I received for what I did. There must be another Marine out there who paid the ultimate sacrifice to save his buddies, I can't accept this," Chris said.

"The Marines want one of their own to receive the highest award since the other upgrades went to Army personnel," the general explained.

"Please let the Pentagon know I don't want an award that others died for. I don't want to live with the guilt."

Chris never mentioned the letter to anyone. He hoped another Marine would be honored for his service.

A few months later, when the president presided over a ceremony in the White House, two Army families posthumously received the Medal of Honor and a Marine's wife accepted the award for her late husband's heroism.

Chris knew he did the right thing for himself and the Corps.

Printed in the United States
by Baker & Taylor Publisher Services